Much Ado About Magic

SHANNA SWENDSON

ALSO BY SHANNA SWENDSON

Books in the Enchanted, Inc. Series:

Enchanted, Inc.
Once Upon Stilettos
Damsel Under Stress
Don't Hex with Texas
Much Ado About Magic

CONTENTS

CHAPTER ONE

I was lost in an underground maze, getting more turned around at every corner. A sea of dead-eyed zombies surrounded me, making me feel like I was swimming upstream. And the unearthly wailing was *really* getting on my last nerve.

I didn't remember the Union Square subway station being this confusing, or had I been gone from New York too long? It had only been about four months—four months of driving to work, aboveground, in an old pickup truck and with no traffic to speak of. Was that long enough to lose my subway navigation skills?

I started to head down a flight of stairs, only to realize they went to the uptown tracks. I needed downtown. Morning commuters swarmed past me, ignoring my frustration in their mindless, relentless journey to work.

I caught my bearings and headed back the way I'd come, past the woman responsible for that creepy keening sound that sent chills up my spine. It was way too early in the day to have to listen to a musical saw, I thought.

Finally, I found the right set of stairs and headed down to wait for a train. I checked my watch, then remembered that I wasn't running late because I didn't technically have a job. I was merely going to see if my old company would take me back, and for that, I didn't have to be there precisely at the start of business hours. They weren't even expecting me.

A train pulled into the station, and I let myself get pushed on board by the flood of commuters. I'd missed a lot of things about New York, but this wasn't one of them. The subways hadn't miraculously become better smelling or less crowded while I'd been gone. The commuters on the train with me hadn't changed much, either. There were the business-suited types heading to the financial district of lower Manhattan, a few downtown hipsters, a couple of fairies, and an elf. Once upon a time, the fairies and elf

1

would have startled me, but now they were just part of the landscape.

One of the fairies smirked—not at anyone in particular, but rather in that way that generally means that someone's up to something or thinks she knows something no one else does. At the same time, a strange tingling sensation made me shiver. Someone nearby was using magic.

I tried to play it cool as I casually glanced around the subway car, looking for any sign of magical activity. A man near me had an odd, glassy-eyed look, but was that from a late night and insufficient morning caffeine levels, or was he under the influence of a spell? My question was answered when he lurched forward and took the wallet out of a nearby man's pocket. The victim didn't seem to notice anything as the thief moved toward the smirking fairy.

I grabbed the unwilling pickpocket's arm and said into his ear, "Hey! Do you really want to do that?" The thief blinked, lost his glassy-eyed look, and stared in shock and horror at the wallet he held.

Before he could do anything, the victim patted his pockets, then his eyes widened and he lunged toward the pickpocket, shouting, "Thief!"

The thief's mouth opened and closed, as if he was trying to come up with an explanation, but he still hadn't spoken by the time the wallet's owner reached him. But then a few other commuters took on that glassy-eyed stare and, moving jerkily like marionettes, they blocked his path.

I moved myself between the unwitting thief and the spell-casting fairy as a fight broke out and then spread from the enchanted people to the rest of the car. In the chaos, I squeezed between fighters, took the wallet out of the still-shaken thief's hand, and then wormed my way to the victim, ducking a roundhouse punch and sidestepping a misguided attempt at a karate chop.

I had to tug on the victim's sleeve a few times to get his attention before I could drag him out of the fight and give him his wallet. "I thought you might want this back," I said.

He started to thank me, but in mid-sentence he went glassy-eyed and before I could react, he had his hands around my throat. I instinctively grabbed his wrists, but he was bigger and stronger than I was, and I suspected his strength was magically enhanced. I hated hurting someone I knew was an innocent victim, but I preferred to breathe, so I kicked him firmly in the shin, then jabbed his ankle with the heel of my shoe.

He let go and backed away. Over his shoulder I saw the trouble-making fairy give me a look that could have set fire to dry grass. I felt a wave of magic hit me, but since I'm immune to magic, it had no effect. The lack of effect definitely had an effect on the fairy. Magical immunes are rare, and most of us who are in on the magical secret (instead of in mental institutions, where people who think they see fairies and elves tend to end up) work for the good guys of the magical world, a company called Magic, Spells, and Illusions, Inc. MSI doesn't sanction using magic for harm or for doing things like making other people steal for you.

The theft victim went after another guy, who pulled something that looked like a keychain out of his pocket and waved it in the air. Everyone—including the theft victim—lost the glassy look and most quit trying to kill each other, though the fight had taken on a life of its own and some people were still throwing punches even without the magical trigger. The would-be thieving fairy rolled her eyes and sighed, then slipped out of the train when it stopped at Canal Street.

The guy who'd stopped the fight must have noticed me staring. "This is coming in handy," he said, holding up the keychain-like thing. "I got it at Spellworks, and it helps counter these influence spells people have been using lately. You should get one." Spellworks was the rival to MSI, and their spokesman, Phelan Idris, had been Public Enemy No. 1 for MSI until he surrendered the week before. Obviously, losing their spokesman hadn't slowed them down, but I was surprised that they'd actually sold something that used magic to help or protect people. That wasn't their usual style, so I smelled a rat. They had to be up to something.

"I'll look into that," I said, edging my way toward a door so I could escape at the City Hall stop. Couldn't he have used his gizmo *before* someone tried to strangle me?

Once I was safely aboveground, I took a moment to collect my breath. I wasn't even back at work yet, and I was right in the middle of the magical war. It was a good thing I had a history with the company, I thought as I inventoried the damage to my appearance. I'd have been sunk if this had been a real job interview. My hair had been neatly pinned up, but pieces had come loose around my face and neck. I had a run all the way up one leg of my pantyhose, the sleeve of my blouse was ripped, and I could feel bruises forming on my neck.

Yes, this was *exactly* the way I wanted to present myself to my former employer and ask for my job back.

With a sigh, I limped across the park and headed toward the castle-like building that was the headquarters of Magic, Spells, and Illusions, Inc. Each step I took toward the building made my heart beat faster, and I wasn't sure if I was more excited or nervous. I'd been dreaming about coming back for months, and while I'd been told there'd always be a place for me, I wasn't sure where that place would be. Would I be starting all over again in the company's depressing verification department, or would I be able to pick up where I'd left off?

Sam, the gargoyle sitting on the building's awning, leaned forward when he saw me coming. "What happened to you, doll?" he asked.

"Commuting was even more brutal than I remembered," I said, giving him what I hoped was a wry smile. Then, more seriously, I added, "I didn't realize things were so bad here. They're openly using those dark spells now."

"Yeah, there's quite the crime wave going on."

"And I thought it would get easier once we caught Idris. But is Spellworks selling protective charms to fight their own dark spells?"

"That's their new thing. They're stirring things up and playin' both sides."

"So they're spreading the virus, and then selling antivirus software to fight it? I guess it's a good business model, if you have no conscience."

"And it's givin' us fits. Looks like you picked a good time to come back."

"Or maybe I picked a really, really bad time." I pushed open the heavy wooden door and went inside.

The security guard in the lobby let me pass without challenge even though I wasn't officially an employee, which was encouraging. I headed up the stairs to the executive suite where my office was—well, had been. "Oh, there you are, Katie," said Trix, the executive receptionist, as I approached her desk to ask if the boss was in. "You're late for the meeting."

"What meeting?" I asked. "I don't work here. That's why I came today, to talk to the boss about getting my job back. Or, well, getting a job at all."

"And you think he didn't know you'd be here? He wants you in the main conference room downstairs. You remember how to get there?"

I thought I did. That was where I'd had my job interview at this company, more than half a year ago. It was also where I'd first learned that magic was real and that I was immune to it, which turned out to be a pretty valuable power. I couldn't zap things into existence or make trains come when I wanted them, but I could see past any illusion, and no one could use magic on me. I headed down the stairs and hoped something would look familiar to me along the way.

If I'd thought the Union Square station was a maze when I didn't quite have my city bearings back, the office building was even worse. It didn't help that I was mentally, as well as physically, confused. How could I be running late to a meeting I didn't know about when I didn't even have a job and nobody was supposed to know I'd be at the office that day?

I apparently hadn't forgotten everything, since I rounded a corner and found myself at the conference room. I took a deep breath to steady myself before opening the door. This conference room was imposing on any occasion. The Knights of the Round Table would have felt right at home in it. The vaulted ceiling with banners hanging from it made the room look regal. It was not a room you wanted to walk into late for a meeting that was already in progress. Most of the seats around the table were taken, with the heads of almost every department in the company present.

Every one of those heads turned to look at me. I was painfully conscious of looking like I'd just been in a fight. That wasn't the best way to enter a meeting of department heads on my first day back at the company. I automatically searched the room for the person I most wanted to see, Owen Palmer, who usually represented the Research and Development department at meetings like this. He was there, looking his usual ridiculously handsome self in a dark suit. Owen was one of the company's resident geniuses and overall magical whizzes. He was also my boyfriend.

Mr. Mervyn, the boss, crossed the room to greet me. "Miss Chandler, I am so pleased to have you back with us," he said, clasping his hands around my right hand. Ambrose Mervyn is his name in modern English, but he's best known as Merlin. Yes, *that* one, King Arthur and all. I'm not sure exactly how true any of the legends are, but I do know that Merlin is real, that he really is a wizard, and that he spent about a thousand years in a magical coma before he was brought back to run the company he started all those centuries ago.

"It's good to be back, sir," I said, glad he hadn't asked why I was such a mess. Then again, this was Merlin, so he probably already knew. I had a ton of questions, namely exactly what job he thought I was doing and what role I had in this meeting. It wasn't the sort of question I wanted to ask in front of all these people. Merlin escorted me toward a seat as I discreetly tried to tidy my hair. Once seated, I was grateful for the cover of the conference table so my ruined stockings didn't show.

Owen caught my eye, smiled, then frowned and gestured toward his neck. I unconsciously mirrored his gesture and winced when I touched the developing bruises from the subway incident. I gave him what I hoped was a reassuring smile and mouthed, "I'm okay." He nodded in response, but still looked worried.

Kim, the magical immune who'd taken my place as Merlin's assistant, was seated behind the boss, her steno pad and pen at the ready, so I guessed my role in this meeting wasn't to take notes and capture action items. What, then, was I supposed to do? I'd heard about expecting new employees to be able to hit the ground running, but they usually got a job description first.

The door opened, and a tall, broad-shouldered man strode in like he owned the place. Merlin rose to greet him. "Mr. Ramsay, what a surprise," he said, his tone coolly cordial.

Most of the people in the meeting looked up with welcoming smiles, like they knew and liked the new guy. He worked his way around the table, shaking hands and exuding good-hearted warmth. In a group full of unusual-looking beings, Ramsay stood out. He appeared to be in his sixties, though considering that Merlin was at least a thousand and didn't look a day over eighty, that didn't necessarily mean anything. He wore his thick white hair slicked back into a ponytail fastened at the nape of his neck, and his fingers were covered in heavy silver rings. He'd look at home in Western wear at a Santa Fe art gallery or in a slick, European-tailored suit at a sidewalk café in Milan. In generic—but expensive—American business attire, he looked a little out of place.

When he reached me in his circuit around the table, he stopped. "I don't believe we've met," he said, holding his hand out to me. "I'm Ivor Ramsay."

"Mr. Ramsay is my predecessor as chief executive," Merlin explained. "Ivor, this is Katie Chandler."

Ramsay smiled at me in a way that made me feel he knew more about me and my role in the company than I did. "Ah, the famous Miss Chandler. I've heard so much about you." He gave my hand a firm squeeze as he shook it.

"All good, I hope," I said.

"Oh, most definitely." He gave another of those knowing smiles, this one tinged with amusement, as if he was laughing at some private joke. "It sounds like you made a big impact in the time you were here, so it's good that you're back." He finished his circuit and someone quickly moved out of the way so he could sit next to Merlin.

Merlin began with a quick overview of Spellworks's latest gambit to sell protection against their own dark spells. Then he turned to me and said, "Miss Chandler, it appears that marketing may remain our best immediate strategy to hold off their attempts to gain inroads. Do you have any ideas?"

I shook my head to clear the confusion. Being asked for a plan in a meeting I didn't know about was the kind of thing I had nightmares about, though in those nightmares I was usually wearing my nightgown—or less.

Okay, marketing, I told myself. I could do this. That was my area of expertise. "I don't have a good sense of the current situation, since I've been away awhile, but we may have passed the point of just saying we've been in business longer and, by the way, don't do bad magic. I'd have to do some research to come up with a plan." *And, you know, find my desk and get some coffee,* but I'd never say that to Merlin in front of everyone.

At that moment, a cup of coffee materialized on the table in front of me. I looked up to see Owen winking at me. Then a bright pink flush rose from his collar to his hairline, and he had to look back down at the table. I'd only dated him a short time, but I'd gotten to know him pretty well and I was fairly certain that he couldn't read minds. He did, however, have an uncanny knack for knowing exactly where I'd be and what I'd need at any given point in time—a handy trait for a boyfriend.

Ramsay leaned back in his chair, making it creak alarmingly. "What we need here is a big idea," he said, gesturing expansively. "We can't beat these guys by being subtle. It's time for an all-out effort to let the magical world know who we are, what we do, and why. We need to find a way to let everyone know this, all at once."

"Do you have any specific ideas?" Merlin asked with an edge to his voice. I knew he wasn't the type to say something like, "Well, duh!" but the concept was certainly implied in his tone.

If Ramsay took offense, he didn't show it. "I'm curious to know what your people have in mind before I offer my input," he said.

"Have you ever done a customer conference?" I asked.

"No, we haven't," said Mr. Hartwell, the company's head of Sales. "What do you have in mind?"

"We'd invite all our major customers and anyone else who's interested, show off our products, have a few educational seminars and some big rah-rah speeches from the executives. The idea is to let everyone see what's going on with the company and maybe hammer in a few marketing messages cleverly disguised as education along the way."

"Do we want to let everyone know what we're doing?" protested the head of Verification, Gregor. He'd very briefly been my boss, and he was a real ogre. By that I mean he was really, truly, literally an ogre when he got angry—horns, fangs, and all. "We don't want to show our hand to the competition."

"But we do want to show our customers what we're doing," I pointed out. "That's the general idea, to give them more confidence in us."

The gnome who headed the accounting department conjured up an abacus and began clicking beads. "It would be expensive, and our revenue is significantly down. Do we want to throw money at something like this?"

"It's worth considering," Ramsay said. "If you don't spend the money now, you may be even more behind later, and unless you've really been squandering cash since I've been away, you should still have hefty reserves." I noticed that Gregor and several other people around the table relaxed at Ramsay's endorsement.

"I think it's an excellent idea, Miss Chandler," Merlin said. "I'd like to see a plan for that, along with some budget figures and a proposed schedule. We should stage this event as soon as possible—at Midsummer, perhaps?"

I took a sip of coffee to stave off a coughing fit. It was early May, which meant Midsummer—if he was actually talking about the first day of summer the way it was referred to in the magical world—was less than two months away. We'd spent most of the year planning my old company's customer conference and had a whole staff devoted to it. "Let me see what I can come up with," I said when I was sure I could talk without gasping. On the upside, we did have magic to work with.

Merlin adjourned the meeting. People rose to leave, but Merlin motioned me to stay seated. Owen gave me a slight wave and a nod as he left, and Rod Gwaltney, director of Personnel and Owen's best friend, shot me a grin along with a thumbs-up. Once everyone was gone, Merlin said, "Now, about your new position."

Finally, a chance to clear things up. "What new position?"

He frowned, then said, "Oh, I suppose you didn't get the news yet."

"Apparently not. I only just got in the door before the meeting started."

"Dear me, you must have been confused," he said with a rumbling chuckle. "You're our new director of marketing. That will be your full-time responsibility. The job is too big to be done on the side. You'll be reporting to Mr. Hartwell in Sales, and you'll have an office there. Of course, there will also be a commensurate salary increase." He named a figure that I'm sure made my eyeballs pop out. It was a real, professional salary, nearly twice what I'd been making before joining MSI.

"Thank you, sir," I said, trying not to show my shock. "I'll do my best."

He stood and ushered me toward the door. "I have every confidence in you."

Mr. Hartwell was waiting for me in the hallway. "I'll walk you to your new office," he said. "I'm looking forward to having you in our department."

The sales department was pretty much what I remembered from my first day at MSI. Compared to the executive suite, it was noisy and chaotic, with voices coming out of all the individual offices up and down the main hallway. Most of them appeared to be talking on the phone or into the crystal ball communicator devices the magical world used in addition to phones. Mr. Hartwell walked me all the way down the hall, almost to where his office was, before opening a door for me. There was a small outer office with a secretary's desk and a door leading into an inner private office. Considering that I'd spent my last few months in a broom-closet-sized office behind the counter at a farm-and-ranch-supply store, this would be like going to work in the Taj Mahal.

"Here you go," Mr. Hartwell said. "I'll leave you to it. Let's meet this afternoon to talk about your customer conference idea. Say, three?" He was gone before I could respond, but I didn't have anything on my calendar to conflict with the meeting, unless there was something else they'd neglected to tell me about my new job.

My pulse quickened as I stepped across the threshold into my own office. I had moved up in the world in a big way. But my executive chair was already occupied by a redheaded elf woman. Her long legs were stretched out and propped on the desk, and her fingers laced behind her neck. She was staring into space, her eyes unfocused.

Apparently, I had the wrong office, which wasn't the most auspicious start to my new job. I turned to sneak out and find Mr. Hartwell, but before I made it out the door there was a high-pitched squeak behind me.

CHAPTER TWO

I whirled to see the woman sitting bolt upright in the desk chair, one hand covering her open mouth, her eyes wide with horror. "Oops," she said. Then she jumped out of the chair and faced me. She was built like a teenage model, half a foot taller than I was and with legs that seemed to go up to her pointed ears. "You must be Miss Chandler. I'm your assistant, Perdita. Sorry about that. I didn't mean to invade your space or anything, but I wanted somewhere quiet to think and you weren't here and I didn't know when you'd be here, so I didn't think you'd mind."

It took a second or two for my ears and brain to catch up with the rapid-fire flow of words. When I was sure I had everything straight in my head, I said, "Hi—Perdita, was it?"

She nodded enthusiastically. "Yes, Miss Chandler."

"You can call me Katie, please."

She nodded again. "Okay, Miss—I mean, Katie." Her mouth then moved silently, as though she was repeating my name several times to herself. "Is there anything I can do for you or get for you, Miss—Katie?"

"Not right now, thanks. I just want to get settled in."

"Okay, let me know if you need anything. I'll be right outside. And I don't mind if you want to shout through the doorway. Or you could call me. My extension's on the list beside the phone. I made a list of important numbers for you."

"Thank you, I'm sure that will be very helpful."

"And your computer's already set up. The computer guy said it was your same e-mail address and password and everything."

"Good. Thanks for letting me know."

"Can I get you some coffee, or something?"

"No, thanks. Not right now," I said, already exhausted by her energy. I hoped she was just nervous about meeting me and starting a new job. I

9

knew I was nervous about a new job and having an assistant.

"Okay. Let me know if you need anything else, because that's my job!" She paused and frowned. "Is there anything I need to be doing?"

"I'm sure I'll have something for you soon, but I have to get myself settled before I have projects to delegate. You can take it easy for a while. We'll be busy soon enough, I'm sure."

"I guess I'll just answer the phone then."

"That'll be great, thanks."

And finally, she was gone. I sat at my new desk and gave myself a moment to calm down. Once I quit feeling like everything might vanish in a puff of smoke, I got out my compact mirror to assess the subway fight damage. Red welts had formed on my neck and I had a scratch on my cheek. My hair was an utter disaster, so I took out the pins, found an elastic in my purse, and made a ponytail.

That taken care of, I was ready to get down to business. I worked my way through a surprising number of e-mails and resisted the urge to call one of my friends to squeal about getting a promotion and having an assistant. I had a feeling Perdita's pointed ears were sharp in more ways than one, and it might diminish my status as boss if she knew how overwhelmed and excited I felt. Instead, I got out a notepad and made a list of things to consider for the customer conference so I'd be ready for my meeting with Mr. Hartwell later that day.

A commotion from the outer office startled me out of my thoughts. Perdita's voice shouted, "Wait, I have to announce you! That's my job!"

A second later, a frazzled-looking Owen stepped into my office, closed the door, and leaned back against it with a big sigh. "I'm going to kill him," he said.

This wasn't quite what I'd expected in our first moment alone since he'd met me at the airport a couple of days earlier, but we were at work, and he obviously was irked about something, so this probably wasn't the time for a romantic reunion. Knowing that didn't stop my heart from fluttering at his presence. "Is that a threat or a premonition?" I asked, trying to sound casual. "And who is this marked man?"

He shoved himself away from the door and collapsed into the chair in front of my desk. "Who do you think?"

"Our friend Idris?"

Owen ran his hands through his hair, leaving bits of it standing on end. "That was too easy."

"How did he earn your wrath? I mean, this time."

"He's decided that he won't talk to anyone but me. I'm a researcher, not an interrogator, but we need whatever information he has, so I'm stuck with the job. And you'll like this part—he wants to talk to you, too."

"How did he even know I was back?"

"I think he's trying to avoid talking by making what he thinks are impossible demands."

I made a show of moving paper around on my desk, like I was terribly, terribly busy. Never mind that most of the paper was blank. "Well, we can't always get what we want, can we? He'll just have to learn to live with the disappointment."

He chuckled bitterly. "I wish I could pass on that message. Unfortunately, we need him to talk, and he won't talk unless you're in the room." With an attempt at sounding upbeat, he added, "It could be fun to shock him if he thinks you're not even in town."

"But I have a job to do! You heard what I have to pull together in less than two months. I don't have time to spend chitchatting with annoying, mildly evil people."

"It's all work toward the same goal, isn't it?" he said with a weary shrug. "We want to stop the bad guys. We might not even need your event if we can get Idris to tell us who he's working for so we can deal with him directly and shut him down. And I'm guessing from the way you looked this morning that you know how important this is."

"Yeah, I got caught in a Spellworks special."

"What was it this time?"

"Influence spell, used to make someone steal a wallet and hand it over and then used to start a fight. A bystander stopped it with a Spellworks charm. I bet it was a setup—a form of guerilla advertising."

"You're okay, though?"

"Yeah, I'm fine. I may have to wear turtlenecks in May to cover the bruises I'm sure to have, but no serious harm was done."

He leaned forward and touched my cheek, a worried frown creasing his forehead. "Does it hurt?"

I'd almost forgotten about it, but his touch brought up a whole new range of sensations that were anything but painful. "It's just a scratch," I said, trying not to swoon.

"Maybe I'd better go back to escorting you to and from work."

Was that a purely practical suggestion, or did he have ulterior motives? "If you think that's necessary," I said, aiming for a mildly flirtatious tone.

"I don't know if *you're* in danger, but with all those influence spells, I may need you to slap some sense into me." His eyes twinkled with humor and a hint of mischief.

"Well, if you insist, but let's hope it doesn't come to that."

"Do you think you're up to dealing with Idris now?"

"This may be the *best* time. It'll be nice to take it out on the person who deserves it."

"Maybe you can terrify him into talking, and then we can get all this over with and go home."

I got up and followed him out of my office. Perdita jumped when she saw us. "Sorry about that, Miss—Katie, I mean. I tried not to let him through, since you were working, but he just barged in."

I silently counted to three and reminded myself that she had no way of knowing that Owen had an all-access pass. She acted like she didn't even know who Owen was. "That's okay, Perdita. This is Owen Palmer, from Research and Development. His department creates the spells we market, so I'll need to talk to him often. You can let him in at any time, and you should always put his calls through." I knew that was safe to say, since with Owen's funny knack for knowing things, chances were he wouldn't ever show up at a bad time.

She gasped an "Oops!" and put a hand up to cover her mouth. "Oh, sorry about that. And sorry, Mr. Palmer. I didn't know." As she turned to him to apologize, she got a good look at him, and then her eyes got a funny glint to them. Owen had that effect on women. He really was quite gorgeous, with his dark hair, blue eyes, and a face worthy of a sculpture.

I cleared my throat to get her attention back to me. "And now I have to go deal with something urgent. I hope it won't take too long, but I don't know when I'll be back."

As we headed down the hallway from my office, Owen said, "So, that's your new assistant."

"Yeah. I'm really moving up in the world. But apparently not up far enough to avoid being assigned a space case." He smirked at that, but then his face quickly went back to neutral. "It's not funny," I insisted. "I'll have to spend all day with her, every day. And if you laugh, I'll call you down for meetings twice a day."

"That wouldn't be so bad." I was still trying to decide how to interpret that when we reached the dungeons.

Since the MSI building looked like a castle I expected a real dungeon—a dark, dank place in the basement, with iron bars and chains and maybe even some really scary guards. The MSI detention facility turned out to be in the middle of the building, two floors below my office. Instead of having slimy stone walls, the place looked more like a laboratory or hospital. The floors and walls were stark, sterile white.

"What, no basement dungeon?" I quipped to Owen as he waved his hand across a blank wall.

"It's too easy to escape through a basement. Here, anyone trying to rescue him would have to get through a good portion of the building, no matter which way they come, and he'd have to go back through much of the building to get out." A doorway opened in the wall, and Owen guided me into an observation room.

A long window showed Idris seated at a table in a brightly lit interrogation chamber. His hands were chained in front of him, and the chain looped through a bracket on the table. He fidgeted and glanced constantly around the room, but then he yawned, so I decided he was more bored than nervous.

Two security gargoyles stood watch next to an area of blank wall that I assumed must be another magical doorway. A tall, thin man dressed in black turned from the window to face us. "Ah, there you are," he said in a voice too deep for a body that thin. "The magical dampening field is in place, so remember that neither you nor the prisoner will be able to use magic," he told Owen. "I will observe and will send the guards if anything untoward happens." He gave a thin-lipped smile that made goosebumps appear on my arms, then waved a hand to reopen the doorway. Owen and I exchanged a look, then he nodded and we stepped forward into the interrogation room.

When he saw me, Idris's jaw dropped in shock at first, but then his face lit up with a huge grin. "Katie!" he called out. "I hope you didn't come all this way just because I asked." His grin faded when I got close enough for him to see my injuries. "Ouch. That looks like it hurts. Maybe you should see one of the healers. Oh, but I guess they wouldn't be able to heal that cut, since magic doesn't work on you, huh?"

Owen ignored him, pulling out a chair across the table from Idris and seating me before taking his own seat. He then fixed Idris with a stern, steely gaze.

Idris squirmed, but with him, you could never tell if he was uncomfortable or just fidgety. After a long silence he blurted, "It's not my fault, you know."

"What's not your fault?" Owen asked, his voice calm and almost casual.

"Whatever happened to Katie. Look, I know I've set some things on her that were not so nice, but she was never really hurt. I only wanted to scare her. I was having a little fun, seeing what she could do, you know? But I've been in here all this time, so I couldn't have made anyone attack her." He broke away from Owen's stare and turned to me with wide, pleading eyes. "You know that, right, Katie?"

I had a feeling his concern was more for the trouble that he was in than for anything he'd done to me. With my best shot at a stern glare, I said, "Actually, it *was* your fault."

He shook his head. "No, no, no, no. It wasn't me."

"But it was someone using one of your spells that caused the incident. And the guy who choked me"—I pointed to the red welts on my neck—"was under the influence of a spell you sold. So, yeah, it was your fault. This is what's happening because of your business."

He stared openmouthed at me. Then he shook his head. "But that's not what I meant."

"Then what *did* you mean?" Owen asked. "What did you expect would happen when you made spells like that widely available?"

Idris looked at him for a moment, then blinked and turned his attention back to me. "What was it like?" he asked. "What happened?"

"That's not what we're here to talk about," I said. "What we need to know is who set you up to do all this. You may not have thought it through, but I'm betting that whoever's behind this did."

Idris leaned back in his chair and attempted to cross his legs, but was hampered by the chains on his ankles. He bent over to investigate and fell out of his chair. The chains on his wrists that were bolted to the table kept him suspended, hanging at an odd angle. He twisted to try to pull himself back into his chair and somehow got the chains tangled up. I wasn't sure how he managed to get into that pretzel-like position. It took real talent to be that inept.

"Uh, guys, a little help here," he called from under the table. "Wow, Katie, you really ripped your stockings. And did you know you were bleeding? Well, not anymore. It's dried. But there's a scab on your leg where your stockings are torn."

Owen jumped out of his seat and went around the table to help Idris. I tensed, suspecting a ruse or a trap, but Idris really was stuck. Owen untangled the chains, then pulled him back into his chair.

Owen rolled his eyes at me as he came back to his own seat. "Now, as we were asking," he said with a sigh of waning patience, "who was behind this scheme to put you in business?"

Still giggling, Idris said, "You two are so great together! And I can't believe you haven't thanked me yet."

Owen and I glanced at each other. He looked as confused as I felt. "Thanked you for what?" I asked Idris.

"For getting you two back together. If I hadn't been teaching Katie's brother magic—and I didn't know he was your brother until you told me— then Owen wouldn't have had to go to Texas, and you two wouldn't have worked things out."

The tips of Owen's ears turned red, not in the adorable bashful way, but more in a "Mount Vesuvius is about to erupt" way. Owen tended to focus on a single thing to the exclusion of everything else—including food and sleep—if there was something he wanted to accomplish. That made Idris, who couldn't sustain a single thought for more than a minute, very frustrating for Owen to deal with. "Who. Are. You. Working. For?" he asked through clenched teeth. If it hadn't been for the magical dampening field, I had a feeling that the room would have been vibrating with barely controlled magic. As it was, I still detected a slight magical tingle.

Idris flinched. "I told you, I don't know. I dealt with the money lady. She's the one who might know who the boss is."

We knew who "the money lady" was. The trick was finding a way to capture and question her. She was a highly respected magical banker—not someone you could drag off the street and throw into the backseat of a car. She knew how to work both the magical and mundane systems.

"Do you know why they set you up in business?" I asked.

"To make money. Duh."

"But have you made money?" Owen asked. "You've had a lot of expenses, setting up those retail locations and buying actual advertising space instead of just using illusion. What were sales like?"

"Those ads were really cool, weren't they? And they all have my picture, so I'm famous!"

Before Owen could blow a gasket at yet another digression, I hurried to ask, "But did they work? Did you have a lot of customers?"

Idris shrugged. "I don't know. I just developed the spells." He turned to Owen. "I mean, do you know how much money each of the spells you come up with makes?"

"I keep spreadsheets," Owen said dryly. "I also think about what might happen if people actually use the spells."

"Back to the why question," I said, "there has to be a reason for Spellworks beyond the money. If it was just money, it wouldn't have been this secretive."

"I was just trying to come up with spells that MSI didn't have, and that leaves a pretty limited range, let me tell you," Idris said with a weary sigh. "I was stuck with the things you aren't willing to do, and I figured there had to be someone who'd want something like that, but couldn't find it. And, generally, the people who want something like that aren't smart enough to come up with it on their own."

That almost made sense—which was a change for Idris. It sounded like he didn't know Spellworks had changed its focus to protective spells. I took another approach. "Surely you've tried to guess who was behind it all," I said, leaning forward and dropping my voice to a conspiratorial whisper. "I mean, someone as clever as you are must have some idea, even if you don't know for sure."

I expected him to puff his chest out with pride, sit up straighter, or otherwise react to my compliment, but instead he went deathly pale and shrank into his chair. "No, no, I have no idea," he muttered, shaking his head back and forth.

"Not even a teeny little guess?"

"No!" he shouted.

I glanced at Owen and saw that a little crease had formed between his eyes. He chewed his lower lip for a moment, then said softly, "We can't protect you from him if we don't know who it is." Idris just sat and shuddered. "Or I suppose we could turn you loose since you don't seem to know anything," Owen added with a shrug.

Idris came halfway out of his chair. "No! Not that! I've failed. And I don't think they need me anymore. They've got the spells already, and I don't think it's about the spells."

Owen and I exchanged a glance of triumph. Finally, a slip.

"What is it about, then?" Owen asked.

"I didn't say anything."

"Yes, you did," I said.

"I didn't mean it."

"What are you so afraid of?" I asked. "And why did you agree to work for someone who scared you that badly?"

Idris resumed his usual arrogant posture—part nonchalance and part smug superiority. "Who said I was afraid? You're the ones who are afraid. You're afraid of my spells. That's what all this is about, isn't it, Palmer? You couldn't stand the competition when I worked here, so you got rid of me, and now you can't stand the competition so you try to make it seem like it's illegal. But the truth is, it's time we got past the days of having a monopoly in the magical world."

"He doesn't know anything," I said to Owen.

"Yeah, you're probably right. This has been a waste of time. Want to get some lunch?"

"Lunch sounds good." Without even acknowledging Idris, we got up and left the interrogation chamber. Once we were in the observation room, I glanced at the window and saw that Idris had gone pale and was back to fidgeting.

Owen also looked at Idris through the window. "I'm starting to suspect that the whole thing—him surrendering and all—was just a ploy to drive me stark, raving mad," he said. "And I think it's working. We talked to him for, what, ten minutes? That was enough to make me have violent fantasies—and I'm not a violent person."

"He wasn't that bad," I said, keeping my voice calm and soothing. A really powerful wizard was the last person you wanted having violent fantasies. "This was actually pretty focused, for him. He might not know as much as we think he does."

"I think he knows more than he's telling."

"Maybe he's stalling for time," I suggested. "Right now he's safe. If you got everything you wanted from him, we might quit protecting him. Try letting him stew for a few days. That might panic him into being more cooperative the next time we talk to him."

Owen raised an eyebrow. "Have you always been that sneaky?"

I watched as gargoyle guards unclasped the chains from the table and took Idris away through a hidden door on the other side of the interrogation room. "You know," I said, musing out loud, "I have a feeling that either he really doesn't know anything other than that he got himself into something bigger than he was prepared for, or he knows exactly who's in charge, and he's more afraid of that person than he is of you or Merlin."

Owen nodded somberly. "That's what I'm afraid of."

CHAPTER THREE

After a quick lunch with Owen, I returned to my office to find Perdita out to lunch. I had a feeling this would be the most productive half hour of my day, so I went straight to work, but I'd barely gotten started when she bounced into my office, breaking my concentration. "Got anything you need me to do?" she asked.

"Not yet. Could you please hold any calls and barricade the doors for the next couple of hours? I've got a meeting to get ready for."

"Except for that Owen guy, right?" she asked with a giggle.

"I doubt he'll be back today. He knows I'm busy."

She must not have caught the "busy" hint, since she plopped into my guest chair and draped one long leg over the arm as she twirled a red ringlet around her finger. "He is so cute. What does he do in R and D?"

"He runs Theoretical Magic."

"Oh, so he's smart, too. That's absolutely dreamy. I wonder if he has a girlfriend."

"He does." I tried and failed to hold back a smug smile.

She groaned. "Of course he does. The good ones are always taken. Do you know who he's dating?"

I knew I was probably risking bad karma by enjoying this so much, but I couldn't help myself. I'd never been on this side of a conversation like this before. "Me," I said simply. The color fled from her face, which made the sprinkling of freckles on her nose stand out like new copper pennies. "Oh!" she gasped as a hand flew up to her mouth. "I'm so sorry, Miss Chandler. I didn't think—I mean, you don't seem like—well, he's so hot, and you're— oops, I didn't mean it that way. You're cute, and you seem nice, and you have to be really smart to have your job, so I'm sure he sees something in you, even if you're not magical." Apparently realizing that she was only making matters worse, she shut her mouth and got out of the chair. "I'll hold your calls and keep out visitors," she said as she left, shutting the door behind her. I returned to my work with a sigh.

By the time three o'clock rolled around, I had sketched out a proposed agenda for a customer conference and had a list of questions to ask Hartwell. When I emerged from my office, Perdita was at her desk, filing her nails. She immediately dropped her nail file. "Sorry about that, I just snagged a nail and wanted to fix it before it got worse or caught on something."

"That's okay. I haven't given you anything to do, so I won't bust you for not doing it. I'm going to a meeting with Mr. Hartwell." I started to leave, but turned back. "I don't suppose you know Mr. Hartwell's first name? I don't believe I've ever heard it used."

She swiveled in her desk chair to face the crystal ball communications thingy. After waving her hand over it for a few seconds, her slanted eyebrows shot up even higher than they normally went. "Oh, wow. Yeah, I can see why he goes by Mr. Hartwell," she said. "I'm not sure I even know how to pronounce that. And I thought Elvish was a tongue-tangler."

"Thanks anyway." I'd never been sure that Hartwell was human. He reminded me of an animated Ken doll, molded from plastic rather than flesh. The apparently impossible first name might have been a clue, but given what I knew of Perdita so far, his name might have been "George."

After an hour spent getting the details I needed from Hartwell to plan the event, I said—trying not to hyperventilate at the thought of what I'd have to pull off—"And now I'd better get back to work. I have plenty of it to do."

"It's almost the end of the day," Hartwell said with a genial plastic grin. "You might as well meet the whole gang you'll be working with."

He came around his desk and took my arm, so I didn't have a choice but to go with him. All the offices we passed were empty, though, so there wasn't much of anyone for me to meet. When we got to the other end of the hallway, he threw open a door, and a shout of "Surprise!" erupted from within.

Hartwell turned to me and said, "Welcome to the department, Katie." The rest of the sales staff raised their glasses to me, and then they went right back to enjoying the party that was already in progress.

"Wow, this is, um, well, unexpected," I said. "You didn't have to do this, really."

"Nonsense!" Hartwell said. "We love any excuse for a party."

And it certainly looked like they knew how to party. The conference room had been turned into the setting for a Hawaiian luau. Floating ukeleles played island music, and I could have sworn I heard the sound of the ocean. On the other side of the room, a group of gnomes did the limbo. They had a rather unfair advantage at the game.

Selwyn Morningbloom, an elf salesman I'd met on my first day at MSI, strolled over to me, wearing a Hawaiian shirt that probably registered on a Geiger counter. "You haven't been laid, have you?" he said.

"Excuse me?"

He snapped his fingers, and a fragrant floral garland appeared in his hands. He draped it around my neck. "Lei-ed, get it?" he asked with a wink. "But let me know if you need help with the other version." Fortunately, he danced away from me before I could spit out the response that was on the tip of my tongue. I never thought I'd see an elf in a Hawaiian shirt doing the hula.

Perdita bounced over to me, carrying a drink in a coconut shell with a paper umbrella coming out of it. "Hey, boss! You look like you could use a drink!" she said. Then she stumbled and would have spilled the drink all over me if someone hadn't pulled me aside at that exact moment. I didn't need to look to see who it was. Only Owen had that kind of timing, and I recognized the feel of his arm around me.

"Oops!" Perdita said, waving her hand to make the mess on the floor vanish. Then she handed me the coconut shell. "Most of the drink is still in there, though." She giggled and swayed, and I got the impression she had a head start on me. "Oh, hi, Owen," she said, giggling again. "Want me to get you a drink?" She hiccupped and giggled. "They're really good—nice and fruity. You can barely taste the rum."

"No thanks, I'm good," he said.

One of the sales guys grabbed her arm and pulled her into a dance. I took a tentative sip of the drink and went into a coughing fit. "How much rum would it take for her to taste it? Want a sip?" I held the shell toward Owen.

"No thanks, I'll take your word for it."

"Nice timing, by the way. What brings you down here?"

"I was looking for you. Since the day was nearly over I thought I'd see if you were ready to go, and no one answered the phone in your office, so I came down."

"And you're just in time for the party."

"Yeah." He didn't sound too enthusiastic. I patted him on the arm and looked for a place to stash my coconut shell before the drink ate its way through and got on my skin.

He looked warily around the room. "Are you ready to go?"

"I'm the guest of honor. I probably shouldn't go until I'm sure they don't have something planned."

I had to admit, though, that they probably wouldn't have noticed if I left. The party was in full swing, nearing Saturday night at the fraternity house levels. I edged my way through the crowd toward Mr. Hartwell. Shouting to make myself heard over the gnome standing on the conference table and singing "Tiny Bubbles" into a karaoke microphone, I said, "This was really nice of y'all to do for me. Thank you."

"You're not leaving already, are you?" Hartwell asked. Somewhere along the way, his suit had been replaced by Hawaiian garb, and if I wasn't mistaken, he was a few shades more tan. That made him look even more like the Malibu Ken I used to have.

"Do you need me for anything else? I don't want to run out on my own party, but someone's waiting for me."

He glanced over my shoulder to where Owen hovered in the conference room's doorway. "Palmer's welcome to join us. It would do him good to mingle a bit, get to know the rest of the company instead of hiding in his lab like a mad scientist."

I'd reached the point that I wanted to be out of there before someone conjured up a whole roast pig, and definitely before someone started a fire dance. "I do have some things to take care of," I hedged.

"Okay, then, if you must go, let's do the presentation now." He went over to the gnome singing karaoke, and I made my way back to Owen.

The music stopped, and Hartwell spoke into the microphone. "As you all know, we're here to welcome the latest member of our team, Miss Katie Chandler, our new marketing manager." There was a round of enthusiastic applause. "Katie, why don't you say a few words?"

With a helpless glance at Owen, I reluctantly stepped over and took the microphone. "Wow, um, I wasn't expecting anything like this. Thank you for making me feel welcome, and I look forward to doing whatever I can to help you all be even more successful in your sales efforts. So, um, thanks."

Before I could hand back the microphone and get away, music started up again. Voices from the crowd called out, "Sing for us!"

I shook my head. "Trust me, y'all really don't want me to do that. I'd break your machine." They didn't relent at my warning. I glanced over at Owen, who stood leaning against the door frame, his arms crossed over his chest and a big smile on his face. I considered dragging him up there with me, since he actually had a very nice voice and, unlike me, could even find the tune, but putting him in front of people like that would lead to me having to do CPR, and that would spoil the party for everyone.

I looked around for the screen that had the words to the song, but I couldn't see anything. It occurred to me that they were using illusion, which meant I couldn't see it. I definitely didn't know the song that was playing. In desperation, I said, "Let's all sing together!" and pointed the microphone at the crowd. Several sales department extroverts stepped forward immediately to sing drunkenly into the microphone. I held the microphone for them and swayed to the music, acting like I was part of the group. By the time the chorus started, they'd taken the microphone from me and were enjoying the full spotlight. I slipped away, grabbing Owen on my way out of the conference room. The entire department kept singing.

We went back to my office to shut down my computer and get my bag, and then made it unnoticed past the conference room door on our way to the exit. "No wonder we're losing market share to Spellworks, if that's how they spend their time," Owen said as we left the office building.

"I think this was a special occasion. It was nice of them to welcome me that way."

He draped his arm across my shoulders and gave me a squeeze. "It's not that I don't think you're special, because you know I do, but something tells me that bunch doesn't need much of an excuse for a party. They probably throw a party like that when they open a new box of pencils."

Deadpan, I said, "Yeah, that would be Pencilfest. I saw pictures in someone's office."

"Seriously?"

I nudged him in the ribs. "No. Just kidding. But I wouldn't be surprised."

"If it happens, call me. I have to see that for myself." We went down the stairs into the subway station and separated to go through the turnstiles. Then he took my hand. For Owen, this was a lot of public affection. He must have really missed me.

Rod was already in the station, waiting on the crowded platform. He greeted us with a wave, and I couldn't help but smile. All of us together at a rush-hour subway station was like old times. That was where I'd first seen Owen and Rod, before I met them. So much had changed since then.

"Nice lei," Rod remarked with a grin.

I'd forgotten I still had it on. I pulled it off and shoved it into my bag. "Sales department party," I explained.

"Are you excited about the new job?" he asked.

"Yeah, but why didn't you clue me in? Surely you knew."

"I didn't know until a few minutes before that meeting—not long enough to give you any warning. You know what the boss is like. He lives in a different time stream from the rest of us." Rod gestured toward my neck. "I meant to ask this morning, what happened to you? Those bruises look nasty."

With a sigh, I tried to explain in a way that wouldn't sound odd to any eavesdroppers. "Oh, just the competition in action, but this time I was an innocent bystander."

He winced. "Yeah, there's been more of that lately." Then he said to Owen, "I wonder if anyone will try to fix sporting events."

"*You've* tried to fix sporting events," Owen reminded him.

"I've merely tried to give a friendly nudge or two to improve the accuracy of umpires," Rod argued.

Neither of them noticed a tall, leggy blond woman nearby on the platform giving Owen the eye. That wasn't unusual, as gorgeous as Owen was, but most women gave up pretty quickly when he didn't notice the flirtation. This woman kept staring hard enough for her gaze to burn holes through me on its way to him, and then she grinned and licked her lips.

CHAPTER FOUR

A train arrived, and I herded the guys to the car just behind us. With all the bad magic flying around these days, I thought it was safest to assume the woman was trouble. She was a woman on a mission and shoved her way through the crowd to get on the same car with us.

The train was jam-packed, and as long as the she-wolf didn't have a clear line of sight to use magic on Owen, he'd be safe. She hadn't come close enough to snag anything of Owen's to use to focus a spell, and I doubted she planned to enchant everyone else in the car. Or maybe I was just being paranoid. I wondered if Spellworks offered an anti-man-stealing-bitch charm.

Owen, Rod, and I clustered around a pole, Owen hooking the arm holding his briefcase around the pole while he continued holding my hand. "I bet you didn't miss this," he said to me as the train lurched forward.

"I missed some of it," I said, giving his hand a squeeze.

He smiled, a flush of pink spread across his cheeks, and he opened his mouth as if to speak, but then suddenly he frowned and winced, then shook his head and swayed forward. At the same time, all the little hairs on my arms stood straight up—a sure sign that someone was using strong magic. I turned to see the she-wolf standing at the next pole, her heavily glossed lips moving silently in what was surely a spell.

Owen was susceptible to magic, but what this chick hadn't counted on was that his girlfriend was immune. I repositioned myself so that my body blocked as much of Owen as possible from her line of sight, then I squeezed Owen's hand tighter, in part to give him strength and encouragement and in part to keep him with me.

"You know how I said I might need you to slap me out of it?" Owen gasped, attempting a smile that failed completely. Beads of sweat were breaking out on his forehead.

"What's going on?" Rod asked.

"She-wolf over there sees something she wants," I said, gesturing with my head. I looked Owen in the eye. "I'm trying to play human shield, but you're bigger than I am so I can't block it all. Can you fight it?"

"I'm doing my best. I should be stronger than she is." He swayed toward her as if pulled by a magnet, then jerked himself back to me.

"Can you do anything?" I asked Rod.

"I'm trying, but there's something odd about the spell. It's getting past my shields."

Owen's palm was sweaty in my grasp, and I felt his grip weakening. His eyes went glassy and unfocused. I was losing him. "Oh, hell," I muttered under my breath. Desperate times called for desperate measures. I released my hold on the pole, grabbed his necktie and pulled him to me for the biggest kiss I'd ever given him. There was more than one kind of magic, and I hoped that a particularly hot kiss from a girlfriend he'd been separated from for months was more powerful than any hocus-pocus.

He resisted for a second or two, then he melted against me, returning the kiss. It wasn't the ideal setting for a heavy make-out session, and the whistles and catcalls from the other subway riders were a little distracting, but my plan seemed to be working.

After a while, someone nearby cleared his throat, then Rod's voice said, "Whenever you two want to come up for air, I got a protective shield to work, and I think your number one fan has given up."

The train jerking to a halt forced me to let go of Owen and grab the pole again. I heard a squeal of feminine outrage from the far end of the car and noticed the she-wolf getting off the train with her arm hooked through the elbow of a glassy-eyed man. She tossed a glare at me over her shoulder as she left. I knew they said that all was fair in love and war, but there had to be *some* limits, and magic definitely seemed unfair.

Owen was still a little shaky when we reached our station, and he walked with his arm tight around me. Once we were aboveground and had some breathing room, Rod asked, "What happened back there, man? Don't tell me that chick was stronger than you are."

Owen shook his head. "I don't know. I don't think she was particularly strong. There was just something about that spell I'd never run into before—like it sapped my will to resist. That was the strongest compulsion I've ever felt. I need to get a copy of that spell so I can come up with a counter or protective charm."

"I've never seen anything like that, myself, and I know attraction charms," Rod said.

It was only then that I realized that Rod must have stopped using his attraction charm. Ever since I'd known him, he'd maintained a charm that made every woman around find him terribly attractive. It didn't work on me, of course, but I had felt its effects when I'd temporarily lost my magical immunity. This had been the first subway trip I'd ever taken with Rod when he hadn't had women eyeing him.

"Speaking of attraction charms…" I said to him.

He raised his hands in mock surrender. "I gave them up entirely. I'm a new man. Turned over a new leaf, and all that."

"And you're afraid of Marcia," I teased. Rod was dating one of my roommates, and I couldn't imagine Marcia putting up with every woman around drooling over her boyfriend.

"Yes, I am afraid of Marcia. Besides, when you've got the best woman in Manhattan—present company excluded, of course—at your side, why bother setting all the other women up for disappointment?"

I wondered if he'd also dropped the handsome illusion he usually wore. He'd certainly continued the self-improvement program he'd started before I left town. Now he had a good haircut, his skin looked better, and his teeth had been whitened.

"Do you think this is another setup for selling protective charms, demonstrating the product in a real-world setting?" I asked.

"I doubt it," Rod replied. "I don't see much of a market for something that keeps hot women from throwing themselves at you. Now, if they were using hags to demonstrate the potential dangers, then you might be on to something."

"Maybe they're marketing a charm to women to help them keep their men from being snared by these spells," I suggested.

Our banter had given Owen a chance to recover, and now he looked more like himself. His eyes were still a little glassy, but from what I knew of Owen, that meant he was mentally analyzing the spell he'd just encountered and was thinking of ways to fight it.

The two of them walked me to the front door of my apartment building, then Rod said, "I'll make sure Romeo here gets home safely without running off with any loose women. Say hi to Marcia and tell her I'll call later."

"Will do. And I'll see you two tomorrow."

I unlocked the front door, checked the mail in the entryway, then headed upstairs to my apartment. I'd missed this dingy old building while I was in Texas, but more for what it represented than for what it really was. Our apartment was far too small for three people, and there was no such thing as personal space. I was relieved to get home and find that my roommates were still out. That gave me a moment of privacy and quiet.

Well, maybe not that much quiet, I thought, wincing at the sound of an argument coming from upstairs. I turned the television on to drown out the noise while I changed out of my work clothes. When I came back to the living room, the TV was showing a live news report from an attempted bank robbery. The cameras zoomed in on a man being arrested while the reporter said, "The suspect, who was identified by patrons in the bank as the robber, surrendered to police, but claimed to have no memory of robbing the bank. Police still have not recovered the stolen money."

I groaned and sank onto the sofa as the newscast returned to the anchorman, who began talking about an unusual crime wave in the city. New York may have the reputation of being a dangerous place, but it's really not that bad except in certain areas. This type of crime wave was definitely unusual.

In a burst of panic, I switched to the national news to see if this was showing up anywhere else. The last thing I needed was my parents knowing about a crime wave in New York when their little girl had just returned to the big, bad city. We needed to put a stop to this as soon as possible before someone really got hurt—and before my parents came to drag me home. It was bad enough that people's lives could be ruined by crimes they hadn't been aware of committing. What would happen if one of these people under influence spells hurt or killed someone and then had to live with that? The magical people could buy the Spellworks charms to protect themselves, but what about ordinary people?

Nothing about a major New York crime wave appeared in the five minutes I had the national news on, and then my roommate Gemma came home. She kicked off her high-heeled shoes right inside the front door, then limped to the bedroom without a word.

"Rough day?" I called after her.

Mumbled cursing came from the bedroom. A moment later, she reemerged, wearing yoga pants and a tank top. "What is it with people these days?" she asked.

"What happened?"

Instead of answering, she inspected a bloody patch on her elbow. "Do we have a first-aid kit?"

I got off the couch and ran to the bathroom for the kit, then waved off her hands when she tried to take it from me. "You can't see your own elbow properly, no matter how much yoga you do," I said, grabbing her arm to hold it steady so I could dab the wound with antiseptic. "What happened to *you*?"

"Oh, just some jerk running out of the subway station. He slammed me against the wall." Then she must have noticed my cuts and bruises. "What happened to you?"

"Something along those lines. I got caught in a subway fight this morning." Out of sheer habit, I left out the reason for the fight. I wasn't yet used to my roommates being in on the magical secret.

"So, tell me, Katie, is all this stuff a magical thing?"

"I think so," I said, putting a bandage across her elbow. "We're working on it, but be careful, and if you notice something weird, get out of the way."

The door opened again and Marcia, my other roommate, came in. She, at least, didn't seem to be damaged or disgruntled. As soon as she saw me, she grinned and said, "So, how'd it go?"

"How did what go?" I asked.

With an exasperated sigh, she threw down her briefcase. "Your job? You know, the one you were going to beg for today."

"Oh, yeah, that." So much had happened that I'd almost forgotten I'd started the day unemployed. "The bad news is, I didn't get my old job back. The good news is I got a promotion, and I'm already busy with a big project."

"Congratulations!" Marcia said. "I don't suppose that promotion came with a raise?"

"It did. A nice one."

Marcia and Gemma exchanged glances, then Marcia's grin got even bigger. "Great! That'll work out great."

Gemma jumped off the sofa. "You mean we got it?"

"We got it!" The two of them jumped up and down like cheerleaders after a touchdown.

"What did we get?" I asked warily.

"Katie, honey, don't bother to unpack, because we're moving," Marcia said.

"Moving?" I asked. "Where?"

"One floor down and to the back," Gemma said. "The people in one of the two-bedroom, two-bathroom units downstairs are about to move, and as soon as we knew you were coming back, we went after it. The rent's higher, but if you got a raise, that shouldn't be a huge problem. We could always find a fourth, if we need to. We'd still be less crowded than the three of us are in here."

"I'll pay more to have my own room," Marcia said. "One of the bedrooms is a little smaller and doesn't have a connected bathroom."

"Just think," Gemma said with a wistful sigh, her face glowing, "two whole closets. Two bathrooms."

"What do you say, Katie?" Marcia asked.

The lack of space was one of the downsides to life in New York. "When do we move?" I asked.

"We should be able to move two weekends from now, if we can hire some movers," Marcia said. "That shouldn't be too hard, since they wouldn't need a truck. We just need someone who can carry things down stairs."

"We do all have boyfriends," I reminded her.

"Oh, right. I guess they could do a lot. The sofa bed can be pretty heavy, though."

"We have boyfriends who have magical powers."

Gemma and Marcia looked at each other, then both of them laughed. "I keep forgetting about that," Gemma said. Gemma and Marcia had only learned about magic at the beginning of the year, when they got drawn into all the complications associated with my life. Gemma hadn't known that the guy she'd been dating was actually a wizard, and as far as I knew, she still didn't know he'd spent nearly a century as a frog under an enchantment. Marcia had met Rod before she knew about magic.

"I guess the guys could levitate things down the stairs, huh?" Marcia said.

"Or they could snap their fingers, and everything in our apartment would disappear and reappear in the other apartment," I suggested.

"They can do that?" Gemma asked.

"I'm pretty sure Owen can."

"That is so cool," Marcia said with a grin.

*

Owen was waiting on the sidewalk in front of my building the next morning. He smiled at me, but didn't quite meet my eyes as he fell into step alongside me to walk to the subway station. "Sorry about yesterday," he said, his cheeks flaming as he stared straight ahead.

"Don't worry about it. You couldn't help it. But there is a way you could make it up to me."

He frowned. "How?"

"Do you have a spell for moving furniture?"

"Usually, I just push."

"I meant up or down stairs. When you moved into your place, did you actually carry everything up the stairs, or did you do the abracadabra routine?"

"Abracadabra wouldn't be very effective for teleporting or levitating heavy items. That's more of a rabbit-in-a-hat spell." The crinkles at the corners of his eyes told me he was teasing me. "But yeah, there are spells for moving."

"What are you doing the weekend after next?"

"Let me guess, I'll be moving furniture."

"Only if it's not too hard, and if you're free."

"Who's moving?"

"We got dibs on a two-bedroom unit downstairs in the same building. And I figure that instead of us hiring big, burly men to carry our furniture down the steep stairs, their muscles rippling and shining with sweat while we gaze upon them in admiration, you might prefer to snap your fingers or flick your wrist or whatever the spell calls for while you say the magic words."

"Yeah, Rod and I could move you easily. You don't even have to pack. And if Rod isn't too eager, I bet the big, burly men threat would work on him."

I hugged his arm. "Thanks. You're the best."

The sound of honking horns on a New York City street wouldn't have caught my attention, but when it was accompanied by the sound of screeching tires and loud, metallic bangs, I whipped around to see what was happening. An armored car was careening toward us, knocking aside every other vehicle in its path. I grabbed Owen's arm and shouted his name, but instead of looking at the armored car, he turned to stare at the crowd.

I wasn't sure what he was looking for, but apparently he saw it, for he tugged his arm out of my grasp and moved his hands in a subtle pushing gesture while he said soft words that I didn't understand. I did understand the surge of power that radiated from him. Soon, the out-of-control armored car resumed a reasonable course, gradually moving to pull over without hitting anything along the way.

Before the armored car came to a complete stop, Owen took off, chasing someone down the sidewalk—probably the magical villain. I figured the real action would be wherever Owen was going, so I ran after Owen, abandoning the brewing shouting match between the armored car driver and the drivers whose cars he'd hit.

He had a head start and was much faster than I was, so I could barely see him ahead on the crowded sidewalk. There was a blast of magic so strong that even the normal people who had no idea magic existed paused and shuddered, and then everything came to a total halt.

I groaned and muttered, "You know you're not supposed to do that," while I wove my way through commuters frozen in time to find Owen stepping forward to grab the arms of two young men.

"It's only for a second or two," he said as I reached his side. "And it was necessary."

"You don't have to get defensive," I said, just as time started moving again. Owen's captives jerked in shock when they suddenly found themselves in custody. They struggled, but Owen was using more than muscle power to hold them.

"Hey, man, what is this?" one of them said, playing innocent. "You can't just grab people like this."

"And you can't just hijack an armored car in broad daylight on a busy city street," Owen said, managing to sound calm even though he was breathing heavily.

"You can't prove anything," the other captive said. "Help! Police!" he shouted, then added, "And try explaining this to the police."

"I won't have to. Did you really think I'd let anyone see or hear you?"

Owen asked, raising an eyebrow.

Two men dressed all in black suddenly appeared in the empty space next to me on the sidewalk. Funny, I hadn't noticed any major magic. "We'll take it from here, sir," the shorter man said, waving a hand. Silver chains materialized and looped around the captives' wrists.

Owen released them and stepped back. "Do you need a statement?" he asked. "I witnessed the incident. I'm with MSI."

"We may contact you later," the taller man said. Then he frowned at Owen and asked, "Aren't you James and Gloria Eaton's boy?"

"They brought me up."

A smile broke out on the man's craggy face. "I thought so. You probably don't remember me, but I was at your house a few times when you were a kid. Tell James and Gloria that Mack said hello. It looks like they trained you well."

The shorter man didn't seem as happy to meet Owen. "You're Owen Palmer?" he asked.

"Yes. Why?"

"What is your involvement here?"

Owen shrugged. "I was here when it happened."

"Three more incidents probably happened while we've been here," Mack said impatiently. "We'd better get these two off for a hearing. We're staying busy these days. Thanks for the help."

The men in black and their captives disappeared. I felt a little shiver in the fabric of reality as everything went back to normal. Sirens sounded behind us, arriving to deal with the wrecks in the wake of the runaway armored car. "What was that, *Law and Order: Magic*?" I asked.

"Something like that," Owen said. "They detain and deal with people who use magic for illegal purposes. The mundane court system can't deal with this sort of thing."

We resumed heading toward the subway station. I was still catching my breath after my sprint, but Owen looked like he hadn't even strained himself, aside from the fact that his hair was a bit windblown. "Can they do anything about the innocent people who've been forced to commit crimes?" I asked.

"They have ways of dealing with that."

"Good. That was worrying me."

I noticed as we entered the subway station that everyone looked wary. Not that New Yorkers were normally full of friendly good cheer to strangers, but they usually just went about their business while pretending other people didn't exist. Now they were eyeing each other with suspicion. Even without knowing about magic, they knew that *something* was wrong.

Once we got on the train, I realized that something was different. The Spellworks ads running along the top of the car now promised protection from the magical crime wave, showing off charms like the keychain I'd seen the day before. The ad's tag line said, "Stepping up to protect the magical world," suggesting that they had to step up because MSI hadn't. That took some nerve.

I nudged Owen and pointed to the ads. He frowned as he read them. "I want to get a look at those charms," he said. "Maybe then I could reverse engineer to find out how those influence spells work."

Fortunately, nothing else happened on the way to work. It was a relief to get to my office and find that things were reasonably quiet and calm. In other words, Perdita wasn't in yet. I took advantage of the moment of peace to search the Internet for venues that could hold our conference.

"Whoops!"

The shout from the outer office told me that my peace and quiet were probably gone for the day. I went to the doorway and found Perdita on her hands and knees, an empty paper coffee cup on the floor nearby, and a widening brown stain on the carpet. She looked up at me and winced. "Oh, hi, Miss—I mean, Katie. Don't worry. I'll get this cleaned up in no time. I'm an expert on cleaning spells. I have to be because I'm always spilling things. I guess I shouldn't have tried conjuring the coffee in midair while I was walking. This was going to be a peppermint mocha for you."

"That was very thoughtful of you," I said. "Maybe it would be best for you to conjure it up on my desk—on the side away from the computer."

She waved her hands over the stain, which then vanished. "Good idea, Miss—I mean, Katie. I'll get you another coffee in a second. On your desk."

"Okay, let's give that a try."

She bounced to her feet and followed me into my office, where she snapped her fingers, whispered some words, and a coffee cup appeared on the end of my desk away from my computer. It wobbled and teetered for a second—and I grabbed my planner and notepad to get them out of the way—then it steadied itself.

Once I was sure it wasn't going to tip over, I reached for the cup and took a cautious sip. "How do you like it?" Perdita asked. "I've been trying to duplicate all the seasonal specials so I can have them any time."

"It's perfect," I said. "Thanks."

She lit up. "I'm glad you like it. Now, what do we need to do today, boss?"

I gestured for her to take a seat, then I sat at my desk, took another sip of the surprisingly good magical mocha, and said, "We need to do the impossible."

"That's practically the company motto."

"This time, we have to do real-world impossible. We need to find a place that will hold a couple of thousand people for an event a little more than a month away. Venues that size are usually booked years in advance. We may have to pitch tents in Central Park and then use magic to hide them."

"That would actually be kind of cool."

I leaned forward, resting my elbows on my desk. "Yeah, it would, wouldn't it? And it might be less complicated. If we use a conventional meeting space, they'd get suspicious if we managed to put together an entire exhibit with no need for labor or catering, and I don't see how we could hide that magically."

"Yeah, I guess that's true. I'm so used to hiding magic that I forget about what people must think about what they see."

I chewed on the end of my pen as I thought for a moment. "So, if we used real meeting space, we'd have to hide parts of what we're doing— maybe make it look like a software users' group meeting—without hiding the fact that we're having an event. But if we create something magical, whether it's tents in the park or boats in the harbor, we could just hide the whole thing. Can we do that?"

"My cousin Edlyn had her wedding in the park, and it was totally invisible to outsiders. She didn't want to get married while using an illusion to make herself not look like an elf, so we veiled the wedding and used a compulsion spell to make people not want to go near that area. A couple of my uncles were able to do it, so I'm sure this company could take care of it."

"This could work," I said with a grin. "Thanks, Perdita."

My brief moment of triumph faded when my phone rang and I saw Kim's name on the readout. After steeling myself with a deep breath, I answered the phone. "You need to come up to the president's office right away," she said. "It's about the incident this morning."

CHAPTER FIVE

I assumed that Kim meant the armored car incident, but I didn't know why Merlin wanted to talk to me about it. All I could think of was that Merlin wanted to know about Owen and that time-stopping spell, which he wasn't supposed to use.

"I have a meeting upstairs. Don't know when I'll be back," I told Perdita as I left. Heading up to Merlin's office, I felt like I was back in elementary school and had been summoned to the principal's office, and even though I knew I hadn't done anything wrong, I still got a sick feeling in my stomach. If this was about Owen, I wasn't sure what I should say.

When I reached Merlin's office, I was surprised to find Ramsay there. "Ah, there you are, Katie," Merlin said when he noticed me standing in the doorway. He sounded friendly enough, so I let myself relax slightly. Merlin gestured and the door shut behind me. "Please, have a seat," he added.

"What's going on?" I asked.

"Far too much," he said. "I'm sure you've noticed the many criminal incidents associated with magic use."

"Yeah. It's getting pretty wild west around here."

"And I understand you were present for one of these incidents this morning."

I glanced from Merlin to Ramsay. Neither of them looked angry or more concerned than I'd expect them to. Ramsay was leaning back in his chair, one booted ankle resting on his knee in the masculine version of crossing his legs. "Yes. But I walk down Fourteenth Street to get to the subway, and that's a pretty busy thoroughfare. That increases my chances of being present for an incident."

"You were with Owen Palmer, weren't you?" Ramsay asked.

I couldn't read his face at all. He seemed so casual and neutral, but suspiciously so, like he was trying not to show anything. "Yes, Owen lives near me, so we usually go to work together," I said, trying not to sound confused or irritated by his question.

"And I understand you two handled what could have been a serious situation."

"Owen did. I just shouted a warning."

"Do you know how he caught them?"

I fought to sound just as casual as Ramsay. "He figured out who was doing the spell and blocked it, then chased the people responsible. Someone sprinting down the sidewalk was a dead giveaway."

If I wasn't mistaken, Merlin was intensely uncomfortable with this questioning. He even fidgeted, which was something I'd never seen him do. That turned my confusion about these questions into suspicion. "There have been questions raised," Merlin said with an overly bland neutrality that conflicted with his body language, "and it is best if we know the answers before they're asked officially."

Ramsay leaned further back in his chair. "I tend to hear things in an unofficial capacity, so I thought I'd give you people a heads up. With all the incidents going on, and with as much trouble as the company has had countering these spells, it's interesting that Owen was able to counter this one on the fly."

He made it sound like an accusation. I shrugged. "I'm not the one to talk to about how magic works. I just see hands waving and feel the tingling. You'll have to ask Owen what he did."

Ramsay turned to Merlin. "I'd be interested in hearing Owen's viewpoint."

Not looking at all happy about it, Merlin nodded and stood up. His shoulders were stooped, like they carried a great weight, as he went to the phone and called Kim to have Owen come up. I'd never seen Merlin act like this. If this Ramsay guy bothered him so much, why was he putting up with him?

"What's your take on these incidents, Katie?" Ramsay asked me. "Maybe what we need here is an outside perspective."

I wasn't sure how much I really wanted to share with Ramsay. "Advertising those protective charms is a good strategy for Spellworks," I said. "No matter what's going on with these incidents, they now look like they're the ones to save us from all the chaos."

"And meanwhile, MSI looks ineffectual," Ramsay concluded. "That is a very good point, Katie. I can see why you're so valuable to this company. I wish I'd had you on my side when I was in charge here." Although it sounded like praise, I got a funny feeling from the gleam in his eyes as he looked at me that what he'd left unsaid was something along the lines of, "so I could have done away with you before you became a problem."

The door opened and we all glanced over to see Owen come in. Ramsay got up to shake his hand and clap him on the back in greeting, as though he hadn't just been questioning Owen's actions. "Good work this morning, son," he said. "Too many of these guys have been getting away, so it was good to get a couple in custody." He guided Owen to the conference table with a hand on his back. "Now, maybe you could help us understand a few things."

Owen looked as confused as I felt. "I'd be glad to help," he said.

"What did you do to stop that spell affecting the armored car?" Merlin asked before Ramsay got a chance to take over the discussion.

"Nothing special. I just blocked all spells coming from that direction until I could tell who was doing it. I didn't really counter the spell."

"How close are you to having some good counterspells?" Ramsay asked.

"Not as close as Spellworks, from the looks of things. I don't have any protective charms ready to go on the market, if that's what you're asking. But then I'm at a disadvantage, since I didn't create the bad spells in the first place."

"That's what you think they've done?"

"I know they created some of these spells because I have the original spells they sold, back when it was an underground enterprise. And now they're selling the charms. It's pretty obvious, even if they're now playing innocent."

"That's a big accusation to make," Ramsay said, leaning forward and resting his elbows on the conference table.

"And one they're sure to deny," Merlin added.

Ramsay propped himself on one elbow while gesturing with his other hand. "I've got to tell you guys, this doesn't look good. The Council is concerned. They're wondering why MSI should get the position of prominence when you can't deal with this situation. You're losing customers left and right. Not to mention the fact that the mundane world is starting to ask questions. I got a call from our person in the mayor's office just this morning." I was totally at sea here. I'd never heard of this Council.

"Our customer conference should help with our image," Merlin said. "How is that progressing, Miss Chandler?"

Oh, great, I thought. Now my event was being viewed as the key to stopping a catastrophe I didn't understand? "I've decided on a venue. That's the first step. Then we'll need to decide what we want to announce or showcase."

"I would be happy to help if you need any suggestions or feedback," Ramsay said.

Merlin's lips thinned, and when he spoke, he faced me instead of turning to Ramsay. "I am sure Miss Chandler is quite capable. Now, unless you have any additional Council gossip to share, Ivor, we should all return to our duties."

If Ramsay felt chastised or took offense, he didn't show it. He just grinned as he stood and said, "Don't worry, I'll keep you in the loop on anything I hear from the Council world."

This sudden dismissal took me by surprise. I'd been sure they were suspicious about Owen's use of unauthorized magic, but they hadn't brought that up at all. What had the interrogation been about, then? It was like Ramsay wanted to see how much we knew, or let us know how much he knew. Whatever it was, my instincts told me there was something fishy going on with Ramsay.

Owen walked with me away from the executive suite. "Is there some backstory I'm missing?" I asked him when we were out of earshot of the others.

"What do you mean?"

"Don't tell me you didn't notice the cold war between Merlin and Ramsay. I felt like I needed to put on a sweater, it got so icy in there."

Owen frowned and tilted his head in thought. "It wasn't that bad, was it? As far as I know, there's no bad blood between them. Ramsay suggested we bring Merlin back, and he retired voluntarily."

"You know, he would be ideally placed to indulge in a little industrial espionage," I mused.

"Don't be ridiculous, Katie," Owen said, sounding truly annoyed as he came to an abrupt stop on a landing and faced me. "I know he can seem overbearing, but I've known him most of my life, and I've never had reason to doubt him. Ramsay's not on the Council anymore, but he's still really well connected."

I backed off by changing the subject. "What is this Council, anyway?"

"The 'law' part of the magical law and order, assuming you consider the people doing the enforcement on the streets the 'order' part. The Council makes the rules about the use of magic and deals with violators."

"Then where have they been all this time? They should have stepped in long before now instead of leaving it up to us."

"It's not quite the same as the mundane justice system. It's hard to explain—it's more like the United Nations and their enforcement of international law."

"So they pass resolutions, but don't do anything serious until it's a crisis that leads to an international outcry?"

He gave a wry smile. "That's pretty much it. MSI has always been the de facto ruling body of magic, in a practical sense, backed by the Council, and that mostly means they leave us alone until things are really bad, and then they get in the way."

I groaned as we resumed walking down the stairs. "Maybe I should go back to Texas."

"Only if I can come with you."

"You wouldn't be able to use much magic there."

He held the stairwell door open for me. "Right now, I don't care. I'd find something else to do. I've got money, and I'm good with the stock market." His voice took on a dreamy quality, as though this was something he was seriously contemplating.

"But could you really leave everyone here to deal with all this? And that's if you could even get away without it following you. Remember, I tried that, and it didn't work."

He sighed. "Of course not. It was just a thought. So I guess I'd better get back to work. We need to develop our own protective charms so it at least looks like we're addressing the situation."

"And we'll need something to demonstrate or announce at the conference."

He came to a dead stop in the middle of the hallway. "What?"

"The centerpiece of an event like that is usually a big announcement of something the company is launching, so there's at least one thing everyone will be talking about. Do you have anything up your sleeve?"

His forehead creased as he thought. "Well, there's a stain remover spell. I guess you could have some fun demonstrating that."

"Only if you want to look like a magical laundry commercial. That's it?"

"Some recipes using conjured ingredients, a few upgrades of earlier spells, adjusted to use less power or to last longer."

"How about your dragon-taming spell?"

"Most people don't have much use for that."

"There are dragons living under the city, so you never know when it might be necessary," I reminded him. "You could announce the threat— you know those legends about alligators in the sewer system? They're not alligators! And then you announce the solution to it."

"Those dragons aren't really a threat."

"Yeah, because you tamed them. You're still checking on them and playing with them, aren't you?"

He turned red enough that I was sure I could feel the heat radiating from his face. "I feel responsible for them. I've been researching dragon refuges to find a good home for them. I'd feel bad about using them for something like this."

"Well, if you can't give me something splashy, I might make you give a speech."

All the color drained from his face. "I'll see what I can come up with," he said a moment later, his voice faint. "And that means I *really* have work to do."

*

I had plenty of my own work, which would have been easier if I worked in a department that believed in work. Even when there weren't official departmental parties, everyone went up and down the halls, visiting with each other. I knew you had to be somewhat outgoing to be good at sales, but this was ridiculous. I resorted to having Perdita veil me and tell people I was out when they wandered by to chat.

Life gradually settled down into something that passed for normal, relatively speaking. Though, the way things were going lately, it wasn't that much weirder inside the walls of the magical corporation than it was outside. City officials were having press conferences and talking about task forces to look into the unusual crime wave. Those of us in on the secret didn't feel like we had much of an advantage.

I was used to being targeted by the bad guys, but now I was in less danger than the average person because those awful influence spells didn't work on me. While I had the occasional scary moment, I was never forced to commit a crime. All I had to do was get out of the way the moment I felt magic at work and hope that someone with a Spellworks protection charm was nearby. Even some of the MSI employees had started carrying those charms.

Owen's workload and obsessive tendencies meant he was working crazy hours, and I didn't even see him going to and from work anymore. The times I ran into him at work, he looked tired, distracted, and more rumpled than he usually let himself be in a business setting. Given the current crisis, I was afraid I'd sound petty and selfish if I insisted on him paying attention to me. When your boyfriend's trying to save the world, it's no time to whine, "But what about us? What about *me*?" no matter how much you miss him.

A week after I'd come back to work, I got a phone call at the office from him. "So, you're still alive," I quipped, trying to keep my voice from sounding too bitterly sarcastic. *Supportive, not snarky*, I reminded myself.

"Sorry, I've been busy."

"I know. But I miss you."

"Then maybe you'll want to see me now. Can you come by? I've got something I want to show you."

"It wouldn't involve something splashy with dragons, would it?"

"Dragons in the office? Even I'm not that crazy. But I can show you something that will give you the picture."

"I can't wait. I'll be there in a moment."

I was heading down the hallway toward the department exit when Hartwell stepped out of the conference room and shouted in a magically amplified voice that rang throughout the entire department, "All hands! Conference room! Now!" I sprinted toward the exit, hoping to avoid yet another party. I got caught by a burst of streamers flying from the conference room, but nobody called me back.

When I got to Owen's lab, Owen and his assistant, Jake, were leaning over something on the lab table. Owen looked frazzled enough that I felt bad for resenting his recent distance. He pulled a metallic green streamer out of my hair. "Let me guess, another sales department party?"

"Yeah, but I narrowly escaped." I gestured toward the streamer he held. "They only winged me."

"How come we don't get parties?" Jake asked.

Owen looked at him with one eyebrow raised. "Can you imagine this department at a party?"

Jake nodded knowingly. "Yeah, now that I think about it, I guess it would be a bunch of people lined up along the walls, looking uncomfortable. But I think they'd like it if you showed movies. They wouldn't be forced to talk to each other."

"I'll consider it, if we ever get to a point when we're not so busy. We can celebrate once we've beaten the bad guys." Then he turned to me and said, "And you're not here to talk about parties."

"In a sense, I am. A really, really big party. What have you got for me?"

"You said you wanted dragons."

"I said I wanted something splashy to show off."

"And what's splashier than dragons? Wait right here." Grinning ear-to-ear, he ran into his office.

I turned to Jake. "What's he up to?"

Jake, also grinning, said, "Just wait. You have to see this."

I wasn't sure quite what I expected Owen to come back with—maybe a giant old magical tome, or perhaps a miniature dragon. Instead, he held a small white cat with a spattering of big, black spots on her body. It was his cat, Eluned, who'd been dubbed Loony by Rod.

"I didn't realize it was Take Your Cat to Work Day," I said.

"I'm using Loony to demonstrate proof of concept. She's a lot smaller and a lot less messy than a dragon. You see, that spell I used to tame the dragons could be used in a modified form for pet obedience training. You could end indoor accidents and keep Fido from chewing your favorite shoes."

"I could see where that might be popular."

"Allow me to demonstrate. You know how notoriously untrainable cats are—there's a reason we refer to wrangling a bunch of people who all want to do their own thing as herding cats. But with the right touch of magic, that all changes." He handed Loony—who looked utterly bored by these proceedings—over to Jake. Jake took her to the opposite side of the room and put her down. She immediately yawned and stretched, then began grooming herself. Owen said some magic words and did a few complicated hand gestures, then called, "Loony, come here!"

The cat interrupted her grooming to shoot across the floor and hurl herself at Owen's legs, where she purred and gazed adoringly up at him.

"Ta da!" Jake said with a flourish.

Owen knelt to scratch behind Loony's ears. "Making a cat obey is actually quite impressive on a conceptual level, even harder than dragons, really. However, cats aren't big enough to demonstrate to a large crowd. But we can demonstrate it with the dragons, which looks a lot more impressive than making a dog sit, fetch, and roll over. You can do that even without magic."

"But you've been training your cat like a dog her whole life. She obeys without magic," I said. To demonstrate, I knelt and said, "Hey, Loony! Come here, sweetie!" She came straight to me and rubbed her face against my ankles.

"She likes you," Owen said. "That doesn't mean the magic doesn't work. You saw what happened with those dragons—one minute they were trying to roast us, and after I did the spell they wanted to play. Now they even do tricks. I did that spell in a panic, with probably a bit too much power behind it. Since then, I've analyzed what I did and figured out a way to control it better. If the spell works on dragons, it should work on household pets that don't breathe fire. Is that what you wanted?"

"It should get their attention," I said.

"We have a few other things to announce, but I'm working on ways to make them look more spectacular."

"Keep this up, and you'll turn into P. T. Barnum in no time. I take it that's why you've been so scarce lately."

"No, not really. This was just taking a break. There wasn't much work to do on this spell. But coming up with protective charms that work against the influence spells is killing me. The whole department's on it, and we can't make anything work consistently, not even when we reverse engineer the Spellworks charms." He called Loony back, scooped her up into his arms, and stood up. "And now I'd better get back to work." I waited for him to say something else, like maybe making plans to see each other. My birthday was the next day, and I'd have thought he'd make time for me then, no matter how busy he was. Surely he'd know. After all, he had ESP and his best friend ran the personnel office. I reminded myself that the current crisis trumped my birthday and forced myself to give him a big smile. "Thank you for coming up with something splashy for me."

He was already back at work before I left the lab.

*

I got to work the next morning to find that Rod must have put out a memo on me. Perdita had decorated my office with birthday balloons.

She'd gone a bit overboard, as there was barely room for me to squeeze in, and I had the strongest feeling I would suffocate. Once I got rid of a few of the balloons, I found a vase full of long-stem red roses on my desk, alongside a giant box of Godiva truffles. The card with the flowers and candy said "Happy Birthday" with a P.S. saying, "Don't even think about sharing the chocolate. It's all yours." It wasn't signed, but I recognized Owen's handwriting, since he was the only person I knew in my generation whose writing looked like something out of a Victorian penmanship primer. My eyes grew suspiciously watery as I realized he hadn't forgotten, after all. I chose a favorite truffle, then put the box in my bottom desk drawer, under a layer of empty file folders.

Late that afternoon, there was a light rap on the frame of my office door. I looked up to see Mr. Hartwell. "Can I borrow you for a second?" he asked.

I didn't think that he needed to borrow me if I reported to him, but what I said was, "Sure." I got up and followed him down the hallway.

He talked the whole time about the upcoming conference and some people in the department he thought might be helpful, and I wished he'd let me know before he scheduled a meeting so I could have been more prepared. Then he opened the conference room door, and there was a loud shout of "Surprise!"

A Mexican-style fiesta was in full swing in the conference room. The banner hanging from the ceiling wished me a happy birthday, and a mariachi band made up of self-playing instruments played the birthday song, to which the entire sales department staff, along with Merlin, Trix, Owen, Rod and his assistant Isabel, and a few other friends from the rest of the company, sang along, mostly off-key. When the song ended, confetti and streamers materialized in midair and descended on us.

Owen came up to me. "Sorry about this," he whispered. "I wondered if I should have warned you."

"It's okay. In fact, it's kind of nice." I smiled at him and added, "I like surprises. Especially surprises involving flowers and chocolate. Thank you." He blushed adorably.

Perdita walked over with exaggerated care and handed me a frozen margarita. "See, I didn't spill a drop," she said proudly, and then she accidentally tilted her paper plate, sending a pile of nachos to the floor. A quick-thinking Owen made them vanish into thin air before they hit the ground. "You'll have to teach me that spell," Perdita said, batting her eyelashes at him. "I could get a lot of use out of it."

Although I had grown weary of the near-daily parties, I was impressed with the attention to detail. Someone had gone to a lot of effort to do all this. Even if it required only a snap of fingers to make it happen, there was still thought and planning. "Do you know who put this together?" I asked

Owen.

"No idea. Perdita called and told me to be here and to invite anyone else you were friends with."

"Oh. Can you excuse me a second?" I meandered over to Melisande Rogers, who, from what I could tell from my previous experiences with this department, involved herself in everything. "This is a great party," I said to her. "Do you know who does all this?"

"Hartwell's admin, Rina," she said with a twitch of her head in the general direction of the woman in question. "She lives for this stuff." She dropped her voice. "To be totally honest, it's driving us all stark raving insane. We can barely get our work done with Hartwell wandering the halls the way he does. Throw in a daily party, and it's a miracle we accomplish anything."

"If she can do this, then what's she doing working as an administrative assistant?" I asked. "Don't you have caterers and party planners in the magical world?"

She shrugged. "Beats me. We smile, say thanks, and go along with it because it keeps her happy."

That explained a lot. I noticed people gradually drifting away and realized I wasn't the only one who'd been trying to escape the constant parties. Then, as I sipped my margarita, I got an idea that would probably benefit all of us. Rina was the perfect person to put in charge of a theme, decorations, and food for the conference, and that should keep her busy enough not to plague the rest of us with daily parties.

Unfortunately, most of my friends left the party before I had a chance to talk to them. That was a downer. They couldn't even stick around to talk to me at my birthday party? "Where'd everyone go?" I asked Owen.

"They had places to be. We should probably get going, too."

"Going where?"

"It is your birthday. Don't you want to go out to dinner?"

"I didn't know we had anything planned."

He looked a little sheepish. "I was afraid to make plans. With us, making plans is like tempting fate. Just making a reservation is asking for disaster. Who knows what might happen?"

I grabbed his arms in mock panic. "Don't even think it. If we get attacked by a roving gang of wild monkeys in the middle of a restaurant, it'll be your fault for having said anything."

We both laughed, but the scary thing was that in our dating history, the wild monkey scenario actually wasn't that far-fetched. We'd already had dates involving a magical restaurant fire, a mysteriously appearing hole in an ice rink, dragons, and a celebrity fight in an upscale restaurant. Wild monkeys would be business as usual for us. "Then forget I said anything," he said.

Once we'd left the office building and were in the subway station, Owen went on the alert, as though he was watching for an incident and ready to step in if necessary. "How many of these guys have you busted so far?" I asked him while we waited for a train.

"About one every other day, I think. Mostly, I counter whatever they're doing and hold them until the enforcers show up. I hate to admit it, but those charms do seem to be helping. They don't stop the actions, but they keep things from getting out of control."

We got off at our usual stop, and he led me in the direction of his house. "Where are we going?" I asked.

"You'll find out when we get there."

"Am I dressed okay?"

"You'll be fine. Can you imagine me choosing to go somewhere too fancy for what you're wearing now?"

He did have a point. He was wealthy and classy, but too much fuss usually made him intensely uncomfortable. Before I could respond to him, there was a loud bang nearby, something that sounded like gunfire.

CHAPTER SIX

Owen shoved me against the nearest brick wall and shielded me with his body. We both held our breath as we waited for the next shot. Then he laughed when the noise turned out to be a delivery van backfiring. "Maybe I'm a little jumpy after seeing all these magical incidents," he said with a crooked grin and a flush spreading across his cheekbones.

"If you think the threat's magical, maybe you should let me shield you," I reminded him. "They can't hurt me that way. But I do appreciate the chivalrous thought."

"I wasn't sure if it was magical or not. It could have been someone influencing someone with a gun to shoot," he said, then added, somewhat defensively, "I put up a shielding spell."

"Well, okay then, as long as you were thinking."

"I never stop thinking," he said with a wry roll of his eyes. "That's my problem."

I looked up into his eyes, which were just inches away from mine. He gave me a roguish grin that was somewhat out of character for such a nice boy, then bent and gave me a thorough kiss that a moment later was disturbed by a hooting call from nearby.

"Hey, you two, get a room!"

Owen immediately pulled away from me while turning bright red. I looked up to see a gargoyle perched on a shop awning.

"Oh, hi, Rocky," I said, feeling my own face grow warm. "What are you doing here?"

"On patrol. This is my sector."

"Has it been busy?" Owen asked.

The gargoyle shrugged. "Eh, not so much today. Things seem to be taperin' off. But I'd better get back on the beat. You two be careful. Save the canoodlin' for when you're safe at home." He flew back to his post.

45

We headed in the general direction of Owen's house, but before we got to his place, he opened the door to the neighborhood's historic tavern. The hostess directed us up the stairs at the back, and as soon as we reached the top of the staircase, a cry of "Surprise!" rang out. This had to be a record, two surprise birthday parties in one day.

"Don't hate me," Owen whispered in my ear as my friends came toward us. "I didn't know until the last minute that they were doing anything at work, and this was all Gemma's idea."

Gemma greeted me with a hug and put a glass of wine in my hand. "You looked like you were really surprised," she said. "He must have done his job without spilling the beans."

"And one day I may even forgive him for that." But I laughed and kissed him on the cheek to show that there was nothing to forgive, even though I wouldn't have minded spending some time alone with him. That was a precious commodity these days, and I had a feeling it wasn't going to get better anytime soon.

*

I barely saw Owen during the week since both of us were so busy, so I was looking forward to our move on Saturday because it meant I'd actually get to see him. "Are you sure we don't need to pack?" Marcia asked on Saturday morning as we waited for the guys.

"That's what Owen said," I told her reassuringly. "He and Rod have something planned."

Owen showed up first with a satchel slung over his shoulder, from which he took a folded booklet that I recognized as a retail version of an MSI spell. "Wait, you're actually using a spell?" I asked.

"I always use spells. I just usually don't need the instructions because I'm one of the people who developed them in the first place. But this one is from before my time—a real classic—and it's not one I use often enough to have memorized."

Gemma pulled the booklet out of his hands and flipped through it. "This is what a spell looks like? It's not what I was expecting."

"The big leather tomes with parchment pages are inconvenient to carry around," Owen said dryly, taking his booklet back from her. "And scrolls tend to get squashed."

Rod arrived next. "Oh good, you got the spell," he said to Owen. "Do you have all the other stuff?"

Owen patted his bag. "Right here. When Philip gets here, we can start. It'll go faster if we combine power."

"This all sounds so exciting," Marcia said. "We'll get to see some real magic being done."

"It's not as exciting as you'd think," Rod said.

"Maybe not for you, but, hello! It's magic! That's exciting for me."

When Philip arrived, he greeted us all with a bow, then kissed Gemma's hand. "I presume you're providing leadership in this endeavor," he said to Owen. "I will be happy to provide power, but it has been a long time since I have worked magic of this nature."

"Yes, I'll guide the spell and draw on you two," Owen said. After a quick tour of the new place, he took a large sheet of paper out of his bag and sketched out a floor plan of that apartment, then made notes as he asked us where we wanted things to go. We went back upstairs, where he took several vials out of the bag and handed them to me, along with a sheet he tore from a notepad. "I've written which colors go with which rooms," he said. "I need you to go down there and sprinkle the right color of powder around the perimeter of each room." When I got back upstairs after carrying out my task, the guys were using a similar powder to color code the items to be moved.

When they were done, the three wizards went over to the corner where Owen had his floor plan laid out. Owen dabbed colored powder on the floor plan, with the colors corresponding to the way I'd sprinkled the powder downstairs. The three guys joined hands, Owen murmured foreign words, then I felt the surge of power. The powder on the floor plan glowed and rose to hover above the paper, then the powder on or around the furniture began glowing. Owen said something else and gave a wave of his hand, and then there was a loud pop. We all blinked, and when I opened my eyes again, everything was gone.

"That's it?" Marcia asked, blinking furiously.

"You wanted it to be more difficult?" Rod asked.

"I put a bandanna around my hair and wore my old clothes," she said. "I thought it might be easier than usual, but I thought it might still be a little like moving."

"I can bring something back up if you want to carry it down for yourself," Rod offered.

I was about to suggest that I treat Owen to lunch when his cell phone rang. After a short conversation, he said, "I hate to run out on you just as the real work is starting, but I've got to go. There's been an incident involving a spell I haven't countered yet, and they can't get in and do anything about it until they get the spell stopped."

"This is more of that weird stuff that's been going on?" Gemma asked.

"Yeah, more of the same."

"Do you need my help?" I asked.

I could tell from his expression that he was about to automatically say no, but then he paused to reconsider and said, "I might, since you wouldn't be affected by the spell."

Philip stepped forward, but Owen shook his head. "No, too big a risk. I know they're gunning for you, and if anything happens to you, then there's no way we're getting that money out of their hands." The bad guys were using Philip's family's financial business to fund their work, after the current owner's ancestor had turned Philip into a frog to get him out of the way. We were still working on getting the business back for him. "You and Rod stay here and keep an eye on Marcia and Gemma. I'll call you if I need you."

I was halfway down the stairs when I realized I was still dressed for moving. Whatever was going on, I hoped I didn't die or make the news because I didn't have time to change.

When we got to the Diamond District uptown, I saw that you wouldn't have to be in on the magical secret to know there was trouble. The street was lined with police vehicles, their lights flashing. A couple of fire trucks blocked traffic, and there was even an ambulance. People hovered behind the official vehicles, trying to see what was going on.

"Come on," Owen said as he tugged me through the crowd. "And don't worry, no one can see us."

Just inside the police perimeter we came across one of the men in black who'd handled the armored car incident. I felt like we should have flashed badges at each other as we entered the crime scene, but he and Owen just nodded in greeting. "Hi, Mack," Owen said. "What's the situation?"

Mack gave a world-weary sigh. "Some idiot decided it would be fun to knock over a jewelry store by getting an innocent delivery guy with a hand cart to crash through the glass door, bust open a display case, and grab the ice. Only problem was, that glass is pretty damn hard to break. It went into shards, injuring the delivery guy, who's still inside. When the perp's victim couldn't pull off the crime, the wizard panicked and blocked the whole place magically so no one can get in or out. The cops think it's a hostage situation."

"Which is the part you're having trouble with?"

"That damned blocking spell. We can't get past it, either."

"Is the wizard inside or out?" I asked.

"We think he's inside. That spell isn't coming from anywhere out here."

I turned to look at Owen, and he immediately shook his head. "No. No way. No how."

"What?" Mack asked, watching us with narrowed eyes.

"I'm a magical immune," I said. "I could get in there."

"Oh, now this gets interesting," Mack said, scratching his chin as a smile twitched his lips. "Very, very interesting."

"What good would it do for you to go in there?" Owen asked.

"For one thing, I could get a first-aid kit in to that injured deliveryman. And for another, doesn't generating a magical field like that require constant effort and attention if he hasn't laid all the groundwork for a continuous ward?"

"You've spent way too much time with me," Owen said, pride and dismay warring on his face.

"Think about it, Owen. I could distract him, which gives you a chance to break his spell, and we could end this thing."

"Sounds like a good plan to me," Mack said with an expansive shrug. "You got anything better?"

Owen ran his hands through his hair and glared at the scene for a while before turning to me. "You'll be careful?"

"No, I'm planning to recklessly endanger myself just to annoy you."

That almost made him smile, and he had to fight to keep looking stern. "Okay, then. How do you plan to explain your ability to get in?"

"The nonmagical people will think I'm a medic, and the wizard should be baffled, which is what we want, right? Then when it's all over with, I can slip out with the other hostages and you can make me disappear. You'll be cleaning all this up anyway, won't you?"

"Oh, yeah, we'll be cleaning up," Mack said. He waved his hands and an EMT jacket and hat appeared in them. He helped me with the jacket, then waved his hands again. A medical bag materialized. "You know what to do with this?"

"I know basic first aid—Dad made us all take a course at the store, since we work with sharp objects and poisons. The main thing is to stop or slow the bleeding—I mean, aside from coming up with a way to distract our wizard, which is my primary objective."

"How do you plan to do that?" Owen asked. He still looked intensely unhappy about the whole situation.

"I'll have to improvise," I said with a shrug that I hoped looked more casual than it felt. In spite of my show of bravado, I was going shaky with the realization of what I was about to do. "It all depends on the wizard himself."

Mack took my arm and said, "Let's get this done," but before he could lead me away, Owen stepped forward and kissed me fiercely. As Mack led me toward the besieged jewelry store, I glanced over my shoulder at Owen, who looked like he was contemplating sending me back to Texas, and then I was standing in front of the shop.

I had to clear my throat a couple of times before I could get enough sound to my voice to call out. Not that I really needed to say anything. I felt like my heart was pounding loud enough that they could hear me inside. "Medic!" I shouted through the broken glass of the door. "I'm here to see the injured man. I'm not armed. I'm just here to help." When there wasn't a response, I took a few deep breaths, and then with a trembling hand, I reached out and opened the door.

It was a tiny store, but with the merchandise they sold, they didn't need a lot of space. Once my eyes adjusted to the dim light, I saw that there were four people inside: an older man in a perfectly tailored suit, an equally well-dressed young woman kneeling on the floor next to a uniformed delivery man who was lying still, and a wild-eyed young man wearing a hooded sweatshirt.

I figured the agitated young guy had to be our wizard. He backed away from me as I made my way into the shop, one of his hands crooked in an odd position—maybe as part of doing his spell. "How–how did you get in here?" he stammered. That verified my assumption—only the wizard would know that it should have been impossible for anyone to get inside.

I gave him the blankest, most innocent look I could muster and raised the medical kit. "The police let me through, since I'm a medic," I said. While he was still stammering and trying to find a way to say that wasn't what he meant without revealing that he was using magic, I knelt beside the injured man. "How is he?" I asked the woman tending to him.

"I–I put my scarf on that wound on his arm," she said. Then she glanced over her shoulder at the wizard and whispered, "He's got a gun. Aren't you afraid?"

Ah, so that's what that funny hand position was about. He'd conjured an illusion of a gun and was "holding" it. I didn't see illusions, so I just saw his hand bent in a way that looked very uncomfortable. "I don't think he'll shoot us," I whispered to the woman.

Just then, she ducked and screamed, and the deliveryman jerked as though he was reacting to something loud or frightening, I turned to see the wizard holding his gun hand out in front of him, like he was taking aim. "Next one won't miss," he said, breathing heavily.

"Oh, did you shoot?" I asked. "I didn't notice." He frowned and brought his gun hand up to his face, inspecting it. I shrugged and went back to the injured man.

I carefully peeled back the scarf—which had a designer logo and probably cost more than my entire outfit—and saw that the gash on the man's arm was bloody, but not deep and not bleeding badly enough to be life-threatening. I wouldn't have to stretch my first-aid knowledge to play medic. "The bleeding seems to have slowed, so I'm not going to put much pressure on it, in case there's some glass in the wound," I said, making my voice calm and reassuring. I wrapped the wound in gauze and handed the scarf to the woman. "Soak it in cold water, and the blood should come out," I told her. "If that doesn't work, try club soda."

"I don't know what happened," the deliveryman mumbled groggily. "I just suddenly went through the glass door."

"Someone must have pushed you," I said as I bandaged the other cuts on his arms and legs. Considering the amount of glass he'd gone through, I thought he was extremely lucky not to have a severed artery.

That part of my mission dealt with, I tried to think of something I could do to distract the wizard. He was obviously disconcerted by my arrival—pacing anxiously, his hands shaking, and his shoulders twitching—but since Owen and Mack hadn't yet stormed the place, I figured he wasn't distracted enough.

The wizard loomed over me. "How did you—" he began, then shook his head. "Why are you –"

"I told you, I'm a medic," I said, standing up and facing him. "There's an injured man here. You may be willing to sit around all day, but I figure he appreciates the help. It would be even better if you'd let him go as a sign of good faith. They might be less likely to shoot you as a way of resolving this."

"They can't shoot me," he said, rolling his eyes.

"Oh, okay," I said in the exaggeratedly soothing tone you use with crazy people. "But what are your plans? I mean, you're not going to spend the rest of your life here. You'd run out of food. And, believe me, they're not getting bored out there. They're not going to just wander off when the game comes on and let you sneak away."

"Shut up!" he screamed, pointing his non-gun finger at me. I felt a wave of magic, but it didn't do anything to me. He frowned at his finger and gave it an "is this thing on?" shake before whirling to point it at the older man. The older man's eyes went glassy, then he squawked like a chicken.

"Father!" the young woman cried out, rushing to his side.

The wizard turned back to me. His breaths came faster and more shallow. If he kept this up, I wouldn't have to worry about a distraction because he'd pass out. To help that along, I said, "You do know the Special Situations squad is out there, right? You don't want to go up against them. They can handle all kinds of stuff, if you know what I mean, and I'm pretty sure you do." I hoped he wouldn't know I'd made that up.

He raised his imaginary gun at me and braced it with his other hand. "Shut up! You don't know anything! I'm more powerful than everyone out there!"

"Everyone?" I asked, raising an eyebrow and allowing myself the slightest hint of a smile. "Really? Are you sure about that?"

"I'm not talking about guns!"

"Neither am I."

His eyes went so wide, they seemed to be mostly whites, and his breathing sped up to sharp little pants. Momentarily forgetting his hostages, he turned to look out the window, and I figured that was my chance.

I spun with a high kick, hitting his hands and, I hoped, knocking away the imaginary gun. He knew the gun was just an illusion, but the other hostages didn't. The older man threw himself on the floor, grabbing thin air and then holding his hands up as though aiming at the wizard. While the wizard was still shaking his hands and cursing, I dove at him in a flying tackle that would have made my brothers proud, knocking him to the ground and digging a knee into his stomach. *Okay, Owen, is that enough distraction for you?* I thought.

It must have been, for a moment later, the door flew open and Owen and Mack ran into the shop, both of them wearing official-looking police jackets. At the same time, two other guys wearing FBI jackets burst in through a back door. Both of them held their wrists up, showing wide rubber bands like those fundraising and disease-awareness bracelets. They weren't carrying guns, which led me to believe that they weren't real FBI agents. They looked more like TV FBI agents. That or the Swedish water polo team. They were blond, and brawny, with toothpaste-commercial smiles.

The non-FBI guys seemed surprised to see Owen, Mack, and me. For a moment, they lost their pretense of authority as they looked at each other in confusion. "How did you get in here?" one of them blurted before the other could elbow him in the ribs and give him a stern shake of the head.

The second man then glared at Owen and Mack. "We'll take over here," he said. "FBI. I think we outrank you local guys."

"It's not your jurisdiction," Mack said.

"It's part of an ongoing investigation," the fake FBI guy shot back.

His partner cleared his throat and said, "I think they know what we are. I recognize them. One of them's with the Council and the other one is that Palmer guy from MSI."

"What the heck?" muttered our suspect, and I remembered that I was still sitting on him. I figured I was light enough that it wouldn't kill him if I stayed there until we worked all this out.

"Since you seem to know who we are, who, exactly, are you? You're obviously not FBI," Owen said.

"We're here to help," one of the blond guys said. "We were able to get through the barrier with these." He pointed to his rubber bracelet. "So we thought we'd help with the situation."

The delivery guy and the store staff were all looking at us like we were nuts, and I could hardly blame them. "Um, guys?" I said to the four pseudo officials who were posturing above me. "We have an audience. You can work out who the hero is later."

"I'll take it from here," Mack said, stepping forward. "I'm the real official here. Thank you for your assistance."

They looked like they might argue, but then the apparent leader shrugged and backed away. "We'll leave it to you," he said. The other guy frowned before following his lead.

I eased myself off the wizard and let Mack yank him to his feet. While

Mack bound the wizard's hands with silvery cords, the older man who worked at the store said, "He had a gun, and I got it when the medic kicked it away, but I must have dropped it in all the excitement. It doesn't seem to be anywhere."

"We'll search the scene, sir," Owen said, sounding very official. "Now, I need you two to leave. There are police waiting for you."

The woman kneeling by the injured deliveryman asked, "What about him?"

"We'll see to him, don't worry." Owen stared at the two of them for a long moment, then both of them blinked and looked a little foggy. The woman went to the older man, who put an arm around her, and with a last anxious glance over her shoulder, they went outside. The two fake FBI guys went with them, acting like they were the ones who'd rescued the hostages.

As soon as they were gone, Owen knelt beside the injured man, placed a hand on his forehead and whispered a few words. The man's eyes fluttered closed. "Okay, you can go," he told Mack. Mack nodded and disappeared with his prisoner.

"The police are still out there waiting for him," I said. "How are you going to explain the robber who set off the whole hostage situation just vanishing?"

"We've got it taken care of," Owen said. He went to the door and called out, "We're clear in here. Bring in the gurney."

Real medics in fire department uniforms came in and went to work on the injured man. While they worked, Owen took my arm and walked me away from the shop. As we left the scene, I took off my jacket and cap and Owen made them disappear. "Now do you mind explaining how you dealt with all that?" I asked.

"The hostages will remember the robber shooting himself. The police will find a magically created body. None of them will remember us."

"That's too bad," I said with a sigh.

"What do you mean?"

"No one will remember my kick-butt action heroine moment."

The strain on his face faded as he grinned. "What did you do? That shield spell dropped like that." He snapped his fingers.

"I kicked an imaginary gun out of his hands. It was much cooler than it sounds."

He put his arm around me and pulled me to him in a hug so tight it squeezed the breath out of me. "It sounds cool enough," he whispered. "Thanks."

When he released me and I caught my breath, I asked, "Who were those other guys? Did you believe them about just wanting to help?"

"Not really. I'm guessing we had more Spellworks plants, setting up a situation where they could save the day. I wish I could have grabbed one of those bracelets. I bet that would help in figuring out that barrier spell."

I ducked behind Owen as a TV news crew went by. "Are we still invisible?" I asked.

"Why?"

"My mother would never forgive me if I ended up on TV looking like this."

Not that I had to worry about that. The Spellworks FBI guys were busy giving interviews and being praised by the hostages they'd supposedly rescued. The reporters didn't even notice us.

CHAPTER SEVEN

The Spellworks guys were splashed all over the front pages of newspapers the next day, those rubber bracelets clearly visible in every photo. They wouldn't mean anything to the average reader, who'd probably just think they were supporting some form of cancer research, but I had a feeling that anyone who'd gone to a Spellworks shop would know exactly what those bracelets were.

Sure enough, when I headed back to work after the weekend, the ads on the subway were all about how Spellworks spells had saved the day, and I noticed the brightly colored bracelets on a number of wrists. It was infuriating, to say the least. I'd risked my life going in there and distracting the wizard long enough for Owen to break the spell, and here they were claiming to be heroes for rushing in after the spell had been broken. They hadn't needed the bracelets. I wondered if they even worked, or if they were just stealing the credit. It was a real shame that Owen wasn't around for me to gripe to. All I could do was fume silently.

I was actually glad to see Perdita already at her desk when I got there, but before I could say anything to her, she looked up at me with enormous eyes and gasped, "Is it true?"

"Is what true?"

"About Owen?"

My fraying patience came dangerously close to the breaking point. "What about Owen?"

"It's all over the network—he tried to rob a jewelry store."

"What? Where did you hear that?"

She waved a hand at the crystal ball thingy on her desk. "That's what people are saying. There are pictures of him coming out of the store after some guys from Spellworks stopped the incident."

"That's not what happened. I was there. The robber was arrested by the magic police, and Owen was the one who broke the barrier spell the robber was using. You people need to get some real magical journalists so you can get decent reporting. What you've got is no better than most of the Internet for spreading rumors."

"But—but that's what people are saying, and there are pictures. He's also been at a lot of those other magical incidents."

"People are wrong. There are pictures because he was there to break things up—or they were Photoshopped, or whatever it is magical people do. Would he be here at work if he had tried to rob a store?" At least, I assumed he was at work. He'd become scarce right after dropping me off at my new place.

With his usual impeccable timing, Owen stepped through the doorway at just that moment, causing Perdita to yelp in fright. Owen gave me a baffled look, and I sighed heavily in response. "Have you checked the crystal network lately?" I asked.

"No. I've been working, and it's a bunch of rumors anyway. Why?"

Perdita said, "You probably ought to see this." Then she jumped out of her chair and moved well out of the way so that Owen could go behind her desk and look at the crystal ball. With my magic immunity and inability to do magic, those things were nothing more than paperweights to me.

As he read, Owen's eyebrows raised, and then he straightened and said, "You've got to be kidding. Where do these people get this stuff?"

"I'll give you one guess," I said.

"They're trying to make me into a villain! And it doesn't make any sense because Mack was there from the Council, and he wouldn't have let me go if he thought I was guilty."

"Mack left directly with the prisoner," I reminded him. "They've apparently left out any pictures of you two going into the building together."

"I haven't seen any," Perdita confirmed.

"At least they don't name me," he said. "It's just pictures and rumors about an unnamed wizard criminal—probably because libel laws work in the magical world, too, and naming me would bring in the boss. But still..." He sounded more frustrated and sad than angry, like this was a big disappointment to him. "I've just been trying to help."

"Was there something you needed from me?" I asked him.

"I need to talk to Idris again. I don't know if that barricade was one of his spells or a more recent one, but if he knows something, it could help, and maybe we've let him stew long enough that he'll tell us more."

"You need me for that?"

He shrugged wearily. "He won't talk unless you're there. I don't know why, but is it worth arguing? I know I'd like you there. He's calmer when you're around."

"Then I can't imagine what he's like when I'm not there," I said. As we headed to the detention area, I watched Owen carefully. He had changed clothes since Saturday, and he had shaved, but I wasn't so sure about sleeping or eating. "You're going to make yourself sick if you keep this up," I said.

"You saw what happened Saturday. I don't want another incident where we can't get our people in before the entire police department shows up—or Spellworks takes the credit."

When we got to the detention area, Idris wasn't looking so good. He was pale and shaky and had developed a distinct twitch. "Oh, thank God!" he called out when we entered the interrogation room. "I thought you'd forgotten about me."

"What happened to you?" I asked. He looked bad enough that I didn't have to pretend to be concerned. "Are they not feeding you?"

"Oh, the food's pretty good."

"Are you sick? Do you need medical attention?"

"No, I'm fine. But I haven't had anyone to talk to! Nothing to read! Nothing to watch! Nothing to do! I'm going insane!"

I couldn't help but wince. For most people, that would be awful, but for someone with Idris's attention span, that must have been a good approximation of hell.

"We'll see what we can do about that," Owen said. "Of course, it all depends on how cooperative you are."

"I'll cooperate! I will!"

Owen leaned forward, bracing his elbows on the table. "Did you do any development on the barricade spell?"

"Barricade spell?"

"Quick magical dome over a large area, blocks out not only magic but also physical entry."

Idris frowned in thought, and his fingers twitched like he was mentally typing. "There was something like that—I think the basis had to do with battlefields. I didn't develop it fully because it takes a lot of concentration, but it came from that book in your office, the old one."

"That narrows it down," Owen said acidly.

Idris snapped his fingers as if conjuring the memory. "Oh, you know, the red one, it was about spells for war."

"I think I know the one you mean. Thank you. You've actually been helpful for a change."

Idris leaned back in his chair and clicked his tongue as he smirked. "Glad I could help. Come to me any time you need assistance with magical matters."

With a great demonstration of maturity, Owen ignored the barb. Idris sat up straight and beamed at Owen. "Don't tell me someone actually used that spell! Wow!"

"That's not something I'd be proud of, considering the way it was used," Owen grumbled.

I gave Idris a pitying look. "With all those spells you were developing, you didn't really want to hurt people with magic, did you?"

"Are people being hurt?" My bruises had healed, but I just had to point to my neck to remind him. "Oh, yeah, I guess they are. I only wanted to have some fun."

"I bet there's plenty of room for magical pranks that are safe, right, Owen?"

Owen looked at me like I was crazy, and then he caught on. "Yes, of course! Magic doesn't have to be dull and boring. You can have fun with it. I bet you have lots of ideas for that."

Idris sat up eagerly. "Oh, yeah! I have lots of ideas."

"That might be something we could get the boss to consider—that is, if we could convince him we could trust you," I said.

"You can trust me, honest!"

"Why should we trust you?" Owen asked sternly.

I touched Owen's sleeve. "Maybe we could give him a pencil and some paper to write down his ideas, and then we'd have something to show the boss."

"It would have to be purely theoretical, since there's a magical dampening field in the detention area."

"I'm sure he could still come up with some good theories, even without testing them. He probably even has ideas he's already tested that he'd like to write down."

Idris practically bounced in his chair. "I do! I do! Please!"

Owen took a small memo book out of his suit coat pocket, along with a pen, and handed them to Idris. "I'd like to see what you come up with." Then he stood and gestured for me to follow.

Outside in the observation room, Owen asked, "What was that about?"

"I thought if we threw him a bone, he might be more cooperative. Think of it as nonmagical dragon taming. Did you get what you needed?"

"I believe so. If I have the basis for the spell, it should be easier to counter it. I've got one of those bracelets, but it doesn't contain a true counterspell."

He started to head off, and I called after him, "I am going to see you again someday, right?"

He stopped and turned around. "When this is all over, we'll go where no one can find us and spend lots of time together. I promise."

"I'll hold you to that," I said. The question was, what would really count as "over," and would it ever really be over?

As if to prove my last thought, the guard in the observation room glanced at his crystal ball, then said to us, "The boss wants to see you both right away."

For a change, I found myself hoping that the sudden meeting was to discuss the conference and my progress in planning it, but I had a sinking feeling that it would be about the weekend incident. Merlin wouldn't believe what they were saying about Owen, but he'd want to look into it.

When we got to Merlin's office, Ivor Ramsay was there, looking irritatingly smug. Merlin looked uncharacteristically stern. "We need to talk about the most recent situation you've dealt with," he said.

Owen looked confused, and while he was still thinking of how he should respond, I jumped in. "The rumor mill is getting out of control. You people need a legitimate news source within the magical world—you know, someone who actually checks facts."

Owen gave me a "stifle it" glare and said coldly, "I gave you my report. The security team called me for help, and Mack from the Council's enforcement branch was with me. I'm not sure what the problem is beyond the misinformation that's being spread."

Ramsay gave a low chuckle. "Easy, son," he said, making a calming gesture. "No one is accusing you of anything—at least, no one in this room is. But we do need to consider the reputation of this company and do some damage control. The Council is very well aware of the role you played in resolving the situation, as well as the interference by others who might be affiliated with Spellworks. However, the magical community is hearing a different story."

"It's slander," I said, backing Owen up. "All we can do is deny it and present our own evidence."

Ramsay leaned back in his chair. "And denial looks guilty. It's a no-win situation." I was really starting to dislike this guy. He almost seemed to be gloating, like he was enjoying this. He paused, making a great show of deep thought, then said, "I suppose all we can do is put Owen here front-and-center in the good things we do so people can get to know him beyond the rumors." He gave Owen a warm smile. "No one who really knows you could suspect you of these things."

Yeah, I thought, and putting him front-and-center was a good way to kill him. Owen could be okay in meetings and one-on-one with people he knew and trusted, but anything beyond that and he'd be paralyzed by panic, which could make him look cold and aloof and give the wrong impression. Even now, just raising the topic had made Owen go horribly pale. We'd been standing in front of the conference table like kids called on the carpet, but I tugged on Owen's sleeve to get him into a chair before he passed out, then I sat beside him, keeping what I hoped might be a calming hand on his arm.

"Again," I said, "It might be handy to have a real news outlet for him to talk to. What else can he do, start blogging?"

"He could be a presence at this conference you're planning."

"I'll be demonstrating some new spells," Owen said quietly.

Ramsay beamed. "Excellent! Then you're ahead of me already. How are the plans going, otherwise?"

I provided an update of everything I had set up thus far. Merlin nodded and smiled the whole time I spoke, which I found encouraging.

"You'll need a keynote speaker," Ramsay said.

It was an obvious request for an invitation, but I ignored it. "We have Merlin. I'm sure that name still means something in the magical world, and this is your first major public appearance since returning, isn't it?"

"I have met with customers, and I have been at Council meetings, but no, I have not made an official public appearance," Merlin said.

"How are you planning to address Spellworks?" Ramsay asked. "It is the elephant in the room. I'm not sure that just talking about what you're doing will be enough. You need to take on the competition directly, maybe even accuse them of wrongdoing."

"And how would you propose we do that?" Merlin asked. "We have only the slightest concrete evidence of their evil intent."

"You have the person who was the face of Spellworks in your custody," Ramsay said. "He could repudiate them and admit that they were the source of all these negative spells that they're now selling charms to fight."

Before I thought about what I was saying, I blurted, "That's insane! *He's* insane. I wouldn't put him in front of any audience. You never know what he'd say." I turned to look at Merlin, sure he'd back me up, but if he thought the idea was crazy, he was showing a lot of self-control in not visibly freaking out.

"I'm sure he could be coached," Ramsay said mildly. "And it is in his best interests to cooperate with us. I understand he's terrified of his former masters."

"He has been a little more cooperative lately," Owen said, and I whipped my head around so fast to stare at him in shock that I felt something in my neck pop. "He even gave me the source for that barricade spell, and he's interested in helping create a line of safe joke spells."

While I was still goggling at Owen and wondering what alien entity had possessed him to make him want to put a wild card like Idris in front of an audience, Ramsay said, "You have to admit it's bold, daring, and a definite stake in the ground." He pounded his fist on the table in emphasis.

"But potentially dangerous," Merlin murmured, as though he was speaking to himself. "Very, very dangerous." Addressing us, he said, "It would certainly get everyone's attention, wouldn't it?"

"It would have the biggest impact as a surprise," Ramsay said, "so we wouldn't have to announce him as a speaker in advance. That way we can wait until the last second to decide if we want to trust him. And we can ensure there are consequences if he doesn't cooperate. The terms of his surrender already mean he can't magically harm this company or anyone who works for it. If he agrees to speak, we could make it part of the contract that he can't profit from Spellworks, so he has an incentive to stay with us."

Merlin nodded slowly, then said, "Miss Chandler, please prepare some brief remarks Mr. Idris might be encouraged to make on our behalf. I will make the final decision on the day of the event."

Before he could adjourn the meeting, Ramsay stopped him with a gesture. "One more thing, Ambrose," he said. I couldn't recall anyone ever using Merlin's English first name like that. Merlin gave Ramsay a "go ahead" nod. "If you don't mind, I'd like to speak, as well. The continuity of leadership would make us look like we're presenting a stronger united front."

"We would be honored to have you participate," Merlin said with a slight bow and a thin-lipped smile.

"Fantastic!" Ramsay said. "Well, it sounds like your event is thoroughly under way, and everything is going according to plan and schedule. It's sure to be a huge success."

I could barely wait to get away from the executive suite before I grabbed Owen's arm and said, "I know illusions don't work on me, so you can't be someone else wearing an Owen disguise, but who are you, and what have you done with Owen Palmer?"

He looked at me like I'd grown a third arm. "What do you mean?"

"I mean thinking it's a good idea to let Idris talk to anyone."

"You were just trying to make him more cooperative."

"Yeah, but to talk to *us*, not to talk to all our customers out in public where we can't put a muzzle on him. I can't believe you and Merlin agreed with Ramsay about that. It was like Attack of the Pod People in there."

"You have to admit it makes sense," he said with a shrug. "He's the best evidence we have that Spellworks isn't what they seem to be." He resumed walking, so I had to walk with him if I wanted to continue the conversation.

"And you still trust Ramsay?" I asked.

"Of course. Why wouldn't I?"

"Well, aside from the fact that he wants to give our rather squirrely enemy a microphone at our event, don't you think it's a little weird that he always shows up to gloat whenever you being involved with saving the day gets misinterpreted?"

"No, because he's not gloating. He's trying to help."

"How did that back there help, in any way, shape, or form?" I glanced around to make sure there was no one else in earshot before continuing with my voice lowered. "Think about it, Owen, who else is better situated to be behind all this? He gets inside info from us and inside info from the Council. He's got access to money. He's got the magical skills."

"But why? He was already the president of MSI and on the Council. He gave that up when we brought Merlin back—and bringing Merlin back was his idea. If he wanted to rule the magical world, he was already there. He's famous enough that if he did want to start his own company, he wouldn't have to go through all of this to do so. He'd have put his name on it instead of wasting time with Idris."

"I know I'm missing some of the backstory," I admitted, "but he just bugs me, and I think there's something seriously wrong with his idea to let Idris speak."

"Merlin thought letting Idris speak was a good idea."

"Merlin has, quite literally, been living under a rock for hundreds of years."

"Don't be ridiculous, Katie," Owen snapped so forcefully that it took me aback.

"Come on, you're not even the tiniest bit suspicious?"

"I deal in facts, not suspicions. And I need to get back to work."

I was left blinking in his wake as he headed down a corridor to his office, wondering if we had just had our first real fight. The two of us weren't exactly high-conflict people, and we'd generally agreed about most things other than his working habits and my safety. This, though, seemed like a fundamental disagreement, and I couldn't understand why he was being so pigheaded. It was like he was under a spell.

I gasped at the thought. That had to be it. Maybe Ramsay was using some kind of influence spell, like Rod's old attraction spell, that made magical people trust him, and it didn't work on me. That would explain everything. I still wasn't sure why Ramsay would do these things or what his real goal was, but I thought it was worth looking into.

And if I was right, I'd have to go this one alone, without Owen's help.

CHAPTER EIGHT

I wasn't sure where to start researching Ramsay. Owen had always been my source for info on the magical world, but I couldn't turn to him this time. If Ramsay was using influence spells to keep people on his side, then that ruled out everyone magical, which ruled out most people who'd know anything about Ramsay. That left the magical immunes, and only one of the immunes I knew was in a position to have the kind of information I needed: Kim.

She'd hated me from the start because I got the job as Merlin's assistant that she'd been aiming for, and the fact that she'd replaced me in that job hadn't made her like me any better. She was the last person I wanted to turn to for help. I'd rather have organized an Ivor Ramsay Appreciation Festival.

I stayed late that evening searching the company archives from my computer, but the only relevant item I found was an internal notice about Ramsay's retirement about a year earlier. It didn't go into much detail, mentioning only his long tenure with the company and many unspecified contributions. The photo with the notice was the usual corporate portrait.

I finally admitted to myself that Kim really was my only option. The next morning I did everything else on my to-do list, in hopes that some other solution would miraculously appear and I wouldn't have to talk to her. Was it too much to wish that Owen would suddenly snap out of the spell and call to tell me I was right?

Apparently it was, because I still hadn't heard from him. With Owen, that wasn't all that unusual. I couldn't tell if he was deliberately not talking to me or just being his workaholic self. Finally, I couldn't put it off any longer and trudged upstairs to the executive suite. Trix wasn't at her desk, so I went to the small office off to the side that used to be mine.

"What are you doing here?" a voice behind me screeched. The owner of the voice whipped around to block me from going further into the office.

I had to swallow a couple of times before I could speak because just thinking these words put a bad taste in my mouth. "I need your help."

She snorted in disdain. "That conference is your job. If you can't handle it, don't ask me to clean up after you."

"This isn't about the conference. I just need some information." I decided to try flattery, much as it pained me to do so. "You've worked here a lot longer than I have, so I thought you'd have some perspective on company history."

Putting one hand on her hip, she sneered and asked, "Don't you have your boyfriend for that?"

I gritted my teeth and forced myself to take a few deep breaths. She seemed determined to make this as difficult as possible for me. "I actually need a nonmagical perspective—an immune perspective." That surprised her enough that when I stepped forward into her office, she didn't block me. I shut the door and asked softly, "What do you think about Ivor Ramsay?"

I never thought I'd see Kim go speechless, but she did. Her mouth hung open, and she lost her usual haughty air. With a furtive glance at the closed door behind me, she whispered, "Please tell me I'm not the only one who can't stand that man."

"I think we need to talk," I said.

"Want to go get coffee?" she asked, suddenly sounding so perky that I was afraid the body snatchers had invaded again.

"Sure! Let's go!" I replied, matching her in perkiness and hoping that the invitation was about talking away from the office rather than a plan to kill me and dump my body in the Hudson River.

We went to a coffee shop around the corner from the office building. I didn't even have to ask a question to get Kim started. "He's driving me crazy!" she said as soon as we got our drinks and sat at a table in the corner. "He just shows up, with no appointment, and Trix lets him in without even checking with the boss. But the boss doesn't complain, either, and it messes up the schedule for the whole day. I'm the one who then has to rearrange everything."

"That must be annoying," I said, grateful for once that I didn't have my old job back. "Does he show up often?"

"Practically every day."

"And how long has that been going on?"

"It started just before you got back—before the boss went to Texas." She frowned suddenly. "Why do you want to know all this?"

"He's getting the boss to agree to things I never would have expected."

She glanced around the room, then leaned forward and dropped her voice into a whisper that barely carried across the table, even though we were both carefully avoiding using names. "Do you think it's a spell that makes people do what he wants?"

"Maybe. Did you know him earlier, when he was in charge?"

"I didn't work closely with him, but I was often asked to provide verification at his meetings." Most magical immunes at the company worked as verifiers who made sure that magic wasn't used to hide or change things in business interactions. She sat up straighter and gave me a haughty look that reassured me that this was still the same old Kim. "He asked for me by name."

"What kind of president was he?"

"He was hands-on—he did a lot of walking around the company, checking in on every department, even Verification. But in a friendly way, not micromanaging. He really did seem to know everyone, all the way up from the mailroom."

My suspicious mind thought that was a good way to conduct industrial espionage on his own company in preparation for a long-term scheme he was developing, but even I thought that sounded a little far-fetched. "What about after the boss was brought in?"

"He stayed on for a few months until the boss figured out the language and had a sense of what was going on with the company, and then he retired. I know they were both in many of the meetings I went to for a while, but the boss didn't say much then."

"Was the idea always to turn things over to the boss?"

She frowned and tilted her head, took a sip of coffee, then said, "I don't think so. The boss was just supposed to deal with the rogue who'd come up. Taking over the company wasn't discussed ahead of time, as far as I know. It did seem like a surprise when it happened. But it makes sense. The boss founded the company, so he should be running it." She dropped her voice again as her eyes widened in alarm. "Do you think he's after his old job and trying to get rid of the boss?"

I wondered how much I should tell her about my suspicions. True, we'd found this one area of agreement, but I didn't trust her as far as I could throw her. If she thought there was any way to benefit from ratting me out, she'd take it without a second thought. I figured she'd be more helpful if I could convince her that helping me was to *her* advantage. "Maybe," I hedged. "That's what I'm worried about."

Her eyes took on a steely gleam. "Well, he won't get away with it, not while I'm around. That's my job—I mean, it's the boss's job, and I won't see him tricked into losing it." A flicker of a smile crossed her lips. "We could sabotage him, make him look bad so that the boss won't listen to him anymore. I know! I'll tell the boss he's hiding things magically."

"Let's hold off on that until we're sure," I said, worried that I might have unleashed a monster. "Just keep your eyes and ears open and let me know if you see or hear anything odd. We may be the only people in a position to do something who aren't affected by him, but we'll have to be careful because the rest of the company may be under the spell."

She drained her coffee cup and picked up her purse. "Don't worry, I won't let him win."

*

After another day of silence, I caved and sent Owen an e-mail, a chatty "how's it going?" message, but I got no response. Under any other circumstances, I wouldn't have been at all alarmed, since he had a habit of falling into his work, neglecting his in-box, and losing all track of time, but because he'd actually snapped at me the last time we'd spoken, I was starting to worry. A weekend without a word from Owen made me want to call police stations and hospitals. I decided it would be saner to call him, but I got no answer at his home or office.

I got to my office on Monday morning to find Perdita sneezing her head off. With each sneeze, strange things appeared in her office—soap bubbles, flower petals, white feathers. "Sorry about that, Katie," she said, dabbing her nose with a lace handkerchief and waving the bubbles, petals, and feathers away with her other hand. "I don't know what got into me."

"Are you okay?"

"I may be coming down with something," she said with a sniffle, which she followed with a cough.

"Do you always sneeze up bubbles and flowers?"

She sneezed some glittery confetti and groaned. "Yes. It's so embarrassing. It's like I totally lose control of my magic when I sneeze. I never know what will appear."

"Why don't you go home and get some rest?" I suggested. I liked having her there to veil me from the overly friendly sales staff, but she looked utterly miserable, and I was worried about what she might sneeze up next.

It was a sign of just how awful she felt that she didn't argue with me. She just sneezed again, creating another cluster of bubbles, coughed, then said in a raspy voice, "I think maybe I will, if you don't mind."

I braced myself for a stream of constant interruptions, but was left in relative peace. In fact, every call I made went straight to voice mail. That afternoon, the subway was reasonably peaceful, compared to the chaos of the last few weeks. The crime wave seemed to have broken. A number of people were sneezing and sniffling, which made me wonder if a cold was going around or if there was some allergen affecting a lot of people.

I felt fine the next morning, but there was still a fair amount of wheezing and coughing on the subway. I got to the office to find a note saying that Perdita was out sick. I wasn't surprised because she really had been in bad shape the day before.

Although I'd had many a moment when Perdita tried my patience and when I'd wondered if not having an assistant would be easier or safer, when she wasn't in the office, I realized how much I needed her. For one thing, her absence meant I had to find another source for coffee. In any other business, there would have been a break room with a coffeepot, or even one of those vending machines that drops a paper cup before shooting out a stream of coffee that doesn't quite hit the cup. There might even be a Starbucks in the lobby. But at MSI, where most of the employees could conjure whatever they wanted to drink with a flick of their wrists, there weren't a lot of places where a nonmagical person could find caffeine. The only coffeepot I knew of in the entire building was in the verification department, and as I recalled from my brief stint there, that didn't exactly qualify as coffee.

I left my office and went in search of anyone who could conjure me some coffee. By the time I reached the end of the hallway and hadn't found anyone present who wasn't making alarming hacking and coughing sounds, I wasn't even hoping for one of Perdita's lovely concoctions. I'd have been happy with a cup of instant, as long as it was hot and contained caffeine.

I headed up to Rod's office because Isabel did good coffee, and she might also know how widespread the flu was. "He's not seeing anyone," she whispered when I stepped into her office.

"He has it, too?"

She nodded sadly. "And he's being a big baby about it."

Just then, a hoarse shout of, "Isabel!" came from the inner office. "I need more tea!"

"Hold on a second, Katie," Isabel whispered before raising her voice to say, "With honey and lemon again?"

"Yes, please."

Isabel raised her hand and flicked her wrist, then Rod coughed and said, "Thank you!"

"You should go home," she said.

"I'm too—" he went into a coughing fit "—busy."

"Men, they're such babies when they're sick," she whispered to me. "Was there something you needed?"

"Coffee, please. I think everyone in my department is out sick. I'm desperate, Isabel."

She waved her hand, and a cup appeared on her desk. I picked it up and practically inhaled the brew. "Oh, you're a lifesaver. Thank you."

"Most of the company is either sick or coming down with something. Germs spread as fast as gossip around here. You should have seen this place in January. The few people who were still standing practically came to work in hazmat gear. You'd better watch yourself."

"Don't worry, I will. But don't you have an anti-illness spell? You'd think a place like this could fight the flu."

"You'd think, but no, we sometimes even get weirder varieties that the flu shot doesn't help with, since our bugs get filtered through the other races, like the fairies and gnomes." I'd always been curious about her lineage, since she was far larger than the average person, but I couldn't think of a polite way to ask if she counted herself among the other races. Instead, I just said, "I may be back for a refill."

Before I made it to the door, I paused. Isabel was the best source for company gossip and information, since working in Personnel meant she knew all the comings and goings within the company. She might know something that could help me, if I could ask without sounding suspicious. I turned back to face her. "One good thing about this flu is that I haven't had to deal with Idris in a couple of days."

She laughed. "I can imagine that's a relief. He always got on my nerves."

Yes! She'd taken my opening. "Did you know him well when he worked here?"

"He and Ari were off and on, and since Ari was a friend, that meant I had to put up with him."

"The more time I spend with him, the harder it is to imagine anyone feeling like he was a danger worthy of bringing Merlin back. Was he really that big a threat?"

"I don't think they knew exactly who was causing trouble at the time, so they couldn't tell how bad things might get. After the last time, I guess they weren't taking any chances."

"What last time?"

"I was just a kid, but it was pretty bad, from what I've heard."

I remembered reading something about an earlier attempt to seize power magically. It was in a reference book Owen had let me borrow so I could get the quick-immersion Magic 101 primer right after I joined the company. Unfortunately, I didn't remember the details, and I didn't think I could ask Owen for that book under the current circumstances.

I grinned at Isabel. "Well, he's not a threat now, and while the flu is going around, he's not even an annoyance." I headed back to my office, trying to think of another way to find out about the last threat.

*

The next day, the absentee rate was even worse. I was getting hundreds of responses to our conference invitation, so there would be people at the conference, but I was starting to wonder if there would be a conference for them to attend. That was the downside of doing everything magically—I was entirely dependent on other people being able to do magic. I didn't think I'd be able to find a circus to rent tents from and get them set up in

Central Park without anyone noticing. There was no nonmagical Plan B.

Considering that the subway that evening sounded like a tuberculosis sanitarium, I expected to get home and find my roommates lying on the sofa with boxes of tissues. Instead, they were in perfect health. "Are y'all dealing with the plague at work?" I asked as we ate dinner.

"Are you talking about whatever Rod has?" Marcia asked.

"Yeah, it's going through the company like wildfire. Is that happening at your offices?"

They looked at each other. "A couple of the designers have been out sick," Gemma said.

"At my firm, people come to work when they're clinically dead," Marcia said with a sigh. "And that means we all catch whatever they've got, so then we have to drag ourselves off our deathbeds to go to work." She glared at me. "You'd better not catch your office plague and bring it home to us."

"So far, I don't have so much as a sniffle," I reassured them.

The subway was practically sedate and much less crowded than usual the next morning. The people struck down by the flu must have all stayed home. "Hey, you made it!" Sam said in greeting as I approached the office building. "It's a good thing you look healthy. You may end up running the place."

"Is it that bad?"

"When Palmer calls in sick, that generally means we need to send the coroner out to his place, and anyone weaker has already fallen."

Perdita was still out, and the sales department was like a ghost town. Rina was out, as well, so I didn't know where she was on handling the party side of the event. I went through my checklist for the conference, but nobody I needed was in the office, so I created a new checklist to see what had already been done and what needed doing. Most of it would come down to the last minute in conjuring tents and protective barriers, food, and decorations. That meant I was sunk if people weren't well within a week. I reminded myself that the worst flu I'd ever had lasted a week. I was weak for a while after that, but I was functional.

Of course, with my luck, everyone else would be well by then, and I'd succumb to the illness the day before the conference. Then we'd be left in Perdita's capable hands.

And then we'd be doomed.

I found some hand sanitizer in my tote bag and rubbed it on my hands, then popped a vitamin C lozenge in my mouth. I wondered if putting on a surgical mask would be overkill.

When I still hadn't heard from anyone by lunchtime, I ventured out into the corridors. It was like something out of a science fiction movie, with me as the only survivor of a terrible plague, left alone in the ruins of civilization.

With a growing sense of worry, I hurried up to the executive suite. Kim sat at Trix's desk, looking reasonably healthy. "The boss is sick," she said. "He's not seeing anyone."

Flu was supposed to be particularly dangerous for the elderly, and they didn't get much more elderly than Merlin. My stomach did a flip. "Have the healers seen him?"

"They're keeping an eye on him, but he insists he's got a potion that will cure anything." She gave a sneaky glance around the office suite, then gestured me forward and whispered, "I haven't seen you know who in days. Don't you think that's suspicious?"

I wondered if that was how I sounded to Owen and understood why he'd snapped at me. "Maybe he's sick like everyone else," I suggested.

"Maybe. But he could be going to all the meetings that the boss is missing."

"Is he missing a lot?"

"Not really," she admitted sheepishly. "Most people are canceling because they're sick."

"You and I must be the last ones standing."

I wasn't sure I liked the gleam that came into her eyes. "We'll be running the company soon." I'd have bet money that she'd be sitting at Merlin's desk by the end of the day.

I was on the way back to my office when it occurred to me that with Owen out, this was the perfect chance to look at his reference books. I could find out what really happened the last time, what Ramsay had done then, and if history might be repeating itself.

CHAPTER NINE

When I got to the R&D department, I was stymied. That department was secured. Owen usually anticipated my arrival and opened the door for me, but the point of this visit was that Owen *wasn't* there, so that wouldn't work.

I settled for the tried-and-true strategy of hanging around and waiting for someone else to either come or go and open the door. Anyone who worked in that department would have seen me around often enough to be willing to let me in. After all, I rationalized, if I told Merlin I needed to get something from Owen's office, he'd surely give me access. I just didn't want to disturb Merlin when he was sick or get him involved in this yet.

I didn't have to wait too long. Soon, the door opened and someone in a lab coat came out, carrying a couple of shopping bags. He stopped to sneeze halfway through the doorway, and I jumped to catch the door for him while he groped for a handkerchief. "Thanks," he croaked.

"Bless you," I said, meaning it quite sincerely. Once he left, I headed into the department and hurried to Owen's lab. The lights were out, and there was no sign of Jake, so he must have been sick, too. There were bookcases in the lab, but a quick skim of the titles I could read told me that these were all books about magic itself, not magical society.

Owen kept his office warded, so I felt a slight tingle as I passed through the doorway, but nothing held me back because the wards didn't work on me. I was sure I'd recognize the books I needed when I saw them, but I didn't see them on the bookshelves. That left the desk, which would be a challenge to search because it was so cluttered and because, in spite of the clutter, Owen knew exactly where everything was. Move one thing, and he'd know someone had been in there.

I remembered giving the books back to Owen not long after I'd joined the company. I visualized the scene—he'd taken the books from me, said I was welcome to borrow them at any time, and placed them… *there*, on the corner of his desk. I went around the desk, sat in his chair, and gingerly lifted a few file folders to find the books exactly where he'd put them, all those months ago.

Taking mental note of the books' position, how they were placed, and the order in which they were stacked, I pulled out the one I recalled having the most information on the recent history of the magical world. I flipped straight to the back, where there were blank pages, although there were fewer blank pages than I recalled. The book had updated itself to include events that happened since I'd last read it. I glanced over the article about the growth of Spellworks, out of curiosity, then flipped a few pages back to the story about the last serious threat to the magical world.

It sounded pretty similar to the way this battle had started, with a brilliant and eccentric young wizard named Kane Morgan who was fired from MSI when he and his wife began using dark magic no other wizard dared to tap into. It sounded far worse than today's magical mischief. The book said that the Council had discussed restoring Merlin, but before they had a chance, the Morgans tried to seize power, and it was another young MSI wizard, one Ivor Ramsay, who saved the day by defeating the bad guys in a surprise attack.

"Yeah, that would get you a fast promotion," I muttered to myself. And it would explain the hero worship, as well as Owen's resistance to my suspicions. It was like I'd accused Luke Skywalker of being Darth Vader, even after he'd destroyed the Death Star. I could even see why they might have jumped the gun on bringing Merlin back for something relatively minor this time around. They were afraid of taking too many chances.

There wasn't much more about Ramsay, aside from him being promoted to company president about twenty years ago and being chairman of the Council for a couple of terms. As Owen said, he'd had just about all the power anyone could want. He didn't need to concoct an elaborate scheme to take over when he was already there.

But still, there was something about Ramsay that just bugged me, and if he was behind this, then that meant he had something far more nefarious than normal power in mind.

The part about Merlin's return was still sketchy, like it was a placeholder article that would be fleshed out when enough time had passed to lend historical perspective. Not only did this book get added to, it expanded along the way. I could have sworn some of the information about that last crisis hadn't been there the last time I read this book.

I put the books back where I'd found them, made sure the folders on top of them were back in place, and then left Owen's office, still deep in thought. I went home early because there wasn't much I could do with everyone else gone, and my to-do list of things I needed from other people was haunting me. The subway was emptier than normal—even accounting for non-rush-hour ridership. And then it occurred to me that there were no obviously magical people on board. Not a single pair of wings, no pointed ears, no gnomes, and no one was causing magical mischief. It was as though the entire magical population of Manhattan had vanished.

As soon as I got home, I called Marcia at work. "Is your office still flu-free?" I asked.

"So far, knock on wood."

"My company has been pretty much wiped out."

"Yeah, I know. I'm going to play Florence Nightingale for Rod after work. He's such a big baby. Do we need to quarantine you?"

"I don't think so. I don't know if there is such a thing, but this looks like some kind of magic flu. The only people I know who are sick are magical people, and I don't know of anyone nonmagical who's sick. Owen's sick, too, and I'll be going over there. I'll leave a note for Gemma."

"Keep me posted," she said. "You have my cell number and Rod's number, right?"

"Yeah, I'll let you know what I find out."

If there was a magical flu, I'd need Owen's help to figure out what we could do, even if he was sick. In case I needed to do like Marcia and play nursemaid, I threw some overnight things into a tote bag. On my way to Owen's place I bought a container of hot-and-sour soup from the Chinese restaurant next door to my building and a jug of orange juice from the corner grocery.

Normally, Owen's door just opened for me when I showed up, since his weird brand of ESP told him I was coming, but the plague must have knocked out his magical senses—or else he was mad at me. I had to hit the buzzer, and I hoped I wasn't waking him from a nap. After a long pause, a scratchy voice said, "Yeah?" over the intercom.

"Owen, it's Katie. I need to talk to you. I've got soup."

He didn't respond, and I held my breath. Then the door opened, and I went inside and ran up the stairs. His front door had already opened for me. I found him sprawled on the sofa, his cat staring at him warily from her perch on the sofa arm at his feet.

I couldn't blame her for her wariness. He looked like hell, worse than I'd ever seen him, and I'd seen him after he'd been practically ripped to shreds by a harpy. The circles under his eyes were nearly as dark as his hair, he had a day's growth of stubble on his jaw, which made his cheeks look even more hollow, and he was pale enough to almost be gray.

"You shouldn't have come," he croaked, squinting at me. His glasses lay on the coffee table, and I doubted he'd bothered with contact lenses in the state he was in. "I don't want to give this to you."

"I don't think you *can* give it to me. Not that I plan to kiss you right now, regardless." However, I did have an urge to give him a hug. When he looked like this, he brought out all my latent maternal instincts. I cleared a spot among the books and papers on the coffee table and set down my bags. I opened the soup, stuck a spoon in it and handed it to him. "Here, this should open your head and give you some energy. You can eat while I talk."

He pulled himself to a sitting position and swung his feet around to the floor. I sat beside him, waited for him to eat a few bites, then asked, "Is there such a thing as an illness that strikes only magical people?"

He swallowed, coughed, and said, "I don't know. I haven't heard of one."

"I noticed that it's only the magical people who seem to be sick. The immunes at work are the ones still going, and Marcia said nobody is out at her office. So either there's an illness that only affects magical people or there's some massive spell being cast all over Manhattan that makes magical people sick."

Owen groaned and leaned back against the sofa, like the effort of eating a few spoonfuls of soup and listening to me had utterly exhausted him. I reached over and took the soup from him before he spilled it on himself. "I really don't need this right now," he said.

"I suspect that's the point. We won't get anything done while all our people are sick."

"But whatever they're doing is probably making them sick, too."

"Unless they have a way to block it from particular people. It might be interesting to see exactly who is still up and around right now." I started to say that Ramsay hadn't shown up at the office, but then I wasn't sure what that proved. It meant either that he was sick or that he wasn't sick and didn't want anyone to see that. Either way, this wasn't the time to stir up that particular argument.

Owen rubbed his temples wearily. "If only I could think," he muttered.

"I wonder how far-reaching this is—is it only Manhattan, or does it affect all magical people everywhere?"

He fluttered a hand vaguely in the direction of his desk in the front corner of the room. "Could you bring me the phone?"

I got up and brought the cordless to him. "I should make you talk," he muttered as he dialed. "She'll know something's wrong with me, and I'll never hear the end of it." Then he cleared his throat and forced himself to sound normal as he said, "Gloria, it's Owen. I wanted to see how you're doing." He winced as he listened, then said, "Yes, I am a little under the weather, but are you and James okay? What about anyone else? Yes, that was what Katie suspected. Okay, thanks, let me know." He disconnected and handed the phone back to me. "They're feeling, as Gloria put it, 'a bit peakish,' which probably means they're barely getting out of bed. They have heard from neighbors who work in the city that they feel sick at work, but get a lot better when they get home. Oh, and she said you were very clever. That's about the highest compliment she can give."

"If we want to see just how widespread this is, I could call Dean or my grandmother." My family has an odd genetic quirk that left most of us either immune to magic or magical, though we'd only just discovered that. My brother Dean was the wizard in the family, and we seemed to have inherited this trait through my grandmother.

"Call them," he said, picking up the soup again.

I called the family store. Dean's wife, Sherri, answered the phone on the second ring. "Chandler Agricultural Supply," she sang out cheerfully.

"Hi, Sherri, it's Katie. Is Dean around?"

"He's out on a delivery. Can I take a message?"

"No, don't worry about it. Is he doing okay?"

"Sure is."

"That's good to hear."

"And how are things in New York?"

Of all times for my sister-in-law to decide to have a conversation with me, I groaned inwardly. "Just great. I'm having a blast."

"I'll tell Dean you called. Want me to have him call you back?"

"Don't worry about it. I'll send an e-mail."

I managed to get off the phone after another minute of chitchat, then told Owen, "The magical plague doesn't seem to have reached Texas. And Sherri says hi."

He shivered and pulled a knitted afghan off the back of the sofa to wrap around himself. I reached over and put a hand against his forehead. "You're burning up. And I don't know what to do about it if this is magical. Something tells me that your average cold-and-flu medicine won't help."

"It doesn't," he croaked. "Believe me. I've tried them all."

"It seems to me that what we need to do is get you far enough away from the city that you'll be able to think, and then we can come up with a solution."

"I'm all for that, believe me. We probably ought to bring the boss, as well." He pulled the afghan tighter around his shoulders and shivered again.

"Then we'll need a car." I knew of one person who had wheels and who might be in any shape to drive: Ethan Wainwright, the magical immune who was our corporate attorney, and whom I'd briefly dated just before getting together with Owen. I found my little address book in my purse and dialed his cell number.

As I expected, he was game—he was always up for a magical adventure. "It'll be like old times!" he said. "It may be a few hours before I can get there, though. I've got a couple of things to wrap up before I can leave the office, and then I'll have to swing by and get Merlin. I should be there around seven."

While I was talking to Ethan, Owen had fallen asleep. I felt his forehead again and found that the fever was even higher. I wasn't sure what to do for him. Would a magically induced fever really hurt him, or did I need to try to bring it down?

I decided that too hot was too hot, no matter what caused it, and the last thing we needed was Owen's brain melting. I got a washcloth in the bathroom under the stairs, soaked it in cool water, then brought it back and placed it over his forehead. He moaned and stirred a little in his sleep, then caught my hand and held it, but didn't wake.

I sat by him for the next couple of hours, rewetting the cloth when it dried or warmed up. I had a whole new appreciation for what my mom must have gone through when we were kids. As I held his hand and watched him sleep, I realized just how much I'd missed him lately. He hadn't acted like he was angry with me when I came over, but he was probably too sick to fight. I knew I didn't want us to be fighting. I liked him too much—maybe even loved him. I gave his hand a squeeze and whispered, "You'd best not abandon me, in any way, shape, or form."

When he woke around six-thirty, he seemed surprised at first to see me there, but then I saw the memory return to his eyes. "Is it almost time to go?" he asked in a hoarse whisper.

"Just about."

He forced himself upright and said, "Then I guess I'd better pack. I might need help with the stairs." He leaned heavily on me as we walked up the stairs to his bedroom, then I went back downstairs and put out some food for the cat.

He didn't come back down, so after a while I went up to look for him and found him asleep on his bed, but at least his bag appeared to be packed. I nudged him awake and helped him back downstairs, where he lay on the sofa and told me which reference books to bring.

When I saw Ethan's silver Mercedes pull up on the street below, I hooked our overnight bags and Owen's bag of books over one shoulder and half carried Owen down the stairs. He was looking worse and worse, and Ethan would need to turn the car's air conditioner to "arctic" to keep Owen from overheating the car with his mere presence.

Ethan already had Merlin in the front seat, not looking quite as bad as Owen did, but almost looking his age, for once. Ethan got out of the car and took the bags from me while I maneuvered Owen into the backseat. He wasn't a big guy, but he was pretty heavy when he was practically deadweight. Once we were all settled in the car, Ethan asked, "Which way do you want to head?"

"I don't know."

"West," Owen rasped. "Into the mountains. That might block

whatever's coming from the city."

"Okay, then, west into mountains," Ethan confirmed. Owen was sound asleep on my shoulder before the car reached the end of the block.

When we'd been driving a couple of hours, I thought Owen's temperature had dropped, and his color looked better. Merlin stirred in the front seat, showing signs of life. "It seems to be working," I said. "Let's keep going."

By the time we pulled into a roadside motel that wasn't the least bit scenic or picturesque, which probably explained why it was the first we came across that didn't have the "no vacancy" sign lit, both our patients looked more human. Ethan went into the office to get rooms for us and came out with a deeply uncomfortable look on his face, just as the "no" in the "no vacancy" neon sign over his head lit up.

"There was only one room left," he said. "I went ahead and took it because I don't think we'll find anything else in the Poconos on a summer weekend, and I don't think we want to keep driving this late."

"We're not here for sleep and comfort," I said. "We just need a place to work."

"That's what I figured." He began turning pink in a blush worthy of Owen. "And one more thing—it's a honeymoon suite. I don't know if you know anything about the Poconos, but it's a big honeymoon destination, and the honeymoon resorts are known for their excess of what some might call kitsch. Others would call it tacky. I guess this place is the low-budget equivalent of that. Anyway, they think I'm here on my honeymoon, so we'll probably want to keep our other guests out of sight."

"They'll be busy," I said with a shrug.

Fortunately, the honeymoon suite wasn't visible through the office's front windows, so we were able to get Owen and Merlin inside without anyone wondering why I was going on a honeymoon with three men, one of them old enough to be my grandfather. Once we got them inside, Ethan and I took our time unloading the car.

When I got my first good look at the room, I realized that Ethan had understated the situation. "Tacky" didn't begin to describe the place. For one thing, just about everything in the room was either red or pink—or mirrored. The few parts of the walls that weren't covered in mirrors were covered in a pink, shiny fabric. The bed was round, in the middle of the room, and draped in a red satin spread, with piles of pink and red pillows. There was a mirror on the ceiling over the bed. The lighting fixtures must have been found at Liberace's garage sale. They dripped with crystals and fake gilding.

"Oh, my," was all I could say. This really wasn't the kind of place where you wanted to spend the weekend with your boss.

"There's also a kitchen," Ethan said. "And a heart-shaped hot tub. Too bad I didn't bring a swimsuit."

"This is ideal," Merlin said. "Thank you, Mr. Wainwright."

Ethan and I turned to stare at him.

"The mirrors will be helpful in some of the work we have to do," Owen explained while avoiding looking at himself in any of the mirrors. He still looked pretty awful, so I could imagine that facing that image wasn't fun for him.

"Maybe you two should sleep now and get to work in the morning," I suggested. "You still look pretty fried."

"Probably a good idea," Owen agreed, sinking to sit on the bed and rubbing his temples. "Wow, I didn't realize how bad that buzzing in my head was until it stopped."

"So you're feeling better?"

"Yeah, but it's more like the week after you have the flu, when you're not sick anymore, but you still don't feel well."

We let Owen and Merlin take the bed, since they'd been sick and were the ones who'd be working. I tried to convince Ethan to take the sofa, since he'd been driving, but he swore it was too short for him and he'd be more comfortable dozing in a chair. The two wizards were still sound asleep when Ethan and I woke the next morning and slipped out to pick up some breakfast.

They were up and hard at work when we got back, and I thought I'd have to confiscate the books to get Owen to stop working long enough to eat. Hours later, there were pages of notes in Owen's textbook-perfect handwriting scattered all over the room. When he and Merlin seemed to have come to an agreement, Owen said, "We'll need some supplies for a spell to pinpoint what's going on." He handed me a sheet of paper. "I doubt there are any magic supply shops nearby, but you can probably find some reasonable substitutes. Where I thought of obvious ones, I made a note."

"Maybe you should come with me," I said, skimming the page.

"You'll do fine. I've got some things to work out." And then he buried his nose again in his book.

Ethan handed me his credit card. "Here, use this. There's a shop off the motel lobby that seemed to have a good variety of stuff, and they think you're my wife, anyway. I'd better stay here and keep an eye on them." Then he handed me his car keys. "But if you need to go elsewhere, you can take my car." I wasn't sure which was the bigger responsibility, getting the right ingredients for a spell to help save the magical world, or driving Ethan's Mercedes.

I took another look at Owen's list so I could decide where to look. He needed candles and several kinds of herbs, some of which were the kind you cooked with and some that weren't. He also wanted a map of

Manhattan—which, if I knew Ethan, would be in his car's glove compartment—a metallic powder, a compass (something else I suspected would be in the glove compartment, unless it was built into the car's navigation system), aspirin, air freshener spray, several ashtrays, and salt. I couldn't begin to imagine what spell he was going to MacGyver with all that stuff, but I thought I'd first try the motel shop.

I expected the typical motel shop—a cross between a convenience store and a souvenir shop stocked with necessities like aspirin in overpriced small containers, razors, and toothbrushes, as well as travel-related and souvenir items, like maps, postcards, and T-shirts and spoons with slogans about the local area.

This wasn't that kind of shop.

CHAPTER TEN

This was the kind of shop that wouldn't even be possible in my hometown. Let's just say it catered to the honeymooning customer. If you looked in the mirror on the ceiling over your bed and thought you'd look better with body glitter, then you could dash across the parking lot and get it, along with several varieties of flavored lotions and powders, feathers in every color of the rainbow, bubble bath to use in that heart-shaped tub, and, of course, edible underwear, in case you worked up an appetite.

The motel's manager came over from the office, and she noticed me before I could sneak away. "Hi there, how can I help you?" she asked.

I backed away a step or two. "Um, well, I was looking for some things, but this probably isn't the right shop for me."

"Oh, you're the new wife from that couple who checked in late last night, aren't you? Eloped, your husband said. I guess if you were in such a hurry, you must have forgotten something."

Ah, so that was the story Ethan had told about why he wanted a honeymoon suite and hadn't made a reservation. "Yeah, that would be us. And I did forget a few things." I gave the display a sidelong glance and shuddered. "But not those kinds of things."

She laughed heartily. "Don't worry about the up-front merchandise. That's just for show. I've got all kinds of stuff. What do you need?"

I looked at the list again, and there actually was an off chance that this shop would stock some of it. "I need some candles—but nothing scented. White if you've got them."

"Of course we've got candles. Come on over here." She led me to the other side of the store, which looked more like the motel shop I'd been expecting. "Candlelight in all those mirrors is very flattering. It makes your skin glow, and it hides a lot of figure flaws. Just don't burn your room down," she added with a wink.

She pointed at a shelf full of candles in ceramic holders. They all had various bride and groom figures and the legend "Our honeymoon in the Poconos." Oh yeah, that was *exactly* what I wanted to buy to use with my boyfriend, my ex-boyfriend, and my boss, but beggars couldn't be choosers. The woman got me a shopping basket and I put four of the candles in there.

"Do you need some matches?" the woman asked.

Owen could start fires with a snap of his fingers, so I shook my head and said, "No, I don't think that'll be necessary."

"Anything else you need?"

I felt my cheeks burn as I realized that the body glitter might work as the metallic powder Owen had asked for. "Some of that body glitter would be good," I said, unable to meet the woman's eyes.

"What color do you want?"

I had no idea. He hadn't specified. "Oh, I don't know…"

"I bet gold would look good on you, especially in the candlelight," she said after giving me a long, appraising stare.

"Um, okay, sure," I mumbled. Owen would owe me for this, big time.

"Is that all?"

Since I was already there, I thought I might as well see what else I could come up with. "Can I just browse for a while?"

"Sure. Let me know if you need anything. Or if you need any ideas. Trust me, I've been married for thirty years. I know how to keep things spicy."

I was suddenly very glad Owen had made me go on my own. I might survive the mortification, but if he'd been there, I wouldn't have been able to look him in the eye ever again, assuming he survived the stroke he'd have had. I checked the list. Owen wanted fennel, marigold, rosemary, and peppermint, as well as cloves and anise. I couldn't imagine finding all that here, but I might as well look. Among the bath products was a package labeled "Bath Herbs for Lovers." I picked it up and read the ingredient label. It contained fennel, marigold, rosemary, and peppermint, along with a few other things like orange blossom and rose petals. I wondered if that would work and threw the package in my basket.

Owen hadn't specified what scent air freshener he wanted, so I took a bottle of room spray in "mountain fresh." Back in the less embarrassing gift shop part of the store, I found some souvenir bowls of potpourri. One shaped like a heart smelled of anise and clove, so I put that in the basket. I also picked up several "Souvenir of the Poconos" ashtrays. At the very back of the shop was the convenience store that I expected to find in a motel, and there I got a couple of plastic salt shakers and a travel-sized tin of aspirin.

The woman gave a low whistle when I went to check out. "Well, well,

well, you've got some honeymoon planned, haven't you?" she said, waggling her eyebrows. "You didn't need my help, after all. Not that I judge. Whatever floats your boat, I always say. But this is definitely unusual."

"Yeah, well, we are from New York," I said with a shrug.

"Oh," she said, as if that explained everything. "You do know the room is nonsmoking, right? I allow candles, but I draw the line at cigarettes," she said as she wrapped the ashtrays in paper.

"Those are just souvenirs," I said. "Gifts for some relatives."

"Okay, then." She leaned forward across the counter and gave me a leering wink. "Have fun, and enjoy your honeymoon."

My face burning as hot as Owen's fever had been, I fled the store as soon as I had my shopping bags in hand. I stopped by Ethan's car on the way back to the room, and just as I'd expected, there was a Manhattan map and a Boy Scout compass in the glove compartment. Heck, from what I knew of Ethan, I wouldn't have been surprised to find most of the rest of the shopping list in his trunk, because he never knew when he might need gold body glitter and a bunch of herbs.

"Wow, that was fast," Ethan said when I got back to the room.

"I found everything I needed at the motel shop. And before I bring out any of this, I want to make it clear that I don't want to hear *anything* about the nature of the items. I had to get creative, and let's just say the shop goes right along with the theme of this room and leave it at that." I gathered from the alarmed expressions on all their faces that I'd made my point.

I emptied my shopping bags onto the room's table and let Owen inspect what I found. "The herbs are all mixed up, but I'm sure we could separate them, if we have to," I said when I got nervous about the fact that he was taking so long to look at my purchases and hadn't said anything yet.

"We'll have to pull the cloves and anise out of this stuff, but all the rest is fine," he said. He raised an eyebrow at the body glitter and the label on the Lovers' Bath Herbs, but otherwise kept his mouth shut. I thought I caught Ethan smirking out of the corner of my eye, but he schooled his expression into neutrality before I could turn and look. I could tell that Merlin was dying of curiosity about the uses for these items, but he also said nothing.

Owen put me to work sorting the cloves and anise out into the ashtrays while he and Merlin set up the spell. They pulled the bedspread off the bed and covered the bed with a dropcloth Ethan had in the trunk of his car. Then they spread the map out on the middle of the bed and placed a candle at each corner. Once I was done sorting spices, Owen put a pinch of the herbs into each ashtray, along with the spices, and arranged those around the map. He then sprinkled a fine line of salt on the floor around the edge of the bed. He had the compass in his hand, but I didn't see that he was doing anything with the aspirin or the air freshener, so I wondered what role they would play.

"We may want to disable the smoke detector," Owen said as he settled cross-legged on the bed in front of the map. Ethan took a chair and climbed up to remove the batteries. Merlin sat across from Owen on the bed.

"What do you need me to do?" I asked.

Instead of answering me, Owen turned to Ethan. "Do you have a fire extinguisher?"

"Of course."

He ran outside to get it, and Owen turned back to me. "Be ready in case this gets out of control. You two can jump in without being hurt. Put out any flames and scatter the herbs. But otherwise, don't cross the salt circle."

Ethan came back with the fire extinguisher. "I think the manager's been watching me get stuff out of my car. She's got to be wondering what kind of honeymoon I'm having," he said dryly.

I shrugged. "Maybe I've got firefighter fantasies." More seriously, I asked Owen, "Are things likely to go wrong? This sounds dangerous."

"It can be," Merlin answered. "In doing this, we're searching for the negative magical energies at work, and that can leave the door open for them to find us."

"Ah," I said, unconsciously taking a step away from the bed.

"You should also watch carefully and pay attention to whatever you see. Our focus may be elsewhere."

"Now, lights out, please," Owen said, and Ethan hit the light switch, plunging the room into near darkness, the only light coming from around the edges of the heavy curtains.

I realized I was holding my breath while I waited for them to begin, but the room was so silent that breathing might have been disruptive. Merlin started the chanting, and in that moment I fully realized exactly who he was. I knew, intellectually, and I'd seen him do some awesome things. But as he said words that sounded incredibly ancient, that were probably even in his native language, I got the full force of the fact that this was the greatest wizard who'd ever lived and a man who was more linked to some nearly forgotten time than he was to today.

Then Owen joined him, and the sight of him being serious and actually working at the magic made my pulse race. He was usually so casual about magic. It was something he did with a muttered word and a careless flip of his wrist. If he was focusing this intently, this had to be big stuff.

While they chanted, the candles spontaneously lit, one after another. Soon, the room took on a sweet, spicy smell as the herbs smoldered. The candlelight reflecting off Owen's glasses kept me from seeing his eyes, making him look darker and more mysterious. I might occasionally have joked about my boyfriend the wizard, but I got the full sense of what that meant as I felt the power in the room swell. I took another involuntary step away from the bed.

Owen placed the compass on the map and passed a hand over it. I couldn't see from where I stood what had happened, but my guess was that he'd aligned the compass with the map, disconnecting it from the actual orientation. I blinked as my eyes watered from the smell of the smoldering herbs, and I started to feel woozy.

After another round of chanting, Owen opened the container of body glitter, poured it into his palm, and then scattered it onto the map. Merlin and Owen then joined their chants and there was a flash of light as the candles and burning herbs flared. When the flash reflected in the mirrors all around and over the bed, it was nearly as bright as if we'd turned the lights on. Then the candles dimmed, going lower than they'd been earlier, but there was another glow as the body glitter shimmered beyond the manufacturer's wildest advertising hyperbole.

While the glitter shimmered, it also swirled around the map, twisting into curls and shapes that gradually converged onto one point. Once all the glitter had piled up there, it shot into the air, forming a familiar-looking shape before suddenly collapsing and going dim. Owen and Merlin both jerked forward, like they were grasping at something that eluded them, and then the candles died out.

Once again, I was afraid to breathe. It was Merlin who broke the spell when he reached over to pat Owen on the knee. "Owen?" he asked softly, then turned to Ethan. "Mr. Wainwright, the lights, please."

I blinked as the lights came back on, and Owen gradually came out of his trance. He shook his head and stretched his shoulders, then said, "I thought I had him, but I lost him."

"Lost who?" I asked.

"Someone caught us prying and tried to trace back to us," Merlin said.

"And I almost figured out who it was," Owen said. He rubbed the back of his neck. "Did you get the aspirin?" I handed him the little container. "Thanks. Could you please get me some water?" I ran into the bathroom and took the paper cover off one of the glasses, filled it, and brought it back to him. He swallowed a couple of the aspirin, then said, "Doing magic like that always gives me a splitting headache."

"Unfortunately, we were too busy evading detection and trying to determine the identity of our foe to see the result of the spell," Merlin said. "What did you see?"

I then realized what shape that glitter had taken. "The Empire State Building," I said.

"That's what I saw," Ethan agreed.

"That must be the location," Owen said, taking off his glasses to rub his eyes and massage his temples.

"Location for what?" I asked.

"They're transmitting a spell," Owen said. "That's what's causing that illness. It's a spell being sent out from one of the highest points in the city, affecting every magical person who isn't protected."

"But what kind of spell?"

"That will require more research," Merlin said. "But at least we now know what to look for."

They both headed to the pile of books on the table, and Ethan set about cleaning up the remnants of the spell. The air had an odd smell—a mix of sulfur, candle wax, the herbs, and that ozone-like fragrance that the air takes on after a heavy lightning storm. I figured that was what the air freshener was for and sprayed it around the room after opening a window.

Owen looked up from the book he was studying. "There's a precedent for this spell, something nearly identical to what's been happening," he said.

Merlin leaned over to look at that book. "Yes, an interesting case in medieval times that almost went unnoticed because it happened during a wave of the plague."

Owen added, "But it was far more localized, reaching only as far as a particular crystal could spread energy. Now, though, they can combine magic with technology and affect an entire city. That's what they're transmitting from the Empire State Building."

"The question," Merlin said, "is what to do about it."

"Can you counter it?" I asked.

"There are a couple of different approaches," Owen said, turning pink behind the dark scruff on his jaw. He took off his glasses and rubbed his red-rimmed, bloodshot eyes again. "It can be done on an individual basis with a simple amulet that protects the wearer, which is probably how Spellworks—or whoever's doing this—is protecting their people. We could get our entire company back on its feet reasonably quickly, and then we could track down the source of the spell and destroy it."

"But I believe it would be far more efficacious to cancel the spell over the entire affected area," Merlin said. "Our enemies likely have personal protection. That means it's the innocents who are suffering, and we can't hope to get the general magical populace on our side if we don't help them in their hour of need."

Realization dawned on me. "Ooooh. So we take credit for curing the magic flu. Nice. It might help us against Spellworks."

"We'd deserve the credit," Owen muttered.

"Well, yeah, but maybe we can beat Spellworks at their own game. If we can stop this spell for everyone before they start selling anti-flu charms, we win."

Owen raised his hands in surrender. "Okay, you've convinced me. Now we have to find a way to cancel their spell by disabling or altering their transmission device. And we'll have to find someone nonmagical to do it because getting that close to that kind of magic is dangerous. If it made everyone in the city sick from up there, being near it could be deadly."

"Getting into the building and up to the top should be easy," I said. "Gemma's got a friend who works in the Empire State Building. She can get the special access pass, and then we could get to their transmitter without even waiting in line."

Owen grabbed another piece of paper and started scribbling. "Then I guess we'd better get to work."

"And you'd better do it fast, before they can get their own 'cure' going."

*

Ethan and I went out to find dinner to give Owen and Merlin room to work. They might have agreed upon an approach to take, but they disagreed rather strongly about the specific methods. I didn't understand one word in ten they said, and the magical chatter combined with the remnants of smoke from the spell had given me a headache. It was a relief to get out of the room, but I couldn't help but cringe when I saw the motel manager staring at us through the office's side window as we got in the car. "She's really going to wonder about us," I said to Ethan.

"I don't see why," he said calmly, giving the lady a wave as he drove away. "It's not like a honeymoon means all that much these days. If you've been living together for a few years, it's not like you're doing anything new."

"Yeah, but I just bought a stack of candles, some body glitter, and some bath herbs for lovers. That makes it sound like we're at least trying something new."

"Maybe we're saving them for tonight, after dinner, for round two after the fireman follies of the afternoon."

Ethan's cell phone rang as we pulled up at a pizza place. He answered, listened, then said, "Yeah, we can do that, but I think I have one in the trunk." After he hung up, he said, "That was Owen. He needs a transistor radio. I may have one for emergencies."

I followed as he got out of the car and went to check the trunk. "What emergencies could possibly require a transistor radio? You've got a radio in your car."

"What if my car breaks down and the radio won't come on? How will I know the weather forecast?" He dug in a latched plastic box in the trunk. "Aha! I knew I had one," he said, coming up with a small radio. He flicked it on and got a news program. "And the batteries are still good." I could only shake my head. I was all for preparation and liked to be ready for any situation, but Ethan took it to extremes.

We got back to the room with pizzas and drinks to find even more piles of diagrams. Ethan tossed the radio to Owen, then I took it away from him and put a slice of pizza in his hand instead. "Eat something first, then work," I instructed. "You still look awful."

After Owen ate enough for me to be willing to let him have the radio, I left him to the work while I lay on the bed and watched a movie on TV. Owen kept sending Ethan out to the car for supplies, and I worried about what the motel manager would think when he went out to get duct tape and a tool kit. It didn't help that Ethan reported with glee how much time she spent staring out the side window of the office.

Sometime during the evening, I must have fallen asleep. I woke groggy and disoriented from not having the slightest idea how long I'd slept or what time it was. There was light coming from around the edges of the curtains, but I couldn't tell if it was daylight or the parking lot lights. Merlin sat snoring in an armchair and Ethan was curled up on the other side of the bed. Owen was nowhere to be seen.

I jumped and bit back a shriek when the door opened, but relaxed when I saw that it was Owen. He looked tired but a million times better than he had the day before. He'd shaved and his hair was damp, as if from a shower, and he carried a doughnut box and a cardboard holder full of coffee cups. He set the doughnuts and the coffee on the table, and I eased my way off the bed, trying not to disturb Ethan.

Owen took one of the cups out of the holder and handed it to me, took another for himself, then gestured toward the box. We each took a doughnut and went outside, where there were lawn chairs on the walkway outside the rooms. "I suspect they'd rather sleep, and I can reheat the coffee later," he said once we were outside and sitting on the chairs.

"Didn't you need some rest?" I asked. Out in the morning light, the dark circles under his eyes were painfully visible.

"I got a few hours of sleep."

"But not enough. So, what's the plan?"

"I've rigged up a device that should cancel out the spell being transmitted. You, Gemma, and Marcia will need to get it into the Empire State Building. The device should help you locate the transmitter, and then all you'll have to do is set it up. I can talk you through it by phone, but I can't go near the city until you've got it working."

"Are you sure the cell phone will work up there?"

"Marcia's will. I made a few enhancements to it."

"Why were you souping up my roommate's phone?"

"Rod wanted to be sure he could reach her anywhere. It only works between magically enhanced phones, though, so if anyone else calls her when she's in a dead spot, she's out of luck. If you had a cell phone, I'd do the same for you."

"Okay, since you've thought through the communications logistics, it should be a piece of cake," I said, even though it sounded like anything but that. "How will I get back to the city?"

"You can get a train to Manhattan from a station not too far from here. We'll drop you off, then stay here until the job is done and Ethan can drive us back."

I couldn't help but smile. "That motel manager is really going to be curious if the bride disappears during the honeymoon and the honeymoon suite is occupied by three men." Speaking of which, the motel manager went out of the office to sweep the sidewalk, then did a double take to see me sitting outside with a shorter, darker-haired man after I'd checked in with a tall man with sandy-brown hair. I gave her a cheerful wave, and she blinked and shook her head.

"Yeah, we'll have to cross this place off the list for potential honeymoon spots," Owen said with a wry grin. "We probably won't be welcome back."

I had to work very hard not to visibly react to that, even as my heart practically leapt out of my chest at hearing him refer to potential honeymoon spots. It was probably just a joke, I told myself sternly.

After a long silence, he said, "I don't think I've properly thanked you."

"Thanked me?"

"For thinking clearly when nobody else was. I can't imagine what might have happened if you hadn't figured out what was going on."

I thought of and then discarded about a dozen responses, finally settling on, "I guess you'd have had to buy the Spellworks cure."

"I guess so." There was another long pause, and then he said, "I wasn't avoiding you. I mean, before I got sick."

"I was starting to wonder," I said with a weak laugh. "When a guy disappears after you've argued, it's generally a bad sign."

He winced. "Sorry about that. I should have thought about how you'd take it. I got busy trying to fix things in my own way—if we could figure out what was going on, then we wouldn't have anything to argue about."

"Well, maybe in the future you could respond to my messages or send up an 'I'm alive and I don't hate you' balloon every so often."

He grinned at me. "I'll remember that. In case you hadn't noticed by now, I'm not too good at communicating and relationships and all that." His grin gradually faded and he looked more serious. I wondered if I should say something, but then it looked like he might say something, and I didn't want to interrupt him, so I kept quiet and watched him.

And then the motel door opened and Ethan came outside with a cup of coffee. "I don't know who got the coffee," he said, "but I think I love you."

Owen turned scarlet before he broke eye contact with me and looked up at Ethan. "That was me."

"In that case, I meant 'love' in the spirit of friendship and brotherhood. Thanks, man."

"You're welcome," Owen said. "Need a reheat?"

I was left wondering what he was about to say to me, but it would have to wait because we had work to do.

CHAPTER ELEVEN

We went back inside, where Merlin was now also awake. While Merlin and Ethan ate, Owen talked me through what I would have to do. I wasn't sure what he'd done to Ethan's radio, but it was wrapped in duct tape and I felt a faint vibration when I held it. "I've already got it mostly set, but when you find the transmitter you'll have to turn the radio on and rotate the tuner dial until the radio is in sync with the transmitter. Wear your magic-detecting necklace and you'll be able to feel it."

"But how will we find the transmitter?"

"The radio will vibrate more the closer you get, and you should feel it in your necklace."

"Okay," I said, turning the radio over in my hands. It didn't look like anything magical at all, and yet this little thing could affect every magical person in the Manhattan area. "You're sure this will work?"

"Magic is a very uncertain art, my dear," Merlin said. "We always have to leave room for the unexpected."

As soon as Ethan had finished his coffee and doughnut, he drove me to the nearest train station. While he drove, I used his cell phone to alert my roommates that we were being called to action so Gemma could get her friend's building pass. As I'd expected, they were more than eager to take part. I'd be lucky if they hadn't created clever disguises by the time I got home.

And I wasn't lucky. They met me at the door of our new apartment wearing Bermuda shorts and loud Hawaiian shirts. "See? We're tourists!" Gemma said.

"You've got a pass to the building," I reminded her. "That means you aren't a tourist."

Her face fell. "Oh. Right."

"You can be the local showing us around. But I refuse to wear a

Hawaiian shirt."

"And Bermuda shorts make my thighs look fat," Marcia said. "I'm changing."

"Or maybe black catsuits," Gemma mused.

"No!" Marcia and I vetoed her, and I added, "We're going in legitimately. Looking like cat burglars would probably draw unwanted attention. Unless you *want* to scale the outside of that building at night."

She finally decided that she was the local who worked in the building showing around a foreign friend (Marcia) and her country cousin (me). I didn't think anyone would much care what our cover stories were, but it kept her from asking too many questions about the magic, so I let it go.

Marcia's phone had a Bluetooth headset, and I hid the earpiece under my hair. While I looked for Owen's cell number in my address book, Marcia pulled it up on the phone's screen. "Why do you have my boyfriend on speed dial?" I asked her with a raised eyebrow.

"It made it easier to nag him about remembering to eat and sleep while you were gone," she said. "Rod deputized me."

"He was that bad?"

"He was that bad. Not that it was all you. He's also a workaholic."

"Tell me about it. He did say that when all of this is over, we'd go away somewhere. Of course, I'm not sure what 'over' means." Then because I couldn't resist, I blurted, "And he made an offhand reference to honeymoon plans. It may have just been a joke, and I don't think he's planning to propose any time soon, but still, guys don't bring up the subject of honeymoons unless they're thinking along those lines, do they?"

Gemma adjusted the scarf she'd tied around her neck to accessorize her otherwise all-black "Really, I'm a local!" outfit. "Yeah, it's generally a good sign if a man ever mentions anything to do with weddings or families. Most guys don't even think about that stuff. So, are we ready?"

"I guess so," I said.

"Communications check?" Marcia said.

I hit Owen's cell number on Marcia's phone. When he answered, I said, "We're about to head out. Any last-minute advice?"

"Be careful. Look out for anything that feels like magic. After that spell we did, they know we're up to something, so there could be some danger."

"I was planning to be reckless. Putting my life on the line is fun!"

"You don't have to be sarcastic about it."

"I know, it's because you care. Anyway, I can hear you loud and clear. I'll call you back when we get there."

Marcia made a tick mark on her list. "Okay, that's a communications check. You've got the gizmo?"

I patted my shoulder bag. "It's in here. And it looks just like a transistor radio, so it shouldn't raise any suspicions."

"Though people may wonder about anyone with a transistor radio held together with duct tape in an age when everyone else is using MP3 players," Gemma said.

"But can you listen to a baseball game live on an iPod?" I asked. "Though I think Ethan had it for weather emergencies. Or maybe alien invasions. With him, you never know."

"That's a check on the gizmo. Other supplies?"

"I've got the duct tape," I said. "And I'm wearing the magic-detecting necklace. I'm good to go."

"I have my obnoxious tourist camera," Marcia said, holding up a huge, practically antique thirty-five millimeter camera on a neck strap. "Plus, my map and guidebook."

"All right, let's do this," Gemma said, putting her hand out like we were a team in a huddle. Marcia put hers on top of Gemma's, and with a sigh and a shrug, I joined them. "We're like the Charlie's Angels of magic. Let's go kick some magical butt," Gemma said. "Go, team!" Marcia and I echoed her.

Gemma went into character as soon as we left the building, giving us a running commentary on life in Manhattan as though we were tourists who were new to the city. We took the subway to the station nearest the Empire State Building, then Gemma waved her borrowed pass and got us past the line of tourists. We went up in the elevator, then changed elevators to go up to the observation deck.

The higher we went in the building, the more my necklace vibrated. I could also feel the device humming in my bag. Or maybe that was me. My legs were trembling, and I had to hang on to my purse strap to keep my hands from shaking visibly. My friends thought this was a lark, but I knew we could face real danger.

We stepped out of the elevator at the observation level, and I called Owen, hoping that his magical enhancements worked and I would have a cell signal. He answered, and I sighed with relief that things were going according to plan so far. "We're here," I said, feeling better to have his voice in my ear. "Now what?"

"Walk around. Let me know what you feel."

"The necklace is giving me fits."

"See if it's stronger in any one direction."

The observation deck was crowded on a summer Sunday afternoon, so that was easier said than done. On the bright side, having to squirm my way through crowds meant that meandering all over the place wasn't too terribly obvious. Gemma and Marcia joined me, and, giggling, they both leaned over and said into my earpiece, "Hello, Charlie."

I gave them what I hoped was a withering glare and hissed, "Knock it off, you two. This is serious."

"Who's Charlie?" Owen asked.

"My friends are getting delusions of grandeur about being on a secret mission." Gemma stuck her tongue out at me, and Marcia took her picture.

"That better not have film in it," Gemma shrieked, lunging for Marcia's camera. It was a shame I hadn't yet found the magical transmitter because they were creating a nice diversion.

"Are you getting anything?" Owen asked.

"I don't know. I can't tell much of a difference."

There was a tug on my sleeve and an older man said, "Excuse me, miss?"

"Just a sec," I whispered to Owen. "Yes?" I said to the man.

He held a digital camera out to me and gestured toward his wife. "Could you take our picture?" He had a heavier Southern accent than I did.

"Sure." I framed them against the skyline and took the picture, then showed it to them on the camera's LCD screen. "Is that good, or do you want another one?"

"That's fine, thank you." As they walked away, I heard him say to his wife, "See, I told you New Yorkers could be friendly."

"Sorry about that," I said to Owen. "Now, what do you need me to do?"

"Get out the radio."

I pulled it out of my purse and almost dropped it, it was vibrating so heavily. "Oh, is the game on?" Gemma said a little too loudly, even though no one seemed to be paying any attention to us. At least, they wouldn't be if Gemma didn't keep drawing their attention.

"It's going nuts," I told Owen.

"Check the tuner dial. It should move to the right when you get closer to the transmitter."

I went back to my aimless wandering, holding the radio up to my ear like I was listening to it and checking the dial every so often. It was difficult to be sure I was covering the whole deck when I had to dodge families, proposing couples, and just about every youth choir in America, all of which seemed to feel obligated to perform "God Bless America" *a capella* on top of the Empire State Building.

"Anything yet?" Owen asked, his voice edgy with impatience.

"Sorry, things are crazy up here. Maybe we should have waited and gone at night."

"You're there now, so let's get this done. I want to go home. Now, look at the dial and tell me what it's doing."

"It's scrolling to the left."

"Then turn right." I turned right and tried to look like I was ambling casually.

Gemma and Marcia flanked me, Gemma saying loudly, "What's the score?"

Marcia glanced around nervously and added, "What inning is it?"

"I thought you were supposed to be a foreign tourist," Gemma whispered to Marcia. "A foreign tourist probably wouldn't know about baseball."

"No one here knows or cares if I'm a foreign tourist," Marcia hissed back. "That was all in your head."

I cleared my throat. "Um, guys, busy saving the world here." Then I reported to Owen, "The dial's moving to the right."

"Then keep going that way. Stop and change directions when it moves to the left."

I moved steadily toward the northwest corner of the deck, then I saw something attached to the wall there. "I think I've found it," I told Owen.

Marcia and Gemma came to a stop beside me. "What is it? Where?" Marcia asked.

"That metal box there in the corner," I said, fighting the urge to point.

"I don't see anything," Gemma said, and Marcia shook her head.

"It must be veiled," I reported to Owen. "Gemma and Marcia don't see it."

"Then that's probably it," he said. "What does it look like?"

"It's a metal box attached to the wall."

"Can you get the cover open?"

"There's a minor problem with that."

"What's that?"

"There's someone standing right in front of it." A sad sack of a man in ill-fitting clothes and a haircut that looked like he'd done it himself at home in the dark without a mirror stood at that corner of the observation deck, holding a wilting red rose and a teddy bear with a red bow around its neck. He shifted his weight anxiously back and forth, from one foot to the other, while he craned his neck to study every woman who walked past. "I think we've got a *Sleepless in Seattle* situation here," I told Owen.

"A what?"

"It's a movie, probably not something you'd have seen. The important part is that the romantic happy ending involves two people meeting at the top of the Empire State Building. It seems like a lot of people who've met online think this is a good place to meet in person for the first time."

"It makes sense. It's a very public place, and you have to go through a security screening to get up there."

I tried not to sigh. He could be so hopeless when it came to this sort of thing. "I think the idea is that it's romantic, and it makes for a good story when people ask how you met."

"So, your situation is that one of these people is waiting for his cyber girlfriend to show up, right in front of the magical transmitter?" There was a strong note of skepticism in his voice.

"Yeah, sounds fishy to me, too."

Gemma interrupted. "Did you find it?" she asked.

"Maybe. I want to check it out. You two go to the gift shop. I may need you in reserve."

"Got it." She grabbed Marcia by the arm and the two of them disappeared into the crowd.

I ambled over to stand at the railing near Sleepless. He gave me a sidelong glance, then asked, "Are you Becky?"

"Nope, sorry," I said. My magic-detecting necklace hummed against my skin, but I couldn't tell if that was from the transmitter or from him.

"We were supposed to meet up here," he continued. His voice had a pathetic, whiny quality, but his eyes were flinty.

"That's nice," I replied, trying very hard to sound like I wasn't at all interested in him or in anything he happened to be standing right in front of.

"She's late," he continued.

I shrugged. "The lines are pretty long."

With an exaggerated sigh, he went back to leaning against the transmitter. I turned my back to him and walked away, saying to Owen, "I'm pretty sure that's our guard. I have to give them credit for coming up with a plausible reason for someone to stand around here all day. What do I do now?"

"Get rid of him."

"They've got barriers to keep people from being pushed over the edge."

"That wasn't what I meant. Think of something."

I found Gemma loudly explaining the American custom of the snow globe to an eyerolling Marcia. "That's definitely the thing," I said softly to them, "but they've got someone guarding it." I led them to where we could see Sleepless standing there with his drooping rose.

"That guy's a guard?" Marcia asked, her tone dripping with disdain.

"Yeah, I'm pretty sure, and he's got a great cover, you have to admit."

"What we need is a diversion," Gemma said, frowning in thought.

"What I need is to get him away from there and keep him away long enough for me to get the job done. I'm worried that he already suspects me."

"Why would he suspect you?"

"Because if he's magical and any good he'd have sensed this gizmo I'm carrying around."

Gemma said, "Looks like it's time for the reserves to step up." She straightened her back, tossed her hair and said, "Leave him to me."

Marcia and I watched from behind a choir singing "God Bless America" as Gemma walked past Sleepless, glancing shyly in his direction and nervously biting her lower lip. Finally, with a deep, steadying breath, she approached him, gesturing to the scarf knotted around her neck as though it was something she expected him to recognize.

"Oh, good call," Marcia said with an approving nod. "No sane man would say he's waiting for someone else after she claims to be his date, especially when he really isn't waiting for someone else, and when it looks like the closest he comes to being near someone like her is when he sleeps with the *Sports Illustrated* swimsuit issue under his pillow."

Gemma and Sleepless had the kind of conversation full of nervous laughter that tends to happen at first meetings, then she took his hand as though to lead him away, but he shook his head and held his ground. "He's definitely the guard," I said.

Just as the choir ended their song, Gemma's voice rose above all the hubbub, screeching, "You pervert! You never said that was the kind of relationship you were looking for!" Every head on the observation deck turned to stare, and a security guard came over.

"Miss, what seems to be the problem?" the guard asked.

"This–this freak just exposed himself to me!" Gemma sputtered in righteous indignation.

"Sir, we can't have behavior like that up here. I'll have to ask you to leave," the guard said.

Sleepless put up a protest, but that only made the guard more stern, and he grabbed the guy roughly by the upper arm to haul him away. Soon, the guard released him and backed off, rubbing his hand like he'd been zapped. I tried to think of something to do, then remembered that I had a wizard on hold. "Owen, our supposed cyber dater is using magic to keep the security guard from taking him away," I whispered. "What do I do?"

"Is the way clear to the transmitter?"

"For a moment, yeah."

"Get over there. He can't do anything to you while guards are around."

I moved as quickly as possible toward the transmitter while Marcia blocked me from view. The security guard had called for reinforcements, so Sleepless was busy for a moment. After another angry outburst, Gemma joined Marcia. "Okay, I'm there," I said to Owen.

"Now, see if you can open it," he instructed.

I got out my Swiss Army knife and pried open the cover, then as soon as I did, I gasped in pain and had to pull my necklace off and drop it in my purse. "There's some serious magic coming off this thing," I said.

"Then that's definitely what we're looking for. Turn the tuner until it stays on five when it's close to the box." I did what he said, then he told me, "Now, turn the radio on and tape it to the inside of the door. Will it fit when you close it?"

"It should."

"And what's that sound? Is it singing? It's terrible."

"Gemma and Marcia are singing 'New York, New York.' I think their theory is that it's so embarrassing that no one will come over here. Sleepless can't come back, either—even if he's escaped from the guards."

"That's actually pretty clever."

"I'll tell them you said so." I ripped off a strip of duct tape and secured the transistor radio to the inside of the metal box, then closed the lid and stood up. "Mission accomplished," I reported to Owen.

"Good work. Are they still singing?"

"Yeah. And everyone on the observation deck is studiously ignoring them."

"Make them stop and then get out of there before that guy does something."

"I don't see him." Gemma and Marcia finished their song with a flourish and a couple of high kicks, then I asked, "Are you two quite finished?"

They turned around. "Are you?" Marcia asked.

"Ages ago." I walked past them toward the elevators. "Honestly, I can't take you two anywhere."

Once we were out of the building and heading home, Gemma said with a groan, "I may never be able to show my face around that building again."

"You were brilliant," I assured her.

Gemma and Marcia were still rehashing their adventures when we got back to our building, so they didn't notice the young Indian woman leaning against the wall beside the front steps. She jumped up when she saw us coming. "Surprise!" she said.

CHAPTER TWELVE

It was my best friend from high school, Nita Patel, who had been working at her family's motel in our hometown the last time I saw her. "Nita!" I blurted before my brain could think of anything more diplomatic to say. "What are you doing here?"

"I got a job at a hotel here in New York! Isn't that great?" she said.

"Wow, yeah, that is great!" I said, fighting to sound enthusiastic as I stepped forward to hug her, even while I was inwardly groaning at the remarkably bad timing. I was glad to see my friend, but she wasn't in on the magical secret and that could make things complicated. Then I remembered my manners. "You remember Gemma and Marcia, don't you?"

"Of course! Hi!"

"Hi!" they chorused.

Nita clapped her hands in glee. "I can't believe I'm really here!"

"How long have you been here?"

"I got in this afternoon. I guess I should have called you, but I wanted to surprise you. I said I was getting out of that town, and now I have!"

"Why don't we go inside to talk?" Gemma suggested.

"Yes, of course," I said, stepping up to unlock the front door. "Come on up." I led the way up to our apartment and ushered Nita inside.

I could see her trying to keep the dismay off her face. "Wow, it's, well, um, cozy," she managed.

"It's a lot bigger than where we used to live," Marcia said.

Nita's eyebrows raised. "This is bigger?"

I patted her on the shoulder. "I told you, it's not nearly as glamorous as on TV. This is the way real people live."

"At least we all have actual bedrooms now," Marcia said, sitting on the sofa. "I used to sleep on a sofa bed in the living room."

Nita nodded. "The hotel rooms here are half the size as in our motel,

98

and they charge about six times as much for them. If we could move our motel here, we'd make a fortune."

Gemma sat on the sofa and gestured for Nita to join her. I dragged a dining chair over to join the group. "What did your parents say?" I asked as I sat.

Nita shrugged. "I have no idea. I left them a note. My brother took me to the bus depot, and he gave me a job reference. I'm lucky that the woman who hired me is also Indian, so she knew all about escaping the family business."

My stomach dropped. "You moved to New York without telling your parents?"

"They'd never have let me come. Better to ask forgiveness than permission, right?"

"That's always worked for me," Gemma said with a laugh.

Nita grinned at Gemma and crossed her legs. "I figure they'll come around when I remind them that I've now significantly increased my chances of meeting a nice Indian boy I could marry. You don't know any Indian men, do you? I hear you're quite the matchmaker."

"I'll see what I can find for you," Gemma promised.

"Have you found a place to stay?" Marcia asked.

I was pretty sure where Marcia was going, and I knew she thought she was doing me a favor, but I wished I could think of a way to signal her to shut up.

"I haven't started looking," Nita answered.

"Now that we have the bigger place, you could stay here," Marcia offered. "We'd have to do some rearranging, but you and Katie could take one room and I'd move in with Gemma. We did say we might take on a fourth when we moved here."

"Sounds great!" Gemma said.

They all looked at me, and I forced a smile. "Yeah!" I said. Under other circumstances, I'd have loved to have Nita move in. When we were in high school, we'd talked about going off to some big city together. But it had been so nice not having to be careful what I said around my roommates, and I hated to go back to lying and keeping secrets. I wasn't allowed to tell anyone about magic, and I didn't want Nita to find out the way Gemma and Marcia had, by being put in danger by the magical bad guys.

"You'll barely notice I'm around," Nita promised. "I'll get all the worst shifts while I'm new."

"You'll need to get a bed," Marcia said. "In the meantime, the sofa folds out, and you can sleep there. I'll talk to the landlord about getting you on the lease, and we'll recalculate the rent and the chores list for everyone."

"I'm so excited!" Nita squealed. "It'll be just like *Sex and the City*, except they never all lived together. Maybe we're more like *Friends*, except we don't have guys across the hall—or do we?" She bounced to her feet. "I'll go get my luggage at the hotel. I don't have a lot of stuff. I'll have my family mail things to me once I'm settled—that is, if they don't disown me. But I figure they'll be a lot happier knowing I'm living with Katie."

Marcia went to the cookie jar where we kept a set of spare keys. "You'll need these. The one with the blue dot opens the outside door, and the other one opens the apartment door."

"Okay, got it. Back in a bit!" She hurried out before we could offer to help, her squeal of joy echoing up the stairwell.

Once she was gone, I allowed myself a long, low groan.

"What, you didn't want her living with us?" Marcia asked.

"I do," I said. "It's just that she doesn't know about the M-word, and there's all this crazy stuff going on. I don't want her getting into any danger."

Gemma cocked her head to one side. "Would you ever have told us if we hadn't been caught up in it?"

"It's not my secret to tell, and they have very strict rules about it. I would have preferred to keep you two out of it, but the bad guys had other ideas."

"And now we're practically honorary magic people," Gemma said with a smile. "Carrying out secret missions, and all that."

I smiled, too, but inside I was worried. I wanted to keep Nita out of it. Adapting to the real New York that wasn't anything like what she'd seen in movies would be difficult enough for her. She didn't need to face magic on top of that.

*

True to her word, Nita was gone before we got up Monday morning, but she did leave a note with a smiley face on the dining table. She was so enthusiastic about being in New York that I couldn't begrudge her being here, even if it might complicate my life.

For the first time in ages, Owen was at his usual spot when I came down to go to work. He didn't look completely healthy, but he didn't look on the brink of death, either. "It seems our cure was successful," I remarked before filling him in about Nita's arrival.

The subway station was more crowded than it had been the previous week as many of the people sickened by the magical flu were up and about. The obviously magical people—the ones with wings and pointed ears—had that wan, hollow-eyed look of people recovering from illness, while quite a few otherwise normal-looking humans had a similar look. I could tell who in the station had magical powers based on how awful they looked.

I could also tell by the way they looked at Owen. Usually, he had a knack for remaining practically invisible in public, in spite of his good looks, but all the obviously magical people and the others who looked like they'd been ill were definitely noticing him today. They gave us a fairly wide berth for a crowded subway platform, and they kept tossing suspicious glances in Owen's direction.

"We must have missed the parade," Owen muttered as he looked around at the others on the platform.

"What parade?" I asked, jolted out of my concern about his apparent public enemy status.

"That's what I was wondering. Look how many people are wearing something that looks like parade beads."

I took another look at the people on the platform and saw that most of those who had the recovering-from-the-flu look were wearing necklaces of cheap-looking plastic beads, the kind that get tossed from parade floats. The necklaces all had flat plastic pendants with a quasi-Celtic symbol dangling from them. "Weird," I said to Owen. "None of these people look like they felt like going to a parade."

A train arrived and we joined the crowd pouring into it. At first, it took all my concentration to find a place to stand and then hang on as the train started moving, but then I looked up and saw the latest Spellworks ad. It advertised a surefire cure for the magical flu—an amulet, available for a special low price, that looked like the beads Owen had noticed.

I tugged on Owen's sleeve and pointed to the ad. "Just as we expected," I said.

He groaned. "I need to get one of those amulets so I can see exactly what it is. There go my plans for the day."

When I got to my office, I found Perdita back at work, looking her usual chipper self. "Oh, there you are!" she said. "I was worrying that you'd caught my flu."

"I'm fine. And you're all better now?"

"Just peachy, thanks to this." She pulled a strand of beads out from beneath her blouse. "My mom got these for the whole family, and as soon as I put it on, I felt so much better."

"It wasn't the beads. You'd have been better anyway."

She frowned. "Are you sure?"

"Oh, yeah. That's what I spent my weekend dealing with. Now we need to get a look at those beads. Could I borrow yours?"

She wrapped her fingers around her necklace, then hesitated. "I don't want to get sick again."

"You won't. In fact, you're probably more likely to get sick if you have that on. They come from Spellworks, you know."

Her slanted eyebrows rose even higher. "Really? Mom didn't say that." She pulled the beads over her head and handed them to me. I took them and headed straight to Owen's lab.

"I've got something for you," I called out as I entered. He looked up from where he was leaning over a table, peering at something that I soon saw was another set of the beads. "Oh, never mind."

"Jake had a set."

"I got them because I knew you'd want to analyze them," Jake said defensively. "I never believed they were a cure."

"Are they a cure?" I asked.

"They would counteract the spell," Owen said. "But there's something else there." He gestured toward the line of Spellworks charms he'd been analyzing. "Even though each of these is supposed to protect against a different kind of spell, there's a bit of magic that shows up in all of them. It was so minor I missed it in the charms, but it's strong enough in these amulets to be obvious, and once I knew what I was looking for, I found it in the charms. Now I need to isolate it and figure out what it is. I'm certain that's the important part—the reason they've created the situations to make people want to buy these."

I leaned on the table and watched as he held his hands above the various charms. "They must have a timetable—something big planned that needs as many people as possible to have these things," I mused out loud. "That would be the reason for the flu. It affected absolutely everyone who's magical, even inside MSI. Before, probably only people who'd been directly affected by the magical crime or who were prone to paranoia would have bought protective charms. This way, they get a lot more people, all at once."

Owen frowned, closed his eyes for a moment, then shook his head. "I think there's a conduit here. It's hard to tell because nothing's being transmitted right now."

"What does that mean?" I asked.

He looked up from the charms and faced me. "Most of the time, affecting someone magically requires either line-of-sight contact or possession of something belonging to the subject. These things—if they're what I think they are—work like having something belonging to the subject, only in reverse. The person who created these things would be able to magically affect anyone in possession of one. They form a link between the creator and the holder."

"That doesn't sound good."

Owen called to Jake, "I need containment chambers, right away."

"On it, boss."

Owen turned back to me. "I can set these up to monitor anything they receive without it affecting us. Then I may be able to do something to feed back into the system and cancel any spell that's sent out. Unfortunately, I won't be able to do much until they use the link, and then I'll have to act quickly."

"In the meantime, you'd better make a company-wide announcement about getting rid of these," I said. "We don't want our people to be affected."

"I'll get Sam on it."

He sounded so discouraged, I patted him on the shoulder and said, "Look on the bright side. Us shutting off the flu spell may have helped. If people who didn't buy them immediately felt better anyway, fewer people may have bought them, and that means fewer people will be affected by anything else they do with these."

"We can only hope," he said with a weak attempt at a weary smile as he headed into his office to call Sam.

While he was gone, I watched Jake place glass domes over the charms and amulets and tried to think like a magical megalomaniac. I didn't know if I was flattering myself by amplifying the importance of my conference, but that was something coming up quickly that might have influenced the timetable for getting those conduit charms into the hands of as many people as possible. If someone wanted to bring MSI down, that would be a great place to hit.

Owen came back into the lab. "Sam's making a company-wide announcement that these things are a security risk, and people are supposed to turn them in or they'll be confiscated."

"Good," I said with a nod, then I asked, "When you get your bursts of foresight, how does it feel?"

He frowned in thought. "It's an odd sensation, like a shiver and a brief bout of queasiness. Why?"

"It's probably too late to call the whole thing off, but I suddenly have a very bad feeling about the conference, like it's all going to go horribly wrong."

"That's not precognition. That's logic. I don't see how they'll be able to resist hitting the conference, and that could be good for us. That may be what flushes the person behind all this out into the open so we can deal with whomever it is."

I tried to hide my growing sense of unease with a smile that probably looked maniacal. "Well, that's certainly a new way to think about it. The best-case scenario is that everything will go horribly wrong." With a sigh, I added, "And now I'd better get back to planning the final details of the maiden voyage of the *Titanic*. I need to make sure we hit that iceberg."

On the way back to my office, I passed Sam in the hallway. He was flying at breakneck speed, with several of the amulets dangling from his feet as an angry woman chased him. "Can't talk now, doll," he said as he flew by. "It's contraband!" he shouted down the hallway at the angry woman. "You're not gonna get the flu without it."

I hoped the rest of the company was more cooperative about giving up the charms, or we'd be in big trouble.

CHAPTER THIRTEEN

The last few days before the conference suddenly became insanely busy. The crew creating the enchanted pavilions in the park set up the venue, then Rina took care of the decorations. I went uptown a few times to check on progress and make sure everything on the to-do list was getting done. I tried to anticipate every possible thing that could go wrong, hoping I could prevent a disaster.

"You're sure no one nonmagical can see this?" I asked a building crew leader on one of my visits. It looked like an old-fashioned circus had set up in the middle of Central Park, and I couldn't imagine that no one would notice.

"Not only can no one nonmagical see it," he replied, "but no one who's not on the guest list, either. That's why we need to get the latest version of the guest list and keep it updated."

"Yeah, I could see where that would be important," I said, making a note. It would be awful if someone showed up and wasn't able to find the place. And if anyone did wander in off the street because they saw the set-up and wondered what was going on, then we'd know we had a new magical immune to recruit. I hoped the spells were enough to keep out unauthorized bad guys, but I still suspected that the main bad guy was one of our speakers. I wondered if I could get away with "accidentally" removing Ramsay from the guest list.

The morning of the conference dawned bright and sunny, with a slight hint of a breeze and lower humidity than normal. The beautiful weather could have been a good omen, but it didn't make me feel much better. I was afraid it only meant we'd have a pretty backdrop for the magical showdown or whatever else happened. When I got to the park, Rina was putting the finishing touches on the décor and on the welcoming breakfast. "How does it look?" she asked.

"It's fabulous," I told her, in all honesty. She'd really outdone herself. The assembly area looked like a forest, with the food and drink stations set up on large fallen logs or massive boulders. Magical medieval instruments hovering overhead provided a lilting soundtrack, and ethereal nymphs floated around the scene, carrying trays. I was tempted to find some little thing to mess up so that could be the worst thing that could happen and I could relax, but I knew it wouldn't work. Whatever was going on was far bigger than Murphy's law.

We still had about half an hour before the guests were due to arrive and I needed someone to shake me back to sanity before I snapped, so I went out to the enclosure where Owen had transported his dragons. The moment I stepped through the doorway, a voice called, "Duck!" and I did so without stopping to question why. A split second later, a gust of flame shot right through where I'd been standing. "Sorry about that," Owen said, running over and giving me a hand up. "They're a little jittery. I don't know if they've picked up on my stage fright or if they're still adapting to the new surroundings."

One of the dragons gave a roar that petered out into a whimper, and then it curled up into a ball on the ground, wrapping its tail around itself. Owen raised a hand and closed his fist, and the light in the tent dimmed. That seemed to soothe the dragons. Then I took another look at Owen. He was dressed in jeans and a sooty T-shirt, not at all like he was prepared to make a presentation. "This is a new look for you," I remarked.

He glanced down at his clothes. "Don't worry, I'll change before I go on, but after I spend the day with these guys, anything I'm wearing will be a mess. Did you need something?"

"I was just checking to see how things are going," I lied, suddenly feeling foolish—not for fearing that something bad would happen, but rather for feeling like I could do anything to stop it other than make sure the conference itself went smoothly. "And it looks like we'll want to dim the lights for the dragon show." I made a note on my clipboard. Then I picked up on what he'd said about stage fright. Apparently, I wasn't the only one with an attack of nerves. "Are you okay about doing this?"

He ran a hand through his hair, and I noticed that the hand trembled ever so slightly. "Well, you know me and talking. I'm sure I'll be fine when I get up there, but thinking about it gives me jitters."

"You'll do fine," I said, patting him on the one clean spot on his shoulder. "You're awesome in meetings. Just think meeting mode. This isn't interpersonal at all. You're presenting your latest findings to fellow professionals. You can do that."

With a big grin, he said, "Yeah, I can do that. I'd kiss you, but I don't want to make you smell like sulfur."

"You know, I think playing with these dragons is your excuse to avoid going out there and interacting with customers."

His cheeks went pink, and he slowly shook his head. "You're getting to know me far too well." Then he gave me an appraising look. "And how are *you* holding up?"

"I'm a basket case," I admitted. "It's terrifying knowing that the best-case scenario involves the bad guys making a move that will disrupt the conference."

"If they do, it's not a reflection on you and your work."

"I know. But even if I hadn't planned this event, I'd be going crazy waiting for the other shoe to drop—and to find out what kind of shoe it will be."

"I'm not just in here to play with dragons," he said, gesturing toward a table set against the far wall, where his set of Spellworks charms lay under glass covers. "I'm monitoring these things, so I'll know if they use the conduits."

"And what happens if they do?"

"Then I'll have to act fast," he said with a grin that bordered on cocky. More seriously, he added, "Don't worry, I won't let them mess things up. I'll put a stop to whatever it is. Does that make you feel better?"

I nodded, then sighed. "I guess so." I attempted a brave grin and said, "Look at us—you with stage fright and me being a nervous Nellie. Is it too late to run away?"

"Probably. But ask me again in a few hours. I might change my mind."

One of the dragons came over to him and rubbed its face against his shoulder, like an overgrown, fire-breathing cat. He scratched it behind the knee, and I felt a surge of affection for him. That image summed up Owen Palmer pretty well, I thought—powerful enough to tame dragons, but still sweet and even a bit vulnerable. If it hadn't been for all the soot and the fact that he had a dragon looming over him, I would have hugged him.

Before I gave in to the temptation, I promised to check on him before his presentation and went back to the front of the main tent, where the customers had begun arriving. The sales staff were circulating and greeting their customers. Food and drink magically replenished themselves, and the nymphs collected empty plates and glasses.

Everything seemed to be going perfectly, but I couldn't help noticing how many of the customers wore those colorful rubber bracelets or the anti-flu amulets. There was no telling how many of them were also carrying the smaller charms. If the Spellworks crowd did want to disrupt the conference, they had the people in place to do so. The question was, what would they do?

I saw a commotion near the entrance, and soon most of the attendees abandoned the food to head in that direction. It was like someone had sent up the Bat Signal—or was it all those charms kicking into action? I followed the crowd to see what was going on and found Ramsay, trailed by an entourage, glad-handing his way through the assembly area. You'd have thought he was a movie star from the way everyone acted. Several took photos with their cell phone cameras, and one guy even asked for an autograph.

It was enough to make my stomach churn. Why didn't they see him the way I did?

On the other hand, why didn't I see him the way they did? I had no actual evidence against him, just suspicion. I studied Ramsay and his fan club, looking for any sign of an influence spell. None of the worshippers had the tell-tale glassy eyes of a serious influence spell, but then the more subtle attraction spell Rod used to use hadn't had that effect. How had I known Rod was using a spell? I tried to remember my early experiences in the magical world. I'd mostly noticed a discrepancy between the way I reacted to Rod and the way all other women did, as well as the discrepancy between their reaction and Rod's appearance.

Based on that, I still couldn't tell if Ramsay's appeal was magical or ordinary. I certainly wasn't under his spell, but I also hadn't grown up in the magical world so that he'd been a lifelong hero to me. I hadn't heard stories about him, didn't know until recently that he'd once saved the magical world from evil rogue wizards.

Still, he just bugged me.

Someone suddenly grabbed my arm and pulled me into the green room, where the speakers went to get ready for their presentations. "He's here," Kim hissed at me.

"Yeah, I noticed," I replied, guessing who she meant. "That's not a surprise."

"Do you think he's up to something here? This would be a good place for him to get his followers to help him take over. I'll tail him throughout the conference, watch his every move, just in case."

Why did everyone around me have delusions of being a secret agent? Before I could respond to Kim, a deep voice behind me said, "Ladies, is there a problem?" It was Merlin.

I was tongue-tied for a moment. I didn't think I yet had enough evidence to tell Merlin about my suspicions, so I brought up something that might be a problem worth discussing in the green room. "A lot of the guests have those charms and amulets that Owen thinks could be used as conduits," I said. "That has me worried."

"I'm sure you have the matter well in hand," he said.

There was a commotion at the doorway and Ramsay swept in. "This looks like an outstanding event," he boomed.

"Ivor, good of you to make it," Merlin said tightly.

"I wouldn't have missed it. We need to present a united front. I've been out there mingling, and the customers have very nice things to say. My compliments to Katie for all her hard work."

"Thanks," I said, trying not to grit my teeth, "And speaking of hard work, I'd better get back to it."

As I hurried back to the assembly area, the attendees were moving into the auditorium tent, where swirling lights and eerie music created a magical wonderland. It looked to me like a prom on steroids, but the guests were eating it up, so I figured it was working. "Great job, Rina," I said as she scurried by me, barking orders into a headset. She flashed me a smile and kept going, and I gave myself a moment to take a deep breath.

As the opening session began, I went back to the dragon enclosure to check on Owen.

"How's it going out there?" he asked.

"Okay, I guess. I had no idea what a celebrity Ramsay is, though."

"Did someone ask him for an autograph?"

"Oh yeah. I thought a couple of those guys might faint."

He grinned, then he frowned and tilted his head as he stared at the charms he was monitoring. "What is it?" I asked.

Instead of answering me, he called, "Jake!" His assistant ran over to join us, and the two of them placed their hands on the glass cases. After a moment, Owen said, "There's a surge coming through," and then his eyes went unfocused, like he was looking within. "Okay, got it, got it, got it," he muttered to himself, then abruptly he said, "Damn!"

"I lost it, too, boss," Jake said, panting. His hair was plastered to his forehead with sweat. Owen looked equally beat.

"What happened?" I asked.

"They sent a signal, but I don't think it was a spell or a directive. It was more like a test, like the magical equivalent of 'testing, one, two, three' with a microphone. I thought for a moment I'd tracked it back to the source, but they stopped the signal before I could disrupt it. I might be able to counteract anything else they send, though."

"What about when you're doing the demonstration?"

Owen and Jake looked at each other. "I'd leave it to Jake, but I need him with me to help handle the dragons."

"Then get someone else to keep an eye out. If I were the bad guys—who seem to know all about who you are—that's when I'd choose to strike."

"I've got more charms set up back at the office," Owen said with a weary sigh. "I'll give them a call and see if they caught anything."

"Delegation won't kill you," I reminded him. "I'll go see if anything happened when that surge hit."

I ran back into the main hall, where a member of the sales team was giving highlights of the year. It didn't look like anything major had happened. The place was still standing and I didn't see any blood. The audience hadn't turned into an army of magical zombies. So far, so good. I went out to the assembly area and poured myself a glass of juice from one of the buffets. I'd eaten breakfast before leaving home, but that was hours ago, and I was already starving again. Before I could drink it, Rina came running over to ask me a question. It went like that all day. The conference was going smoothly, but there seemed to be a conspiracy against me getting anything to eat. By the time for Owen's presentation late in the day, the most I'd managed to eat was a cube of cheese during the afternoon breakout session, and I was becoming light-headed.

I went to the green room to check on Owen and found him pacing nervously. He'd cleaned up and changed clothes, so now he looked like the professional he was, but he also looked like he might bolt given the first opportunity. "Do I really have to do this?" he asked me, his voice sounding strained and not too steady.

"Well, considering that you have to represent Research and Development because your boss is a giant frog and refuses to go out in public, and considering that you're the one who tamed the dragons, yeah, you really have to do this. Now, take a deep breath and settle down."

He closed his eyes and took a few long, shuddering breaths, then shook his head. "No, that didn't work. I can't talk."

"You do it in meetings all the time. This is just a really big meeting."

His eyes went wide and panicky. "But there are a lot of people in there, and they'll all be staring at me. A lot of them may even think I'm the big magical criminal."

"Only the ones dumb enough to listen to rumors. Once the dragons come on, they'll all forget you're even there." That didn't seem to make him feel much better. It was time for tough love. "Look, Owen, this isn't the time for a shy attack. The way the lights are, you won't be able to see most of the audience."

I grabbed his shoulders and pulled him close to me so I could look him directly in the eye. "I'm going out there to sit in the front row, where you should be able to see me, and I want you to give this presentation to *me*. I'm the only person in the audience, and I will like you no matter how it goes. Can you do that?"

He took another deep breath and let it out slowly. "Yeah, I can do that."

"I know you can. I've seen you take on things a lot scarier than that crowd." We stood there for a while, our eyes locked, and I wasn't sure if I was picking up on his stage fright or if something else was going on, but my heart pounded and my mouth went dry. As I looked into his eyes, I decided it wasn't stage fright on my end. It was the dizzying realization that I was in love with this guy. I was about to tell him, with the hope that would distract him from his fear, when Hartwell's voice came from the stage, introducing

Owen. I stood on tiptoes and gave him a quick, hard kiss. "Now go knock 'em dead."

I went into the auditorium and found an empty seat, front and center, just as Owen came on stage. He froze at first, and his voice was soft when he started talking, but once he found me in the front row, he gained confidence and sounded more normal. Then he really got going as he forgot about the crowd and focused on his favorite thing to do: geek out about the science of magic.

Soon, he had the audience eating out of the palm of his hand, and there was little wonder. Take an incredibly good-looking guy with next to no ego and a passion for his subject matter, and you've got a captivating speaker. "But enough talk. Now I'd like to show you something," he said. "I don't know how many of you have pets, but those of you who do probably know that making them behave can be a challenge. We've developed a way to make pet misbehavior a thing of the past. I know this works because it works on my cat—and if you have cats, you know exactly what that means." That got him a laugh, and he grinned as he continued, "But it's hard to do a proper demonstration on something as small as a cat, so I thought I'd show you just how effective this is." The audience gasped audibly when he brought the dragons on stage.

The dragons went through their paces, playing fetch, rolling over, and even toasting a marshmallow on a stick. There was only one minor mishap involving a curtain that got accidentally set on fire, but Jake doused it immediately. I held my breath the whole time, nervous for Owen, but also worried that the Spellworks people would strike at any moment. I got a sense of tension from the audience, but it was hard to tell if it had anything to do with magic or was just because they were in the presence of real, live fire-breathing dragons. When Owen sent the dragons away and ended his presentation, the audience gave him a standing ovation.

Hartwell introduced Ramsay, who got an extended standing ovation and a roar from the crowd. Ramsay basked in the admiration until the applause died down long enough for him to give Merlin a long-winded introduction. The response to Merlin was more subdued, but more from awe than lack of enthusiasm. He talked about the founding of the company and the changes he'd noticed in magic since his return.

I glanced to the side and saw Owen come in one of the doors near the back of the auditorium. Although I had an empty seat next to me, he stayed near the exit, watching the crowd.

Merlin spoke fervently about the importance of using magic for good, and the crowd was totally with him. I felt like I was at an old-fashioned tent revival. I barely kept myself from shouting, "Amen!"

Then Merlin said, "You're probably aware of our competition by now, and there are some things you should know about that company. The man who has served as the face of Spellworks has rejoined MSI, and he can tell you more about what their magical methods really mean. I am pleased to welcome Mr. Phelan Idris."

That brought murmurs of surprise and some tentative applause. Someone had really managed to clean Idris up. He almost looked respectable in a nice suit. It may have been the first time I'd ever seen him in clothes that actually fit him. I held my breath as he started talking. "I'm a big one for fun and, let's face it, mischief," he began, and I relaxed as I recognized the opening line of the speech I'd written for him. "That was the reason I left MSI. I was creating spells that caused trouble, and those spells were the foundation for Spellworks."

He was no orator. He sounded stiff and like he was reciting from memory, which he was, but at least he was more or less on script. "It does seem like every generation has someone rise up to challenge the status quo," he went on, and that wasn't in the script. I held my breath again. "I guess I was this generation's one." His smirk indicated that he was proud of that, and that worried me. "I'm not old enough to remember it, but some of you probably remember the last time we went through this, only it was a lot worse when the Morgans tried to take over the magical world. They used magic—raw power—to stop anyone who got in their way, and it took a lot of raw power to bring them down."

Merlin, who'd taken a seat on stage during Idris's speech, rose slowly to his feet when Idris went off-script, but he hesitated. Anything that looked like censorship at this point was bound to backfire. I had no idea what was coming, but my heart pounded in anticipation.

"What were their names? I think it was something like Kane and Mina. Yeah, that's it, Kane and Mina. They were pretty young, even younger than I am now. Maybe that's a phase particularly powerful wizards go through." He smirked again and shrugged, like he was including himself in that group. "But the good guys destroyed the bad guys, and all was right with the world. There was just one loose end. One very tiny loose end. Like, a baby they left behind. Just think about the power that kid might have, with those parents, and with the amount of power Mina was channeling while she was pregnant. Didn't you ever wonder what happened to that kid?"

The audience was spellbound. I wondered how Idris could possibly have all these details that weren't in the histories, but given his interest in the darker side of magic, I supposed he was likely to dig up that kind of dirt.

"Believe it or not, he's been among us all along, right in the heart of things, hidden by the so-called good guys, and totally trusted, in spite of who and what he is. You'd think as paranoid as these people are, they'd be more careful." Merlin moved closer and closer to Idris, but Idris kept talking. "In fact, you saw him here tonight. Let's see, what was that baby's name? Why, I do believe it was Owen. Only, he doesn't go by Owen

Morgan these days."

I felt like the floor fell out from under me. Instinctively, I turned to where I'd seen Owen last. He was standing with his back flattened against the door, his eyes wide, all the color drained out of his face.

"Yeah, that's right, our Owen Palmer is the last remnant of the darkest magical days in recent memory."

And from the look on Owen's face, I knew it was news to him.

CHAPTER FOURTEEN

I jumped out of my seat and sprinted toward Owen. While I ran, Idris kept talking. "And it sounds like he's up to his parents' old tricks, since it seems like he's always around whenever dark spells are used to commit a crime." Then there was a yelp and a commotion from the stage. I turned to see Merlin stepping forward to grab the microphone while security guards went after Idris. The crowd muttered and mumbled, but so far they didn't seem to be turning into a mob.

Owen was gone by the time I reached the doorway where he'd been standing, and I could hardly blame him for getting out of there. I ran through the outer assembly area, looking for him. Even if he'd gone invisible by veiling himself, I should have been able to see him, but he was nowhere in sight.

I tried the dragon enclosure, but Owen wasn't there. I ran back to the assembly area, where people were pouring out of the auditorium. They entirely ignored Rina's carefully arranged dinner buffets as they hashed over the announcement. From the bits and pieces I picked up, I got the impression that some had decided that MSI wasn't to be trusted and that they'd known all along that Owen Palmer was up to no good. There were a few who scoffed at the accusations, and the MSI sales force was attempting damage control.

Before I could give in to the urge to deliver a few bloody noses for the things people were saying about Owen, I headed for the green room to talk to Merlin and get to the bottom of this. With any luck, I might also be able to get to Idris. His neck was skinny enough for me to wrap my hands around it.

I ran into Rod on the way there. "He's not—?"

I shook my head.

He sighed heavily. "I've already tried his cell phone, but there's no answer."

"Rod, is it true?"

Groaning, he rubbed the back of his neck. "I don't know. I never heard anyone say anything. I do know that when he started school, James and Gloria asked me to keep an eye on him, and they wanted me to tell them if anything happened. I always thought it was because he needed someone to look out for him. He was so small when he was young, and you know how shy he is. But I guess it could have been because they had to keep tabs on him."

"So he had jailers instead of parents? And a magical marshal instead of a best friend?" I said, my voice verging on an outraged screech. "No wonder he's so screwed up."

"Our friendship was always real," Rod insisted, his voice strong and firm. "I never faked that. He's my best friend and might as well be my little brother, and since he's in trouble, I think we have better things to do than argue."

I shook my head wearily. "Sorry. I think priority one is finding Owen. I already checked with the dragons. Do you think he might go talk to James and Gloria?"

"I doubt it. When he's upset, he withdraws. He doesn't go talk to anyone."

"Imagine what he must be feeling," I whispered, tears of sympathy welling in my eyes.

"Okay, you give this place a once-over in case he's lurking, and I'll make a few phone calls, then we'll meet back here and figure out where to go next," Rod said, sounding crisp and businesslike.

I nodded and ran off, though I didn't expect to find Owen anywhere in the vicinity of the tents. While I checked the perimeter of the conference area, Sam flew up to me and landed nearby. "I guess you're lookin' for Palmer," he said.

"Yeah, have you seen him?"

"Sorry, no. And not a sign of Idris, either. He vanished in all the commotion—which was probably his plan all along. You think the kid's okay?"

"He's not okay. He's in shock and he's alone," I said. *Why didn't he wait for me?* I wondered. I would have been willing to vanish with him.

Sam came along when I went back to meet Rod. "Anything?" Rod asked me.

"Not a sign."

"I called James and Gloria to give them a heads up, but they'd already got the word. They haven't heard from him. James offered to come to the city, but I told them to stay put for now. I'm still not getting an answer on his cell or his home phone."

"Can you track his cell phone?" I asked. "He did something magical to that phone, so maybe you guys can find it."

"Let me check." Rod made another phone call, then came back to me. "Got it. Let's go."

"I'm comin' with," Sam said, flying alongside us as we ran from the tents.

It was still daylight, and this was the longest day of the year. At least we wouldn't have to search in the dark for a few more hours. "The phone's in the park, so he may have found a private place to think," Rod said. He pointed the way so Sam could fly ahead, and then we reached a secluded spot in the Ramble, where a cell phone lay abandoned on the ground.

"There goes that idea," I said, kneeling to pick up the phone. I checked the missed calls list, and it was full. Everyone was calling him. No wonder he'd ditched the phone. I turned it off and put it in my pocket.

Rod swore and kicked a rock. "Now what?"

"You've known him longer than I have. Where's he likely to go if he needs to think? Does he have any favorite places or places where he feels safe?"

Rod ran his hands through his hair the way Owen usually did when he was thinking. "You mean other than home? That's where he usually feels safest. Let's see, I know that sometimes when he needs to clear his head, he goes up to the park around the Cloisters. And there's the stadium. I don't think there's a game tonight, though."

"I'll go up there," Sam offered. "I can stop by the cathedral along the way and get a few gargoyles to help." He took off, soaring uptown.

"Anything else?" I asked Rod.

"There's the bookstore. Someone could hide in the Strand for hours— and he's been known to do so."

"Then let's go."

We ran to the nearest subway station to head downtown. I was so distracted by worry that we were halfway to our stop when I noticed that there were Spellworks ads in our car—new ones proclaiming the trustworthiness of the company since it didn't keep secrets. I elbowed Rod and pointed it out. "They had to have planned that," I said. "I wonder if Idris knew all along."

"I wonder *how* he knew. I grew up with Owen, and I didn't know anything."

When we reached the bookstore, I wished we'd kept Sam with us. It would take someone with wings to do a quick search of this place. If you wanted to hide from someone, this was better than a maze. "Do we split up or stick together?" I asked Rod.

"Splitting up might be more efficient, but it's probably best if we stick together since you're the one who'll be able to spot him even if he's used an invisibility spell, and I can stop him from getting away."

We worked our way gradually through the store, level by level, starting with the sections where we were most likely to find Owen and then spreading out. For perhaps the first time in my life, I spent at least an hour in a bookstore without being tempted by even one book. My feet were killing me and I was dizzy from hunger when we finally concluded that he wasn't there.

"There's a diner near here that he likes," I said, unsure whether I suggested that because I was starving or because I thought Owen might go there.

He wasn't at the diner, and the waitress, who remembered me from having been there with Owen, said she hadn't seen him. We got burgers to go and ate while we scouted the neighborhood.

"He's such a homebody that I can't think of too many places where he might go," Rod said. He took out his cell phone and made a call, then shook his head. "Still no answer at his place. Do you think he might have gone to your place?"

"It's a thought. Gemma, Marcia, and Nita wouldn't know or care what all the fuss is about, and he'd know I'd eventually go back there."

We exchanged a glance, then both of us took off running as fast as we could go, weaving through the crowds on the sidewalk. I was out of breath by the time we reached my building, and it took me two tries to unlock the front door, my hands were shaking so badly. Rod ran ahead of me up the stairs, taking them two at a time, then he knocked on the door while I was still halfway up the last flight of stairs.

Marcia opened the door. "Hey, I wasn't expecting you!" she said, giving him a quick kiss. "I thought this was a crazy day for you."

"Crazy doesn't begin to describe it," he said. "You haven't seen Owen, have you?"

By this time, I'd reached the top of the stairs, and Marcia gave me a funny look. "Why, what's wrong?" she asked.

I was about to explain when Nita appeared behind her. "Oh, hi, Katie!" she said. "How'd your conference go?"

I forced myself to sound as breezy as I could. "It was great, just great, but now I need to find Owen. I think we got our wires crossed. In all the confusion after the conference, I'm not sure if we agreed to meet at his place or my place."

"He hasn't come here," Marcia said. She looked really concerned now, but I couldn't explain this situation in front of Nita.

Already turning to head down the stairs, Rod said, "Okay, then it must be his place. I'll talk to you later."

Marcia raised an eyebrow at me, and before I followed Rod I said, "Post-conference debriefing," to which she nodded knowingly.

By the time we were back outside, Rod was completely panicked, his eyes wild and his body twitching, like he wanted to go in every direction at once. "I don't know where else to look!" he said.

"Let's try his place," I suggested.

"But I've been calling there every five minutes, and there's been no answer."

"That doesn't mean he isn't there, and he'll have to go home before long."

"Why's that?"

"You don't think he'd leave his cat to starve, do you?"

Rod let out a long sigh of relief. "Of course not. So he'll be home before it gets too late. Let's go there. We can stake out the place and wait for him to get back. I've got a key, for when he needs me to check on Loony."

I wasn't up to another sprint, so I was glad that he just set off walking quickly, but his legs were a lot longer than mine and I had to practically run to keep up with him. When we got to Owen's street, I saw that the lights were on in his living room windows. "Look, he's home," I said to Rod.

"That, or someone's there waiting for him." He rang the doorbell, and when there was no response, he took his key chain out of his pocket. I caught his arm before he could unlock the door.

"He's probably got the place warded."

He took the key off the ring and handed it to me. "The wards won't stop you. He needs you. He doesn't need to be alone, even if it takes barging in."

There was a flutter of wings, and Sam and several other gargoyles alit in the trees in front of Owen's building. "Looks like you two found him," Sam said.

"I was just about to go up and check on him," I said, reluctantly taking the key from Rod.

"I'll leave some people here to keep an eye on the place, make sure no one tries anything funny," Sam said.

"Thanks, Sam," I said. I glanced at Rod, then held up the key and said, "Well, let's see how this goes."

"Give me a signal to let me know he's okay," Rod said. "I'll wait out here until then."

I unlocked the front door, then went up the stairs. At Owen's door, I hesitated, then rapped lightly on it. "Owen?" I called out. "It's Katie. Rod gave me his key. I need to talk to you. I'm alone." There wasn't a response, so I said a little louder, "Okay, then I'm coming in. If you don't want me to come in, you'd better throw an interior deadbolt or put up the chain. You've got a count of ten." I counted down from ten, then said, "Ready or not, here I come," and unlocked the door. I felt the magic of his wards as a slight shiver when I passed through the doorway, but they didn't stop me.

Loony met me at the door, meowing loudly and twining herself around my legs. I wasn't a cat person, but I could still tell that she was agitated. That made me wonder what I'd find inside. "Where is he?" I asked her. She flicked her tail at me, then ran into the living room.

"Owen? It's me!" I called out as I followed her. "Are you okay?" Then I came to a stop just inside the living room.

The place was always untidy. For such an ordered thinker, Owen could be a real slob, especially with books and paper. This was a different kind of mess. There was a pile of books on the floor in front of the bookcase, like he'd pulled them out one-by-one, then hadn't bothered to reshelve each one when he didn't find what he was looking for and moved on to the next book. He must have finally found the right book because he was leaning over his desk, peering intently at an open book.

I'd anticipated that he might be in a severe sulk or a serious, soul-searching depression. After all, he'd just learned his true identity after a lifetime of contented ignorance, and it was a horrifying truth. According to what I'd read, his alleged birth parents had been worse than anything Idris aspired to be, and now he'd been accused of being a monster like them. That was the kind of news that tended to make people want to slit their wrists.

But he didn't look all that different from any other time when he was focused on a problem. I supposed research mode was a comfort zone for him. He was still wearing the slacks and shirt of the suit he'd worn that day, with the collar undone and the sleeves rolled up. His jacket and tie were thrown across the arm of a chair. His hair fell across his eyes and stood up in every direction, like he'd been running his fingers through it. He glanced up as I entered and said mildly, "Oh, there you are. I was wondering when you'd get here."

I shook my head to clear the fuzz. I felt like I'd just walked onstage expecting to act in one scene and found myself in an entirely different one from a different part of the play—or even from a different play. "Well, you haven't exactly put out the welcome mat," I said. "You're not answering the phone—by the way, I've got your cell—or the doorbell, and you've got the place more heavily warded than Rod's little black book." Mentioning Rod reminded me that I'd promised to signal him. I stepped to the front window, pulled back the curtain and gave a thumbs-up before returning my attention to Owen.

"Like that could stop you," Owen said with a shrug. "And don't tell Rod, but I got past the wards on his little black book when we were in high school. It's very interesting reading. When I was fourteen, I considered it quite educational."

"Are you okay?" I asked. "I've been worried sick about you."

"I haven't had the best day ever, if that's what you mean. But I'll have my existential crisis later."

I gestured at the pile of books. "If this isn't an existential crisis, what do you call it?"

"Fact finding. Before I collapsed in despair, I thought I ought to get to the bottom of things. First, is it true?"

I leaned against the edge of the desk and crossed my arms over my chest. "Is it?"

"Well, since I don't have a handy home DNA test kit or samples from my alleged parents, I can't say with absolute certainty, but the dates do work out. The Morgans died very soon after I was born, so of course I don't remember them." He pointed to a couple of photos in the book on his desk, which looked like an old club membership directory. "There is some resemblance, I guess. I hadn't ever seen a picture of the Morgans before. For all the disruption they caused, they don't get a lot of play in the histories. I'm lucky I bought this old university magical society annual for one of the articles in it, so I have these pictures."

I had to squint and peer closely at the tiny photos. Owen apparently got his looks from his mother. She was strikingly beautiful and dark-haired. His father had a vague, absent-minded genius look about him, and his eyes were similar to Owen's, but I couldn't tell their color in the black-and-white photo. "I suppose if someone merged these two, they might get you," I said.

"The next question is who knew? Was I just some orphaned kid with magical powers, and whoever's behind Idris managed to unearth the truth, or have they known all along behind the scenes while keeping it a secret, even from me?"

I squirmed uncomfortably, then said, "Rod said—" I broke off, unsure if I should share what Rod had told me, but then I decided that there'd been enough secrets. "Rod said that when you were kids, James and Gloria told him to keep an eye on you. He thought it was because you were so little and needed someone to look after you, but now he's wondering."

I wasn't sure how he'd react to that bit of news, but he took it calmly enough, just nodding. "Yeah, I remember that. But I was so little that I was bully bait and I didn't have good control over my power yet. That's a dangerous combination, so having a bigger kid stick with me made sense. On the other hand, I often felt like a prisoner on parole with James and Gloria, so maybe I was." He gave a bitter laugh that was the first sign he wasn't as okay as he was trying to act. I caught his hand in mine and gave it a squeeze, noticing as I did so that he was trembling. "I do wonder who knew."

"And how did Idris know?" I asked. "Then there's the part where they're trying to make it look like you were following in your parents' footsteps and doing all of this negative magical stuff."

"I missed that. I was already out of there."

"I don't blame you."

His grip tightened on my hand as he ran his other hand through his hair. "So, now what do I do?" he asked.

"I think we need a plan."

"A plan? For what?"

"Well, first, we need to definitively answer your questions: Is it true, who knew, and how did Idris find out? Then we have to clear your name—not because of your identity, since it's not like you can help who your parents were and you never even knew them. If you had evil in your genes, surely it would have manifested by now. But we do need to clear you of these accusations about causing magical trouble, and to do that, I think we'll need proof of who really is doing it."

"So, we're right back to where we were." His lips twitched, and it looked like he was on the verge of breaking down in laughter. "Only this time, it's personal." He said it dramatically, like an announcer in a movie trailer.

"Okay, before you go into hysterics on me, what do you need me to do?"

He pulled himself together with a visible effort, then frowned. "I don't think I'll have much freedom of movement for a while. It's safer if I stay here until I know what's going on. That makes it harder for them to accuse me of any future incidents. But you could do some fact-finding at the office. Talk to the boss and see if he'll be honest with you about what he knows, find out who made the decisions and why."

"I'll see what I can do. Maybe you should call James and Gloria. They may know something."

He shook his head as his jaw took on a stubborn set. "No. Not yet. I really don't want to …" His voice trailed off as he shook his head again, more firmly. "No."

I knew better than to push, given the state he was in. "Okay, then. I'll get back to you tomorrow with whatever I find out. Will you be okay?"

"Why wouldn't I be?" He was back to icy calm, but I got the feeling he was barely clinging to that calm and didn't want to lose his grip in front of me, so I released his hand.

"Try to get some sleep," I suggested, patting him on the shoulder. "I know that's probably a tall order, but put on an old movie or read the most boring book you can find. You won't be helping yourself or anyone else if you exhaust yourself."

"I'm fine," he insisted.

"Only if we're grading on a curve." I hesitated, wondering if I should kiss him or give him a hug, but I could practically see the barriers he'd put up, and these weren't the kind my magical immunity would let me through. I settled for saying, "I'll come by again tomorrow." When he didn't respond, I took that as my cue to leave him alone.

*

The next morning, instead of Owen waiting for me downstairs, Rod was there. "How was he?" he asked.

"I don't know. Weird. In shock, maybe. Mostly pretty analytical. He wants proof, and I don't think he's going to do anything based solely on what Idris said."

"That sounds like Owen."

"I intend to get to the bottom of this today," I said, setting off down the sidewalk with a purposeful stride.

Rod joined me. "And I'll be right there with you," he said.

When we got downtown, more people than usual got off at our subway stop. It was a busy station, but there was something odd about the way these people moved that made me nervous. Then I saw a flash of plastic under the collar of one of the people—an anti-flu amulet. If these people were wearing the amulets, bracelets or charms, then we might be about to see what their real purpose was.

When we got across the plaza, we saw where all those people were going. A crowd—really, more of a mob—had gathered in front of MSI headquarters. It seemed to be a cross between a riot and a protest. Rod took my arm and said, "Stick with me," as he led me through the crowd, which parted around us.

Sam eyed the mob suspiciously from his perch on the building awning. "Would you believe this?" he asked when we reached the awning. "I talked to the boss about breaking it up, but he said they weren't doing any harm and to leave them be." He curled and uncurled his foot talons around his perch, like he was forming fists.

A ripple went through the crowd, and they moved as one to turn their attention away from the MSI building and toward the other side of the street. I was about to ask Sam what was going on when I saw Ivor Ramsay rising above the crowd, levitating. They all cheered, and he soaked up the adulation for several minutes before he raised his hands and they instantly went silent.

"My good people," he said, "It warms my heart to see so many of you here today because it gives me hope that the magical world has not turned its back on truth and ethics." Above us, Sam muttered under his breath and flexed his talons. I gritted my teeth and wished I had talons to flex. "I was as shocked as any of you to hear about the secrets our magical leadership has kept from us. When I fought and defeated the Morgans, I never dreamed that their son would be harbored by the same people I served for so many years. And now that same son—the biggest threat our world has known since his parents terrorized us—has been given a position of trust and leadership by Magic, Spells, and Illusions, Incorporated, the very company charged with protecting us from dark magic." The crowd booed on cue.

Now I *really* wished I had Sam's talons. I didn't realize I'd been leaning forward, ready to pounce, until I felt Rod's grip on my upper arm, restraining me. How could Ramsay say those things about Owen?

"I will not be a party to this any longer," Ramsay continued, shouting above the boos. "I will no longer be associated with MSI, and I am happy to announce that I have accepted a position as chief executive of Spellworks, the magical company I believe will lead the magical world into a new era of peace, prosperity, and innovation. I know Merlin is a great wizard, but he is from another age, and I believe it is time to move in a different direction. As the leader of Spellworks, I vow to turn from the old ways and work toward reforming the magical world."

CHAPTER FIFTEEN

The cheers of the crowd drowned out my mutter of, "I told you so." I turned to Rod to see his reaction and was surprised to see a grim-faced Merlin standing just behind Rod.

"Want I should disperse the crowd, boss?" Sam asked Merlin.

"That will not be necessary, thank you, Sam," Merlin said evenly. "As I understand it, free assembly is a right in this society." He gestured toward Rod and me. "Now, if you two would care to join me in my office, I believe there are some things we should discuss."

Rod was pale with shock, and I was sure I was livid with fury as we followed Merlin up to his office. He motioned us to take seats at the conference table and went to the wet bar to make tea the old-fashioned way, without magic.

While Merlin worked on the tea, Rod tried to process what had just happened. "So Ivor Ramsay was the one behind Idris's schemes all this time?" he said, frowning in disbelief. "But that's impossible! He was the one who let Owen fire Idris and had us take action against the threat of dark spells on the open market."

I turned to him. "Of course he let Owen fire Idris. How else could Idris go off and be the initial front man for the new company? And then Ramsay could call for taking action. We wondered how Idris has known our moves all along. He was getting it from the top. Ramsay knew everyone in the company. No one would have thought anything of him wandering in and asking how things were going."

"I'm still not sure I get it," Rod said. "Why would he pretend to help fight against Spellworks, only to go take over? He could have just started his own company to begin with."

"Yeah, but then he wouldn't have been able to take the moral high road," I said. "They'd have been merely a competing company. This way, they're here to save the magical world. Why he needed to do that at another company, I don't know."

Merlin brought tea to us and joined us at the table. "I had hoped that by lulling Mr. Ramsay into complacency, I could encourage him to show himself," he said. "I will admit, I did not anticipate this development. Magical wars were so much easier in my day when we simply attacked our enemies directly. It was all about demonstrating power, not about developing an image and swaying public opinion."

"How did we not notice this?" Rod asked. "Now that I think about it, there were red flags, but I've always thought the guy was wonderful, and I never suspected anything. No one did, except you, I guess."

"And me," I said under my breath.

Merlin gave the slightest chuckle. "You, of all people, should realize what he was doing, Mr. Gwaltney. As I understand it, you're quite the expert on attraction spells."

"You mean he's been manipulating us all along?"

"Yes, and doing it so expertly that even accomplished wizards are not aware that his appeal isn't natural. I discovered it by being analytical, comparing his actual behavior to the way he was perceived. I had no preconceptions and was studying the situation." Merlin pulled an antique-looking watch out of his vest pocket. "And then I obtained this clever artifact that blocks the action of spells like that. I'm afraid in recent weeks it has been more difficult for me to play along and act like I am as affected by his charisma as everyone else, but by then I'm sure he already knew I suspected him."

Rod shook his head. "You'd think I would have noticed what he was doing. And what about Owen? Is what Idris said true?"

Merlin stared into the depths of his teacup and sighed. "I do not know for certain. I have seen no documentation to that effect, but I had my suspicions. When I was brought back, I initially devoted myself to learning everything I could about what had happened in the intervening years." He gave a wry smile. "That was a rather extensive project, as there were a great many years. I was curious about that last threat because I believed it was more urgent than the one I'd been brought to face, so I did a fair amount of study on that. Meanwhile, I was getting to know Owen rather well—he was the one who did the spell to restore me, and he was one of the very few who spoke my language. He served as my interpreter until I learned modern English. I was intrigued by the amount of power he had and was curious about his origins, and even more curious when I learned that he knew nothing about his origins. More research uncovered some interesting parallels."

"What parallels?" I asked.

"It is not public knowledge, but those directly involved in the fight against the Morgans knew Mina had been with child, but she no longer was when she was defeated, and the child was never found. Meanwhile, Owen was abandoned soon after his birth and then adopted from foster care by the Palmer family. He was discovered by the wizard Council when he caused some trouble for his adoptive parents as his powers began to manifest. From the report I read, it would seem that this family did not handle it at all well, and he went back into the foster care system. The wizards got him out of the mundane system and sent him to James and Gloria Eaton, who had the expertise to bring him up with the training and discipline that would be required to manage his great power. The timing and circumstances were such that I thought there might be a connection."

"And no one else put two and two together and figured that this mysterious child who showed up in the home of two magical leaders might be the missing spawn of evil?" I asked.

"That is not as uncommon as you might think," Merlin said. "We lose magical children all the time within the child welfare system, since untrained magical powers tend to create problem children. You can imagine the potential for disaster when a child doesn't understand his power and his parents don't understand what he's doing. In addition, many of the details about the Morgans were not a matter of public record. I had access to privileged information. Very few people would have had reason to make that connection."

"Who else could have known?" I asked. "And did anyone know officially?"

"It is possible that those who were on the Council at the time knew or suspected, but no one has ever discussed it with me."

"You never mentioned this to Owen?" I asked.

Merlin shook his head. "It was nothing more than a suspicion, and I didn't think it mattered. He has more than proved himself to be a good man."

"Yeah, but now Ramsay and Idris have the perfect scapegoat for their crimes, while they can pretend to take the high road and fight him," Rod snapped.

"That's probably the part we need to focus on now," I said. "We need to clear Owen's name and show Ramsay up for what he is."

"But what is he?" Rod asked. "Has he really been behind this all along, and how far back does it go?"

"Do you really think Phelan Idris was worth bringing Merlin back?" I asked. "I'm guessing it has something to do with that. The problem is that he's set himself up in a no-lose situation. He can make accusations against Owen that are impossible to deny through anything short of a DNA test. Meanwhile, Ramsay is acting like the savior of all magic, so if we fight him, then we look like the bad guys. Before we can defeat him, we have to prove that he's been the bad guy all along. It's a PR war more than a magical battle, and I'm not sure how we can fight it."

"We will need evidence of Ramsay's wrongdoing," Merlin said.

"Unless he's been keeping a diary of his evil deeds, I doubt he's left a paper trail," Rod said.

"Maybe Owen's situation is the key," I suggested. "For Idris to make that accusation, he had to have information from somewhere, which was probably Ramsay. I think it's suspicious that Ramsay killed the Morgans and also happens to know Owen's identity, which he hasn't said anything about until now. Was he the one who kept Owen hidden?"

"That will be your assignment," Merlin said. "See what you can learn about Owen's origins."

He stood and gave a smile that was like ice water down my back. "Meanwhile, if Ivor Ramsay wanted Merlin, then Merlin he shall have," he said, his voice taking on an eerie booming quality. He strode to one side of the office and waved his hand over a section of wall. A narrow cabinet popped open, and he took out an elaborately carved staff that was taller than he was. From another cabinet he took robes of an iridescent blue-black. I hurried over to help him settle the robes around his shoulders. He got out a tall, pointed hat, then hesitated. "Is the hat too much?" he asked. "Modern wizards don't seem to hold with the old regalia."

"You're giving them Merlin," I reminded him. "Go all-out with the old regalia."

Rod and I followed close behind as Merlin swept downstairs to the building entrance. I didn't want to miss seeing this, and it looked like Rod was on the same wavelength. We stood in the doorway as Merlin moved out onto the sidewalk under Sam's awning.

The crowd was still there, though Ramsay had gone. Some were actively protesting while others just milled about like they were waiting for something to happen. Merlin struck his staff against the sidewalk and thunder boomed. A burst of wind rushed up the street and swirled around the protesters, who scrambled for cover. As suddenly as the micro-storm had come up, it dissipated into absolute silence. Then Merlin spoke.

"What is your business here?" he intoned in that same eerie, reverberating voice he'd used earlier.

The protesters mumbled to each other and moved away from the building. One brave soul stepped forward and said, "You're Merlin, aren't you?"

"That is what some call me. That was my name in the Latin tongue in the days of Arthur, and that is my name in legend."

An awestruck gasp fluttered through the crowd, and a few people snapped pictures with their cell phones. "So, it's true?" one woman asked skeptically. "You're *the* Merlin, brought back to life from the Dark Ages?"

"Yes, it is true," Merlin said with a little less booming reverberation. "I was brought back a year ago to help face a great threat to the magical world."

"What threat is that?" another person asked.

"You would have to ask Mr. Ramsay, as it was he who saw a threat and made the decision that it was time to awaken me."

That brought a little more muttering from the crowd, and I was tempted to slip among them to act as an audience plant and ask pertinent questions. Just when it looked like they might be reasonable, about half the crowd suddenly froze and then surged forward, practically trampling those who weren't moving with them. I suspected that those amulets had kicked in again, but not everyone in the group was affected. Some had apparently joined the crowd because they honestly believed in the cause, or at least because they wanted to see what was going on.

The unaffected people tried to push back, and a few fights broke out in the mob. Merlin raised his staff over his head and shouted some words, then calm descended. "You may have heard that I am from an ancient era that has no relevance in our time," he said, "but peace is timeless. Sadly, so is strife. But I bring peace while there are others who create only strife—or incite others to strife."

That set off the amulet zombies again as they surged toward Merlin. A couple in the front row looked like they were primed for attack, but before they reached him, Merlin aimed his staff at them and they slumped to the ground as if they'd fainted. The people who weren't in lockstep with the others got out of the way, and even the ones under the influence hesitated.

"I will not harm you," Merlin said, "but I will not allow you to harm me or my people. You should also know that those charms you carry protect you only from specific spells, and none of those spells are in my arsenal. I fight with different weapons."

A few more people dropped out of the mob, but the rest pressed onward. Merlin raised his staff again and shouted more magic words, and then the mob was pressed against an invisible barrier. Merlin watched them for a moment, then turned around to face us. "That should give them something to think about," he said as he came into the building. "And now I need to go impress some customers. Perhaps they will think twice about withdrawing their business after a friendly discussion."

"Have we lost that many?" I asked.

"There have been a number this morning, and I would imagine several more since Ramsay's announcement. So it would be good if you could find anything you can about Ramsay as soon as possible."

I hadn't even made it to my office, but I turned to head out again. Sam flew escort, magically shielding me from the ongoing demonstration.

When I got to Owen's place, a small mob of protesters had formed on the sidewalk. They were chanting about how he should stop using evil magic, and I doubted they'd let me pass. Before they noticed me, I ducked back around the corner and went to the tavern where they'd held my birthday party, bought a meal to go, a souvenir ball cap, and a T-shirt, then put on the T-shirt, pulled the hat down over my eyes, and acted like I was delivering food. Wearing something that looked like a uniform and doing a menial task was even better than magic for making a person invisible, so the crowd didn't pay any attention to me.

I let myself into the stairwell, then knocked on Owen's door before I unlocked it. "Lunch delivery!" I called out as I came inside.

The living room was even more of a mess than normal. Every book Owen owned was out, and a snowfall of paper lay on top of the books, full of scribbled notes that actually looked scribbled, for a change. Owen was equally untidy, still wearing the white shirt he'd been wearing the day before, but now with the tail untucked. He hadn't shaved, and he was wearing his glasses. His eyes were bloodshot and had dark circles under them. I got the impression he hadn't slept and that he was running on a wave of manic energy.

He looked up as I entered and said, "I think I've figured out who's been behind Spellworks."

"Ivor Ramsay."

His enthusiasm deflated a little. "Oh, you knew? Of course you knew. You've been telling me all along. I should have listened to you. But is it anything more than a suspicion?"

"He announced this morning that he was severing his association with MSI to join Spellworks as their new chairman and to usher in a new magical era, or something like that."

"Wow. Yeah, I guess that's proof. But do you know *why* he did it?"

"That's the part that has us stumped," I admitted as I set the bag of food on the coffee table, pulled off the ball cap, and took a seat on the sofa. "Do you know?"

"I think so. The pattern's been there all along, if I could have just seen it. Why didn't I see it?"

"Merlin says he was using a spell—like Rod's old attraction spell—to make everyone like and trust him."

"Oh. I should have seen that. I've spent enough time with Rod to know what that looks like, and of course you'd be immune to it." He looked up at me and winced. "I'm sorry I didn't listen to you. I was a real jerk about that, too."

"There are sometimes real drawbacks to having magical powers," I said with a smile I hoped was soothing. "I may not be able to do all the amazing stuff you do, but I can see the truth."

"And you'd think I'd remember that. Now, about Ramsay. I think he did the same thing with my parents that he's doing with Idris. He found someone young, promising, and gullible, then encouraged and supported them behind the scenes to challenge the magical status quo. The Morgans were his protégés, just as Idris was."

"Owen," I said softly, ready to tell him that there was no proof that they were his parents.

"Don't worry," he said with a shake of his head. "I'm not fooling myself into thinking they were good people who were misled. If they were good, they couldn't have been used that way. But I do think Ramsay was using them. Their story looks a lot like what happened with Idris. They worked for MSI, had some big, unorthodox ideas, they were fired, and then they reappeared in a way that would have required more backing than you could reasonably expect someone like them to have."

"That does sound familiar. But why would Ramsay bother? What did he get out of it? As hobbies go, there are probably better options."

"I don't think he got what he wanted out of it, other than maybe a step up in the magical world. That situation made him a hero, but he didn't achieve his goal, so he had to do it again."

"Again I ask, why?"

He scrambled around in the pile of books on the floor by the sofa and handed one to me, dropping it in my lap. He'd opened the book to a page describing Merlin going into magical retirement, to be brought back at a time when he was needed by the magical world.

I looked up at Owen, who stared expectantly back at me. "It was all about Merlin," he said with a triumphant grin.

"Yeah, I didn't think Idris was an opponent worthy of Merlin, so I've been wondering. But why?"

"The very idea of Merlin has always been a deterrent to anyone who wanted to make a bid for taking over the magical world." He gestured toward the books scattered on the floor. "Over and over again, that's come up, throughout magical history. They know that even if they do take over, that will trigger Merlin's return, and they couldn't hope to win against him. It's used as a threat, like 'Give yourself up now, and we won't bring Merlin back.'"

"So Merlin is the nuclear bomb of magic."

"Precisely. And that means that if you want to rule the magical world in a way that isn't hampered by the checks and balances set up within MSI and the various councils, you've got to get Merlin out of the way, permanently."

"And that's impossible to do while he's safely snoozing in a crystal cave somewhere."

His face lit up in a huge grin, and he patted me on the knee. "Exactly!"

Taking a stab at completing his thought, I ventured, "And so the way to deal with Merlin is to manufacture a situation designed to require him to be brought back. Then you could fight him head-on and get him out of the way once and for all."

"I knew you'd get it!"

"But that would require a lot of confidence. You'd have to believe you could beat Merlin head-to-head, or maybe that you could cheat well enough to win."

"People with low self-esteem seldom try to take over the world."

Suddenly, I realized exactly why Owen's foster parents had practically encouraged his nearly crippling shyness. Someone who had to psych himself up to have a conversation wasn't likely to try to take over the world. I couldn't imagine seeing Owen as a potential threat, but then I wasn't the person entrusted with a frighteningly powerful kid whose early years sounded like the kind of life that often breeds serial killers—even if they didn't know about his parents being evil.

"So, Ramsay comes along, and he thinks that the only thing in the way of his ambitions is Merlin," I said, thinking out loud. "He creates a threat, getting a couple of bright people who work for him to play evil genius. But it must not have worked, since he had to try again, nearly thirty years later. What went wrong?"

He reached for a book lying facedown across the arm of the sofa. "For one thing, he wasn't in charge then. He couldn't bring Merlin back. He had to convince his predecessor that the threat was great enough, and his predecessor wasn't known for being excitable." He pointed at a picture of a stern, gray-bearded man. Remove the beard and give him a pair of glasses, and you'd have had my high-school principal. "That meant he had to escalate the threat. And then—" he blanched and had to swallow hard, as though he was in some discomfort "—it seems my parents rather liked the idea of taking over the magical world and became a *real* threat, one that had to be dealt with immediately, before Ramsay had a chance to make a case for reviving Merlin."

He paused and frowned. "It sounds really weird to say 'parents.' I've never had any, so it's a new concept for me. It's even weirder to say 'parents' in this context. I mean, I'm talking about Mom and Dad trying to take over the world."

I got a sense of imminent unraveling, as though he'd taken about as much as he could and was in danger of losing it at any minute. "Owen, there's something you should know," I hurried to say while he took a breath. "They may not be your parents. It could just be Idris or Ramsay messing with you. Merlin didn't know about who you were. He did suspect this was a possibility, and I'm sure if he did, then James and Gloria also suspected, but there doesn't seem to be any official proof."

"I think it's true," he said softly. "It *feels* true. I should have suspected, if I'd even bothered to think about it or had done any research. But I thought it was healthy for me not to worry about where I came from."

"Even if it is true, no one lied to you. They weren't keeping deep, dark secrets from you, just suspicions. I guess Ramsay suspected, too."

"Or he knew. He was the one who killed my parents, so he could have been the one to drop me off at that fire station and hope I'd be lost in the system. I suppose I should be grateful that he didn't kill me. Anyway, Ramsay had to stop the Morgans before they could be caught by anyone else, interrogated, and be linked to him. He bides his time, builds power, makes good alliances, and then Idris comes along, giving him the perfect opportunity to set up a new patsy, and then we need Merlin, and now the stage is set for Ramsay to take out Merlin." The words spilled out of him like bullets from a machine gun, and when he was done, he let out a deep breath.

"Then he could rule the world," I finished. "Even better, he's got things set up so that if Merlin fights him, Merlin's the one who looks like the bad guy. We'll have to prove to the magical world that he's evil before we can even oppose him."

"It's rather brilliant, when you think about it." He suddenly sank against the sofa, like the mania had burned itself out, leaving utter weariness. "And how do we prove it?"

"You may be the key." I explained what Merlin, Rod, and I had discussed earlier. "So," I concluded, "our next step is to play 'Owen Palmer, This Is Your Life.' You said you were left at a fire station. Do you know which one? Or would James and Gloria have that information?"

He shook his head. "I don't know. And I don't see how helpful digging into it would be. If Ramsay really was trying to hide the Morgans' baby, would he walk right into a fire station and say, 'Hey, I found this on my doorstep'? He'd have probably left the baby where it would be found and where nothing could be traced back to him. That's if he didn't just kill it."

"But we won't know until we ask."

"It's a waste of time. There's someone out there trying to take over the magical world, and I don't think you can stop that by having a few nonmagical firefighters—if you can even find anyone who was working there then—say that someone who kind of looked like a younger version of Ramsay dropped an abandoned baby off at a fire station thirty years ago. Ramsay would probably spin it so he looked like a hero, anyway. We need a better plan than that."

"In other words, you aren't ready to deal with James and Gloria. Or with who you might be."

"No, that's not it at all. I just don't think digging through my nearly nonexistent baby book is going to do any good." But he had turned bright red, so I knew I was on to something.

"Then do you have a better plan?"

"I'm working on it." Making an obvious attempt to change the subject, he said, "And how are things at the office today?"

"Well, there's a protest going on in front and customers are leaving left and right, so obviously the conference was a huge success."

"Customers are leaving? It's not because of me, is it?"

"I have no idea. Merlin's meeting with some of them—in full Merlin mode, which you really have to see. I have a feeling it has more to do with Ramsay putting the whammy on them."

"And?"

"What?"

"There's something you're not telling me."

Apparently, his wasn't the only face that gave away feelings too easily. "And one of Ramsay's reasons for joining Spellworks was the fact that MSI was harboring you—and that you were the one causing all the trouble."

His shoulders sagged and he seemed to wilt. "Oh."

"Yeah. Sorry. He's a real jerk. Which is why we need to bring him down. You're sure you don't want to see if James and Gloria know anything?"

He shook his head. "No. And I'd better come up with a better plan, right away." He began pulling papers together and stacking books.

"Maybe you'd think better with some food and rest," I suggested.

"I don't need another mother," he snapped. "I think I've more than met my quota of mothers."

I stood up and put my ball cap back on as I fought to control my temper. "Excuse me for caring about your well-being. How insensitive of me," I said, forcing my voice not to quaver.

I made it all the way to the door before he called after me, "Sorry about that. I'm just—well, I'm not good company at the moment."

"Yeah, I noticed." I turned to give him a faint smile. "I'll check on you later."

As I headed down the stairs, it occurred to me that Owen wasn't the only one who could talk to James and Gloria. Facing Gloria would be only slightly less scary than going alone into the dragons' lair, but even if getting the information didn't prove to be the key to beating Ramsay, I thought Owen needed the answers about his past before he could move forward.

CHAPTER SIXTEEN

I went home to change into some nicer clothes, fix my hair, and freshen my makeup. Gloria wasn't the sort of person I wanted to face at anything other than my best. I checked the train schedule on Marcia's computer, then took the subway to Grand Central and caught the Hudson line. The little town where I got off the train looked different from when I'd last seen it. I'd been there for Christmas, when there was snow on the ground. In summer, the lawns were lush and green, with brightly colored flower beds.

I hadn't called ahead, so there was no one to meet me at the station, and there were no cabs in sight, but it wasn't too far, just up a steep hill, so I set off walking to the home where Owen had grown up.

The town was a magical enclave, populated with magical people of all kinds, so it wasn't odd to see fairies running errands and gnomes working in gardens. I couldn't help but wonder what these people thought of the rumors about Owen. When I'd been here for Christmas, they'd all adored him. Did they regard him with suspicion now?

My feet had spawned a blister or two and I was slightly out of breath by the time I reached James and Gloria Eaton's home, a brick gingerbread-like concoction on a hill over the town. The house didn't look quite as magical as it had with an icing of snow on the peaked and turreted roof, but the flowers in the garden made up for that. I was tempted to check to see if they were made of gumdrops.

It took a few minutes after I knocked on the door before James came to open it, his elderly black dog at his side. His appearance took my breath away. He seemed to have aged a dozen years since I'd seen him last, and I'd have bet that most of that had come since yesterday. He'd already been white-haired, but his skin stretched tighter across his cheekbones, his eyes looked hollow, and his shoulders were stooped. "Katie! This is a surprise," he said.

"I'm sorry, I probably should have called first, but I need to talk to you."

"Yes, we should talk. Do come inside."

James was being cordial enough, but then he was the easier of Owen's foster parents. Gloria would be another story, I was sure. She was the only person I'd seen really able to scare Owen. There was something about her that made me want to stand at attention whenever I was near her.

That made what I saw next so shocking that I couldn't believe my eyes. Gloria, who was tall, stiff, and quite formidable, lay slumped on the sofa, looking even older and more frail than James did. Her eyes were puffy and red-rimmed, like she'd been crying for days. She may have scared me, but my heart went out to her.

When she saw me, she struggled to sit up. "How is he?" she demanded, only a trace of her usual starch in her voice.

I hesitated, not sure how to answer. Did she want to be reassured, or did she want the truth? Oh, who was I kidding? This was Gloria. She'd want the truth. "I honestly don't know. He's being weird. And stubborn."

"I wonder where he learned that?" James muttered, and I had to fight not to laugh.

"I think it's getting to him, but it's taking a while to sink in," I said. Even though I hadn't been invited to do so, and Gloria was someone who took that sort of thing seriously, I sat on the chair across from the sofa. "The big question is, is it true? If it is, who really knew? Right now, Owen doesn't seem to want to even think about it, but I believe it's important to get to the bottom of this. What did you know?"

James sat next to Gloria on the sofa and said, "The situation is, as you may imagine, complicated. We didn't know who he was, but we did know he was a special case because his abilities were unusually strong in someone that age and because of the difficulties he'd already gone through. That can be a recipe for disaster if the child isn't properly trained."

"The Council wanted us to train and monitor him," Gloria continued. "But we were not supposed to become emotionally involved. Doting, overly permissive parents have been the downfall of many a powerful child. In the nonmagical world we had the rights of foster parents, but within the magical world, guardianship rested with the Council, and they could take him away at any time. We had to remain neutral so we could objectively observe his progress." Her voice cracked. "It was a difficult situation—if we showed signs of loving him too much, we would lose him, and yet we soon came to love him too much to bear the thought of losing him. Our inexperience as parents probably meant we weren't able to strike quite the right balance, and we erred on the side of duty."

"We had always wanted children of our own, but we were not blessed in that way," James said, placing a hand over his wife's. That simple gesture brought tears to my eyes.

Gloria gave a crooked smile. "And then one day they brought us this little boy. He was so small—he was rather sickly at first. He hadn't been taken care of very well. He was so quiet, and we later learned his vision was weak. I was expected to treat him as though he was a pupil at a single-student boarding school, and I was his matron. If I ever seemed too attached to him, then I would have been deemed unfit for my job."

Tears spilled from her eyes, and I was pretty sure my own cheeks had become wet. "That must have been awful for you."

"It was wonderful and awful, all at the same time."

"We were very proud of him," James added.

"It was only much later when we heard the rumors that Mina Morgan had been pregnant and noticed the timing," Gloria said. "Then we figured it out."

"Do you think anyone official knew? Someone on the Council, maybe?" I asked.

James shook his head. "I never got that impression. And I was afraid to ask in case no one did know. We didn't want to be the ones to attach that stigma to Owen."

"We may have been a little stricter with him after we became suspicious," Gloria said, sitting up straighter, "but that was for his own good. We wanted to be sure he was nothing like his parents. If something had gone wrong with him and we hadn't mentioned our suspicions, then we would have felt responsible."

"So, if you didn't know, and the Council didn't know, and Merlin didn't know, then how did Idris and presumably Ramsay know?" I asked. "Does Ramsay have evidence, or is he merely putting two and two together like you did and making a wild accusation?"

"We've known Ivor Ramsay for a very long time," James said. "He knew we were bringing up Owen, and he knew what we knew about Owen's background, but he never showed any signs of suspecting that Owen was anything more than a particularly powerful magical child."

I braced my hands on my knees and leaned forward. "I presume you've heard about Ramsay's announcement about taking over Spellworks?" They both nodded. "We believe he's been behind it all along, and it's all part of a plot to either discredit or do away with Merlin so he can eliminate that deterrent and go for absolute power. I think that if we can show that Ramsay knew who Owen was all along, then we can prove that he isn't the noble, upright guy he's claiming to be, and that's the way to get to him. If he knew, then that means he's been the one hiding that secret from the magical world, and then that brings up the question of why. I was wondering if you have any information on where or how Owen was found in the first place. He said something about a fire station, but that was all he would tell me. He's reluctant to look into this, and I suppose I can understand that, but we need to figure it out."

The life snapped back into Gloria's eyes, and she became the woman who'd nearly frightened me to death when I first met her. She threw off the knitted shawl from around her shoulders and came to her feet with ramrod-straight posture. "I know we have some information. Let's go look."

She moved with a sense of purpose out of the living room and toward the study, with James, the dog, and me in her wake. If the information we needed was in that study, then I had a feeling this could take all day. Owen had learned his organizational skills from his foster father.

Once we were all in the study, James took the lead. "Now, where did I put that file?" he mused out loud. "I haven't looked at it in ages, not since we first wondered about the possible connection between Owen and the Morgans. When was that, Gloria?"

"When Owen was ten. And as I recall, the information we had wasn't of much use in answering the question, so I don't know if it will help you, Katie."

"If you can even tell me where he was found, I may be able to track back and find out how he came to be there," I said, even as I got a sick feeling in my stomach from worry that Owen was right and this was a waste of time. I didn't have another plan.

After trying three different file drawers, James came up with a large document file envelope. The heavy brown paper was faded, and it was closed by a fat rubber band. He swept a clear space on his cluttered desk, slid the band off the envelope, and opened it. There were a few official-looking documents and a sheet that looked like a typewritten carbon copy. "That's the one that had the background information," Gloria said.

James put on his reading glasses, skimmed over the sheet, then said, "Ah, here it is. Children's Services picked him up at the fire station on Broome Street, where the firefighters said he'd been left."

I took a notepad out of my purse and wrote that down. "It doesn't say how he was left, does it? Did someone bring him there, or was he left on the doorstep in a basket?"

"It doesn't say."

"And what was the date?"

James smiled, "July fourth. They used that as his birth date because the doctors who examined him that day believed he was a newborn."

"Then maybe that date is distinctive enough for someone to remember it," I said. I gave each of them an impulsive kiss on the cheek. "Thank you. This really helps."

"You must tell us what you discover," Gloria said. She hesitated, then said tentatively, "Should we perhaps go to him ourselves?"

I understood that she'd want to see him, but I felt like I was treading on thin ice with Owen by going behind his back this way, as it was. Dragging in his foster parents would be too much right now. "He refuses to call you. I don't think he's up for visitors. And I may need to keep you in reserve for when I really need to knock some sense into him."

That evoked a slight smile. "I understand. Then please tell Owen what we told you. He may not be ready to speak to us yet, but he should know."

"I will," I promised. She insisted on feeding me a snack that was more like a meal, and then James insisted on driving me to the train station. By the time I was back in the city, it was the end of the workday, so I went straight home.

I hadn't yet had a chance to tell Gemma and Marcia about everything that had happened, and Nita was already home when I got there, so I wouldn't be able to anytime soon. I'd thought her presence might complicate matters since she wasn't in on the magical secret, but it was nice to have an excuse not to talk about any of this for a while.

Nita went into throes of ecstasy at the idea of ordering in Chinese food. "I've always wanted to do this!" she gushed, gazing at the delivery menu for our favorite Chinese place. "But we don't have any restaurants that deliver back home, unless you count Meals on Wheels for the old people. And we don't have Chinese food."

"It's just takeout," Gemma said with a shrug.

"But I have been living in a world without it," Nita said with the kind of drama that you'd expect to hear about electricity or indoor plumbing.

"Welcome to the twenty-first century," Marcia said, her lips twitching with wry amusement.

Once we had food and were gathered around the dining table, Nita said, "I have the early shift again tomorrow, so does anyone want to go out tomorrow night? We could have a big girls' night out—something very *Sex and the City*." She paused, chewing her lip, then said, "But you all probably have dates."

"No, Philip's got something going on," Gemma said.

"And Rod's barely even talking. He seems upset about something. That reminds me, Katie, I was going to ask you—" Marcia cut off when she caught my slight shake of the head.

The last thing I wanted to do was play *Sex and the City* when my life was more like *hex* and the city, but that wasn't something I could easily explain to Nita, and I knew Owen wouldn't be up for a date night. "Sure, sounds like fun," I said, trying to sound a lot more enthusiastic than I felt.

Nita clapped her hands. "Yay! We could start out at the hotel cocktail lounge. It's very swanky, and I can get us an employee discount and give y'all a tour of the hotel." Then she frowned at me. "Are you okay? You don't look so hot."

That was one of the good and bad things about having Nita as a friend.

She seemed shallow and flighty, but she really saw people, and you couldn't sneak a bad day past her. "I've just had a couple of crazy days," I told her. "There was the conference yesterday, and I had a meeting out of town today, so I spent most of the day on trains. I don't know how people who commute like that every day do it."

"Oh, but starting every day by going through Grand Central is so inspiring!" she said. "I get off the subway one stop early so I can cut through the terminal on my way to work. I feel like Mary Tyler Moore."

"Wasn't that in Minneapolis?" Marcia asked.

"I think she means the feeling of making it in the city," Gemma said. "Too bad they got rid of the old Penn Station, because that's where my subway stop is, and it's not nearly as inspiring as that must have been."

That started a conversation about things that got them excited when they first moved to the city, and I didn't have to answer additional questions about why I was out of sorts. There was only so much claiming to be tired could cover for when the real trouble was that my world was in danger of falling apart.

*

I went to the office the next morning because I needed to do some research before I tried the fire station. Perdita's greeting when I entered the office wasn't nearly as friendly, cheerful, or welcoming as it usually was. "Oh, I didn't think you'd be here," she said.

"Why not?"

"Because of—well, you didn't come in yesterday, so I was wondering if maybe, well, you know." She didn't quite look at me when she spoke.

"After my boyfriend was accused of being the son of the previous generation's bad guys, you thought I wouldn't dare show my face around here, or I might even have been fired?"

She looked up guiltily, peering through the hair she'd let fall into her face. "Something like that. You didn't know, though, did you?"

"*He* didn't know. The boss didn't know. It may not even be true. And he's not evil, I'm pretty sure of that."

"I didn't *think* he was evil, but you can't be sure, can you?"

"I suppose it depends on where you stand on the nature versus nurture issue. I'm a magical immune like my mother, but I hope I don't share all her personality traits. And, as I said, there's not even any proof that it's true."

"Would you like some coffee?" she asked sheepishly.

"Peppermint mocha, please. And make it a big one, extra whipped cream, maybe even some sprinkles."

"Coming right up." It appeared on her desk, and I picked it up. "Is there anything else you need me to do?"

"Not right now. I'm working on something for the boss and I'll probably be out of here soon." I started to head into my office, then turned back. "On second thought, there is something you could do. You're pretty tuned in to the network, aren't you?"

"I get around," she said, twining a ringlet around her finger.

"Then you could start a few rumors—ask where the proof about Owen is or how Phelan Idris knew about that. And you could rebut anything you see that you know isn't true. Get your friends on board, too."

"Oh cool! I can talk to my friends, and it's work! Awesome! I'll get right on that."

At my desk, I looked up the location of the fire station and figured out the best way to get there. Then I searched for any photos of Ramsay from around the time of the war with the Morgans. I figured if he was the big hero, there would have to be something, and sure enough, there was. I printed one. There were no such photos of the Morgans. Owen's pictures of them were tiny and I didn't think he'd share them, anyway, if he knew what I was up to. I went up to Merlin's office to see if he had anything.

Before I could get to Merlin's door, Kim came out of her office and pulled me aside. I was startled when she high-fived me. "Looks like we were right about you know who," she said smugly.

"Yeah, we were. Go, us," I said without much enthusiasm.

"He was talking to Idris before that speech. I'm sure he was the one who told Idris all that stuff about Owen."

"Really?" That was what we'd all suspected, but it was nice to get a little more evidence. Not that a brief chat before a speech was real proof. "Thanks for the tip. Now, I need to talk to the boss." She gave me a "be my guest" wave.

"Have you spoken to Mr. Palmer since yesterday?" Merlin asked as soon as I entered his office.

"No, not since lunchtime. Why? Did something happen?" I sat in the nearest chair before the sudden surge of fear could make my knees go weak.

"His resignation was waiting for me when I returned to the office yesterday afternoon."

"He quit?"

"For the good of the company." Merlin said with a deep sigh. "And I am afraid he was correct. Three more large customers wanted to cancel their contracts this morning, and I was only able to persuade them not to by assuring them that Mr. Palmer was no longer in our employ."

"So you're throwing him under the bus," I said.

"That is a very colorful turn of phrase, but not entirely accurate."

"Yeah, but it works out well for the company," I muttered, leaning back in my chair and folding my arms across my chest. "It makes for good damage control."

"Which was his reason for resigning," Merlin said firmly. "He's putting the good of the company first, which gives us the opportunity to contain the situation." He sighed in deep resignation and sagged against the back of his chair. "I hope you have made some progress."

I told him what I'd learned, then said, "Do you have any pictures of the Morgans I can use for identification?"

"Pictures of them are quite rare."

"I wonder if Ramsay had anything to do with that—keeping his secret until he could use it. Owen found some pictures in an old club directory, and he does look a lot like them. If everyone knew what the Morgans looked like, it wouldn't have been a secret for long."

"That may very well be the case. I don't believe I've ever seen a photograph of them." Merlin got up from his desk and thumbed through a few of the books on his shelf, then shook his head. "No, I am afraid I have nothing."

"It was worth a shot," I said. It was time for Plan B, and Owen looked enough like his supposed mother that someone might be able to make a connection. Unfortunately, I didn't have any photos of my own boyfriend, which probably said something about the history of our relationship. We'd always been too busy trying to save the world to pose for pictures.

I headed for Owen's lab and got Jake to let me into the department. "I don't suppose you have any pictures of Owen lying around?" I asked him.

"Someone once brought a camera to a department party," he said. There was a crowded bulletin board over his desk, with pictures overlapping each other, and he searched through them. "He's bad about vanishing as soon as a camera comes out, but wait, here's one where he didn't get out of the way in time." He unpinned a photo and handed it to me.

The photo focused on Jake and a couple of other guys in lab coats and Santa hats. On the edge of the picture, Owen was leaning over a lab table and had just looked up. It wasn't a shot worthy of a Men of Magic calendar, but it looked enough like Owen to work. "Can I take this?" I asked.

"Sure. No problem."

"I'll bring it back."

"There's no hurry." He worried his lower lip with his teeth, then asked, "How's he doing? Have you seen him—or do you need that because he's gone missing?"

"He's fine, just a bit upset. Next time I see him, I'll tell him you asked after him."

Armed with photos, I caught a subway train uptown and got off near Little Italy, then walked to the fire station. It was an old station that looked a lot like the toy firehouse my brother Teddy used to have. Right next door was a church, and I wondered then if the baby might have been left at the church, then discovered by the firemen. The baby left on the church steps was such a cliché. Did anyone actually do that in real life?

The bay door was open, and a couple of firefighters stood outside, leaning against a wall. "Can I help you with somethin', miss?" one of them asked, and my first instinct was to look up to see if Sam was perched nearby. The voice, accent, and way of speaking were almost identical.

I approached the firemen, feeling suddenly awkward and unsure. "Maybe," I said. "This is going to sound kind of weird, though."

"Ah, try me," the fireman said. I didn't think he was that much older than I was, but his face was weathered. His dark hair was cut in a short, military style, and his nose looked like it had been broken a few times. "I get a lot of weird every day. It comes with the job." He grinned at his colleague, who nodded in agreement.

"Okay, then," I said, wondering for a moment if Sam might have taken human form. "Is there anyone still around who was working here thirty years ago, or do you know of someone who was?"

He turned to his colleague. "Vinnie's been here forever. Think he was here back then?"

"I think so," the other guy said. "He was probably here when they still used horses to pull the engines."

The human version of Sam said, "What do you want with an old-timer?" He winked and added, "Or is it personal?"

"It's about a baby who was left at this station."

His eyebrows rose. "Seriously? That does happen sometimes, but I never found one. And I'm okay with that." He jerked his chin in a "follow me" gesture and went into the fire station. I followed him inside and then up the stairs to the office/living area of the station. "Is Vinnie in today?" he asked the firefighters hanging around in a common room.

"He's makin' lunch," one of the men said.

"Hope you brought the Alka-Seltzer!" another one said, and they all laughed.

"Aw, shaddup," my Sam clone said with a good-natured laugh. "He's a better cook than any of you guys. C'mon, doll, we don't need these losers." As he led me to the kitchen, he said, "Vinnie's mostly retired and doesn't go out on calls, but he comes in and helps out around the station. The job gets in your blood, makes it hard to leave, y'know?"

As we entered the kitchen, he yelled, "Yo, Vinnie! Someone here to see you."

A barrel-chested man wearing a chef's apron and a ball cap turned to see us. "Whaddaya want, Corelli?" he asked.

Corelli gestured to me. "Miss?"

"Katie Chandler," I supplied.

"Miss Katie Chandler, this is Vinnie Marciano."

Vinnie wiped his hands on his apron, then held out his right hand to shake mine. "Pleased to meet you. How may I be of service?"

"She's lookin' for someone who was around thirty years ago," Corelli said. "I figured that would be you."

"Yeah, I was around then. Why?"

With a deep breath, I said, "A baby was left at this station—at least, this is where Children's Services picked him up, though he could have been left at the church next door. It was on July fourth. Maybe that'll make it easier to remember."

Vinnie frowned and nodded. "Yeah, yeah, I remember that. I was workin' that day, had an early shift." He grinned. "That was our little Yankee Doodle Dandy, born on the fourth of July, he was. I've always wondered what happened to that kid."

A lump grew in my throat as I reached for the photos in my purse. "Do you remember anything about how and where he was found?" I asked.

"He wasn't really found. His mother brought him."

CHAPTER SEVENTEEN

My hand froze halfway inside my purse. "His mother?" I repeated. There went my theory about Ramsay.

"Yeah, I'm pretty sure that was the mom," Vinnie said with a shrug. "I mean, the baby was fresh out of the oven, barely even cleaned up, and she wasn't lookin' too good." He knitted his bushy eyebrows at me. "Why do you wanna know, anyhow?"

"That baby is my boyfriend." I launched into my prefabricated cover story. "He's starting to wonder who he is and where he came from—I guess turning thirty will do that to you—but he also seems to be a little scared about what he'll find. My birthday gift to him is to do some investigating and see what I can find out. All he knows is that he was turned over to Children's Services at this fire station."

Vinnie nodded. "Okay. Then let's make a deal. I'll tell you what I know, and you tell me how that kid turned out, even bring him by to see us." He took off his baseball cap and shoved it onto Corelli's head, then took off his apron and draped it over Corelli's shoulder. "You're finishing up on lunch. Just stir the sauce so it doesn't stick or scorch." Then he took my arm and said, "Come on, sweetheart, let's you and me go talk."

He escorted me to a cramped office and showed me to a chair with a vinyl seat repaired with duct tape. He sat on the edge of a metal desk. "So, you say you know our Yankee Doodle?"

I smiled at the thought of that nickname applying to Owen. He'd probably turn red and cringe. "Yes, I think so. As I said, he was turned over to Children's Services on July fourth thirty years ago at this station." I took the photo of Owen out of my purse and handed it to Vinnie. "This is him."

Vinnie studied the photo, creasing his forehead until his eyebrows almost met in the middle. He then gave a long, low whistle. "Damn, but he looks just like his mama."

"So the woman who brought him here looked a lot like this?" I asked, gesturing at the photo.

"Yeah." His eyes took on a distant look as his brain went back thirty years. "I was workin' that morning. We had the bay open, and I was standin' outside, and not long after dawn this girl comes staggerin' up the street, holding a bundle. I think she was aimin' for the church, but it didn't look like she was gonna make it. She almost fainted on me, and I barely caught the kid. We got her and the baby inside, and she kept babbling about needing to keep the baby safe. Strange thing was, she was wearin' a wedding ring. Usually, it's teenagers and unwed moms who leave babies like that, not married women. She had some bruises on her face, so I thought maybe her husband beat her and she was afraid of what he'd do to the kid."

"Did she give you her name?"

"No. And I don't know how she did it, but while we were getting a blanket for the baby and some food for her and calling the police, she just vanished, leaving the baby behind. I mean, I barely turned my back on her, and she was gone. Nobody saw her go. Considerin' that she could barely walk, that was a neat trick."

There went my theory that Ramsay had taken the child of his defeated enemies and tried to hide him in the mundane world. It had been Mina who'd sent her child to safety just before the final showdown. What did that mean? Did she have second thoughts? Had she known she was about to die, or had she discovered what Ramsay was up to?

Of course, it might not have been Mina at all. Women who are planning to take over the world and start a magical dynasty don't generally abandon their newborn infants at a fire station. At least, I didn't think they would.

"There wasn't anything with the baby that identified him or gave any clue about him, was there?" I asked.

"Nah, he was just wrapped up in an old shirt. Tiny little thing he was, too—must've come a bit early. But there was one thing—later that day we found an envelope with a note on it saying to give it to him—and only to him—if he ever came there looking for it. I swear it wasn't there with the baby. We only found it after the police and Children's Services left with the kid." He shrugged. "I dunno, maybe she hid it while she was here, or dropped it on her way in or out. Hell, she may have come back and left it."

"What did you do with it?"

"We filed it." He frowned then, as a memory came back to him. "We probably should have given it to the police, but keeping it seemed like the right thing to do at the time—like that was the obvious thing. Funny, I never even thought of it until now."

I'd been around magic enough to recognize the signs that envelope was enchanted, which meant it was probably important. "Do you know what was in the envelope?" I asked, moving to the edge of my seat. My heart was racing so quickly that I was almost dizzy.

He shrugged—using practically his whole body to do so. "I dunno. I didn't open it. I knew I wasn't supposed to. But it felt like there was something heavy in it beyond just paper, like a key or something."

"Do you still have it?"

"I'm sure it's still here. But like the lady said, it don't go to no one but that kid. He comes here, I'll find it and hand it over. Otherwise, no dice."

I forced myself to slide back in my chair so I wouldn't look overly eager. If it was enchanted, then he didn't have a choice. "Of course. I understand. I'll have to talk him into coming. This is a big step for him."

"So, he's successful now? He's had a good life? He's been safe and happy? 'Cause that's what his mama wanted for him."

I didn't want to tell him about the failed adoption, string of foster homes, and the foster parents who weren't allowed to get too attached, so I focused on the positives. "He ended up with a family that loved him and took good care of him. He went to school, even has a doctorate," I said. "I think his mother would be very pleased." That is, if his mother wasn't disappointed that he wasn't ruling the magical world.

I stood up and shook his hand. "Thanks, Vinnie, you've been very helpful," I said. "I'll try to get Owen to come back and see you."

"His name's Owen?" he asked with a grin. "Yeah, he looked like an Owen. Tell him he can come by anytime and have lunch or dinner with us. He's an honorary member of the company."

"I'll do that," I assured him.

*

I could barely wait to get to Owen's place and tell him what I'd found. Whatever was in that envelope had to be important—unless it was just some "I hope one day you can understand why I had to do this" note and his mother's ID bracelet. In case there were still protesters at Owen's place, I swung by my apartment to get my delivery disguise, then hoped no one noticed that I was carrying Chinese takeout instead of food from the tavern.

The crowd had grown since the day before, and this time I had to push past people to get to the front door. I knocked on Owen's door before unlocking it. I almost didn't recognize the place when I entered. For a moment, I thought I'd accidentally gone into the lower unit, but then I remembered climbing the stairs.

The apartment was clean. All the books were shelved neatly, and there wasn't a single loose piece of paper in sight. The living room could have been a photo in a home-décor magazine. Had Owen moved out?

"Owen?" I called.

Loony came charging into the living room, and then I knew he still lived there. He wouldn't have left Loony behind. "Hey there, sweetheart," I said, kneeling to pat her head. "I bet this doesn't even feel like home for you anymore."

"Katie, is that you?" Owen's voice called from back in the kitchen.

"Yes, it's me," I said, heading in the direction of his voice. I found him standing at the stove, stirring something.

"Have you eaten yet?" he asked.

"I brought Chinese."

"That sounds better than canned soup. I'll save this for later." He turned off the stove and put the pan aside. He sounded frighteningly normal—so normal it was absolutely abnormal for someone in his situation.

"I noticed you've tidied the place up."

"Yeah, I got a little bored, and spending that much time at home made me notice how bad the clutter was."

"It looks great." I unloaded the takeout bag while he got plates out of the cabinet.

I watched him closely as he scooped food onto a plate and started eating, trying to judge his mood before I sprang the news on him. "I'm not about to disintegrate," he said dryly.

"What?" I wasn't sure how innocent I managed to look, but I gave it a shot.

"You're looking at me like you think I'm about to snap or fall apart, or something."

"You mean, I'm acting like I'm worried about you because I care about you and I know you're going through something horrible that's turned your life upside down? Gee, I don't know why I might be doing that."

"I'm fine."

"This must be a new definition that hasn't made it into the dictionary yet. I heard you resigned."

He shrugged casually. "Well, I haven't made it to work in a couple of days and I don't know when I'll be able to go back, so it's not fair for me to stay on the payroll."

"And how many weeks of unused vacation time have you accumulated?"

"I used some of it when I went to Texas."

"Uh huh, so now you only have a month or two left."

"Until this is worked out, I'm no good to the company. Let them do some damage control, and then I can come back after everything's worked out." He sounded freakishly unruffled about this.

"That's pretty much what Merlin said," I admitted.

"See? I'm not crazy or distraught. What I'm doing makes sense."

I ate my lunch while trying to think of a way to tell him what I'd discovered. I doubted he'd be happy about me going behind his back. I finally gave up and just blurted, "I tracked down the fire station where you were found. It wasn't Ramsay who brought you there. It was your mother."

He blinked, shook his head, then said, "What? I told you I didn't want to dig into that."

"And Merlin specifically assigned me to do so. I was just offering you the courtesy of being a part of it. Even without you, I had to do it. I met the firefighter who found you—who found your mother, really. He still helps out around the station." I told him what Vinnie had told me about helping Owen's mother. "She was trying to protect you," I said. "Even if she was scheming to take over the magical world, or was misguided, or whatever it was she was into, she still wanted the best for you."

He sat totally still for a moment, like he was trying to absorb and process the information. He'd gone ashen, and I couldn't tell if he was even breathing. I held my own breath as I worried about how he'd react. When he didn't say anything, I added, "You're an honorary member of that company. The firefighters would love to meet you. They've always wondered what happened to you."

Finally, he said, "I told you it would be a dead end."

"But it isn't, or it might not be." I told him about the envelope his mother had left. "It could be evidence. If she was trying to hide you from Ramsay, then that meant she knew Ramsay was trouble. You have to go to the station and get that envelope. They wouldn't give it to me—I think it might be enchanted, so they can't give it to anyone else. That envelope could be our key to beating Ramsay."

He shook his head. "You're putting too much hope on something some young woman threw together to leave with a baby she didn't think she could bring up. You've got it in your head that Mina had a change of heart or wasn't all that evil to begin with, and her last act of courage was to get her baby to safety and leave a huge smoking gun that would expose Ramsay as the ultimate evildoer. But that's only what happens in books. In the magical world, it tends to work differently."

I crossed my arms over my chest and asked, "How does it work, then?"

"If she was trying to take over the world using magic but was afraid she was about to fail or be doublecrossed, she could have left an enchantment that would then make her son carry out her dreams or that would put her essence into her magically powerful son so her life could continue, or something equally nasty."

I tried not to shudder. "You really think she'd have done something like that?"

He raised an eyebrow. "She tried to take over the world using dark magic. What do you think?"

"Okay, then, you don't have to open the envelope. You have to be there to get it from the firehouse, but then I could take it and open it to find out what it is. It can't affect me."

"It's probably not even something that dramatic. It's probably just some note about how she hoped I would have a better life than she could have given me. We still don't even know if that woman was Mina Morgan."

"You said yourself that it felt true."

"There's a difference between feeling and knowing."

If he'd been one of my brothers, I'd have stuck my thumbs in my armpits and flapped my elbows like wings while making chicken sounds, but I didn't think that would go over very well in these circumstances. "If you go and we open the envelope and it's just a 'sorry for ditching you, kid, but it was for the best' note, then I give you permission to gloat all you want. But at the moment, it's the only lead we've got."

I didn't think it was possible, but he went even paler. He shook his head and said. "I–I don't know if I can face that yet. I just need a little time, okay?"

"I'm not sure how much time we have. You can mope all you want later, but there's a lot at stake right now." When that didn't get a response, I shifted tactics. "You never told me your birthday was July fourth."

"I don't know that it was. That was just the date I was found."

"Oh, it was your birthday, all right. They said you were 'fresh out of the oven' when you showed up at that fire station. The firefighters called you their little Yankee Doodle Dandy."

As I'd expected, he turned red, but he also smiled. "How much will it cost me for you to keep that quiet?"

"A trip to the fire station? They said you had an open invitation to lunch or dinner, and whatever Vinnie was cooking, it smelled really good. The station's in Little Italy, so I'm guessing you'd get some good Italian food there. You like Italian food, right?"

His smile faded and he shook his head. "I can't."

"Then I'll have to tell Rod. Or maybe I'll tell Marcia and Gemma, and Marcia will tell Rod. And I'm sure Jake would find it highly amusing. Of course, we'll have to throw a huge party. It's short notice, but I understand there are already fireworks scheduled."

This time, there wasn't even a flicker of a smile. "I'm sorry, Katie," he whispered. "I can't. Could you, if you were in my shoes? If you found out that there was a chance your parents were someone like Bonnie and Clyde or Lee Harvey Oswald, would you be willing to prove it, or would you prefer to leave the possibility open that it wasn't true?"

"I think I'd want to know. Having that question hanging would drive me nuts."

"You might think differently if it wasn't purely hypothetical for you. I'll come up with another plan, but please, don't ask me again."

"Okay, I won't." I stood to leave. "But I have to admit I'm disappointed in you. I understand you're going through a lot, but aren't you the one who likes to quote that *Casablanca* line about the problems of one or two little people not adding up to a hill of beans? This isn't just about you."

"I said, I'm working on a plan—something that might actually get us somewhere." He spoke through gritted teeth.

"Then you do that," I said. "But you should know that I don't give a damn who or what your parents were. I don't care whether or not you're a wizard. And I don't think anyone other than those idiots with the amulets cares, either. What really matters is what you do, and if I were in your shoes, I'd do anything in my power to stop Ramsay, no matter how uncomfortable it made me."

I'd given up on dramatic exits when I was a kid and I realized my brothers didn't even notice when I flounced out of a room, but I gave it my best flounce and left him sitting alone in his kitchen.

While I was somewhat sympathetic about his position, I couldn't take the risk that we'd have the time it would take him to come to terms with the situation and come around. But if I couldn't persuade him, maybe someone else could. It was time to bring in the big guns, whether or not he was ready to see them.

I still had Owen's cell phone, and I found James and Gloria's number in the contacts list on it. I called and told them what had happened. "We'll be on the next train," James said.

I met them at Grand Central. We took a cab from there to Owen's place, stopping at the end of the block because his narrow side street was nearly blocked by the mob, which seemed to have grown. Gloria's eyes flashed with cold fire when she saw the protesters. "How dare they?" she growled.

James straightened his back until he looked like a general about to survey the troops, and before I could say or do anything, the two of them were striding forward, right into the mob. I may have been about sixty years younger, but I had to rush to catch up with them, and I wasn't sure what I could do to help.

The strange thing was, the protesters backed away from Gloria. I knew she was formidable and that I was afraid of her, but I hadn't thought that absolutely everyone would be that frightened of a tall, thin old lady. She carried an old-fashioned umbrella that wouldn't have been out of place in Mary Poppins's umbrella stand, and she banged it on the ground at her feet as she shouted, "What is the meaning of this?"

Because they were a mob that was probably being magically influenced, there wasn't any one leader to act as spokesman. They all looked at each other, and none of them had a good answer. That did not impress Gloria. "Surely you have more constructive things to do with your time than make nuisances of yourselves. What do you expect to accomplish, standing out here in the street all day? He's not going to come down so you can arrest him, or whatever it is you plan to do, and it's not as though he's even done anything wrong. Are you protesting what someone has told you about his very existence? Is that it?"

They backed farther away from her. One man moved toward her, his lips bared as his fists raised in an aggressive posture, and she barely flicked a finger at him, sending him reeling backward. "If you have a complaint, you can make it to me," she said, sweeping the crowd with her steely gaze.

"To us," James said firmly, standing by her side. "You will leave our boy alone."

One person wandered off with a shrug. Two more joined him. One man moved to block the stairs to Owen's front door, but buckled under the combined glares from James and Gloria. I knew then that I'd made the right call in bringing them here. Owen needed allies like this, whether or not he wanted them.

Since I had guests with me, I went through the formality of ringing the bell and waiting for a response that wouldn't come, then unlocked the front door and led James and Gloria upstairs. "He's got his door warded," I warned them, "so I may have to talk him into letting you in."

"And who do you think taught him to set wards?" Gloria asked. "I'm sure we can find our way past them."

I forced myself to face Gloria and meet her eyes without wavering. "And I'm sure you shouldn't," I said as firmly as I could manage. "He's being this way because he doesn't trust himself. You're not going to help that by going against his wishes and acting like you don't trust him. You'll either go through that door because he lets you, or you'll shout through it."

She held my gaze long enough for it to become a staring contest, then she nodded curtly. "Yes, you do have a point. Very well, then, go and talk him into letting us in. We will wait."

I unlocked the door and passed through the wards, calling out, "Owen?"

He was standing by his desk, looking out the front window. "Why did you bring them here?" he asked without turning around.

"Because your parents want to talk to you."

"They're not my parents."

"Yes, they are. Whether or not the Morgans were your birth parents, James and Gloria are your *real* parents. They're the ones who took you in and brought you up. They're the ones who taught you right from wrong and how to use your power responsibly. They're the reason that in spite of you having just about every possible strike against you, you didn't turn out to be a monster. They care about you. They're the reason you're the man I love." I realized a second after I said it that this might not have been the best time to use the L-word for the first time, but it was done, I meant it, and I might as well go on. "And you're going to hear them out if they have to shout through the door."

I felt the surge of magic that sometimes came when he was angry or frustrated and in danger of losing control. "They may not have known who I really was, but that makes the way they treated me even worse."

"Maybe you should talk to them about why they were that way. And maybe you should get over being afraid of things that have already happened and start worrying about the future. If you want to be public enemy number one, you're making a really good start. Now, if you need me, you know where to find me, but you'll have to be the one to come looking because I'm done trying to talk sense into you."

He didn't say anything, so I turned and left, but as I went through the doorway, I felt the wards shift. "We'll take it from here," James said, bending to kiss my cheek before the two of them headed into Owen's house and shut the door behind them.

*

I didn't want to go home, and I couldn't face the office, so I went to my favorite place for grounding myself, the greenmarket in Union Square. It was my taste of country in the city, and looking at all the fresh fruits and vegetables cheered me up a little. As frustrated as I was with Owen about his reluctance to research his past, I could kind of understand his fears.

While I was still in the market, a few drops of rain began to fall, then it quickly turned into a real downpour. Of course, I didn't have an umbrella with me, though I probably should have known to expect rain, since Gloria had brought hers. I headed for home, jogging so I could get out of the rain sooner.

By the time I neared my building, I'd given up jogging, since I was already utterly drenched and getting there a few seconds faster wouldn't make me less wet. As I drew closer to my front door, I noticed someone leaning against a lamppost, near where Owen usually waited for me in the mornings. I had to wipe the water and wet hair away from my eyes to see clearly. He was as wet as I was—or worse—and wore a baseball cap pulled down over his eyes, but I still would have recognized Owen Palmer anywhere.

He shoved away from the post as I approached and took a hesitant step toward me. I couldn't read his eyes under the cap's brim, but he gave me a hesitant smile before saying, "Sorry."

"It's okay," I said.

Then he stepped into my arms and buried his face against my neck. I hugged him, rubbing his back while he clung to me. "I've been such a jerk," he whispered into my ear. "I have no excuse for treating someone I love that way, and I want you to know that I do love you."

He took a few deep breaths, then pulled away just enough to look me in the eye. "You're right, you know. I have to deal with this, and I can't hide forever. So, do you want to come to the fire station with me?"

"Sure," I said, grinning in a way that must have looked foolish.

He reached out and took my hand. "Okay, then, let's do this. You know where to go, so lead the way."

Just as we turned to head for the subway, there was an odd magical popping sound, and Mack, the black-clad magical enforcer, appeared. His face was set into grim, cold lines, his lips narrowed to a slit in his face, and his eyes were hard. There was another man with him, also wearing black.

Mack stepped up to Owen. "Owen Morgan, also known as Owen Palmer, you are hereby taken into custody for examination on charges of conspiracy to commit magical crimes."

CHAPTER EIGHTEEN

At the same time, Owen and I shouted, "What?"

The men moved to hold Owen's arms, and he wormed out of their grasp. I clutched Mack's arm and demanded, "On what grounds?"

"That is for the Council to discuss," Mack said as he grabbed Owen again, and this time the two men didn't give him a chance to struggle as they conjured a silver cord to bind his wrists.

"But there isn't any proof of anything," Owen protested. "If this is about that jewelry store incident, you were there! You know what happened."

"A complaint has been made, and it must be answered," Mack said stiffly, as if reciting something he didn't entirely believe.

"Come on, this is ridiculous," I said, grabbing Mack's sleeve. "You can't do this." The other man raised a hand at me, and I smirked when his magic had no effect. "Sorry, doesn't work," I said. "Now how are you going to stop me?"

"Katie, don't," Owen shouted, his voice tight with desperation. "Get James and Gloria, now."

I reluctantly released Mack's sleeve, and I'd barely stepped away before all three of them vanished. Then I spun and took off as fast as I could run for Owen's house, my heart pounding in time with my racing feet. I didn't bother ringing the bell before I let myself in the front door with Rod's key, then knocked briefly on Owen's door before letting myself in and rushing inside.

"Gloria? James?" I called out as I stood dripping in the front hall and gasping for breath.

Gloria came running from the direction of the kitchen, while James emerged from the living room. "You're soaking wet," Gloria said, managing to sound stern and concerned at the same time.

"They took Owen," I blurted between gasps. "The men from the Council, the ones in black. One of them was named Mack. He said he knew you. They said Owen had to answer to the Council for a complaint filed against him, something like conspiracy to commit magical crimes."

Gloria's anger was so fierce that I shrank away from her. Her nostrils flared and her eyes blazed with fury. "How dare they!" she said in a whisper that somehow seemed louder and more piercing than a shout. "James, we must stop this."

James had gone so pale that he was almost blue. "We should talk to Merlin," he said. "He surely will not allow this to happen."

"Let me get my umbrella," Gloria said.

It was theoretically impossible to hail a cab in New York when it was raining, but apparently no one had told Gloria. We walked to the end of the block to a major street, and then within seconds of her raising her umbrella, a cab had pulled over. I wasn't entirely sure it was voluntary, but the cab didn't have passengers in it, so I didn't quibble.

We made it downtown in near-record time, which I suspected had something to do with Gloria's influence. I wasn't sure if it was magic or just the fact that she was the kind of person around whom the universe rearranged itself. Sam popped to attention as James and Gloria approached, then came inside with us. "The boss had a feeling you'd be comin'," he said.

"He knows, then?" Gloria said.

"Yeah, and talk about steamin' mad. I thought he was gonna set the building on fire just by glarin' at it."

Kim glanced up at us through her office doorway as we entered the executive suite, but even she knew better than to take on an angry Gloria, no matter how much it threw off Merlin's schedule, and wisely stayed at her desk. Gloria marched into Merlin's office and snapped, "How could you have let this happen?"

Merlin looked nearly as angry as Gloria did. His eyes were hard and stern, and his breathing was heavy. "It was done without my approval, and I was notified after it was done."

"But why?" Gloria's voice became almost plaintive. "There are no grounds. There's no proof of who he might be, so how can he be blamed for that? And surely no one believes he's been behind the magical crimes." She sank onto Merlin's sofa as though suddenly overcome with weariness. Her hands clutched her purse on her lap so hard that her arthritis-swollen joints whitened.

"I can only assume the chairman was unduly influenced in some way," Merlin said. "Ivor Ramsay must hope to create an enemy to take the blame for his own actions, while eliminating a potential threat to his position."

"But what can we do about it?" I asked.

"I'm afraid there must be a hearing," Merlin said with a nervous sidelong glance at Gloria. "Even to drop the charges entirely, the Council has to convene once the complaint has been made."

"When will the Council convene?" James asked as he sat in one of the wooden chairs facing the sofa.

"No earlier than Monday, I'm afraid."

I tried not to groan out loud. Why had they taken Owen on a Friday afternoon, when nothing could be done until Monday?

"Monday?" Gloria asked, raising an eyebrow. If I'd been Merlin, I'd have scrambled to do anything I could to change that before she turned me into a toad, but he showed no fear.

"The Council does no business on weekends, I'm afraid," he said.

"And he must remain in custody the entire time?"

"I am afraid so, but they assured me he is not being mistreated."

She gave a disdainful sniff, as though she was sure her definition of "mistreated" varied greatly from the Council's.

"Can we see him?" James asked.

"Not until the morning of the hearing."

"We need to work on our case, then," I said, pacing nervously around Merlin's office. "We might as well take advantage of that extra time. I don't know how to prove that Owen didn't create the bad spells or use them. On the other hand, I'm not sure how they could prove their case. The charges are bogus, which makes me wonder if there's a chance of a fair hearing. The whole thing is probably rigged."

"That is my fear," Merlin said. "If Ramsay had the influence to get the chair to accept the complaint, I am worried that he might have influence in the hearing."

"Then what do we do?" I asked.

"We prepare as though it's a legitimate hearing," Merlin said. "We have numerous character witnesses. People from throughout the company would be willing to speak on his behalf. Miss Chandler, you will need to be there, as well."

"I am rather biased," I said, sure I was blushing.

"As are we all, but that cannot be avoided in these circumstances. After all, one would hardly be a character witness if one were entirely neutral on the subject. You have seen him work magic on behalf of others and at risk to himself time and time again."

I'd also seen the rare moments when he lost control or did something too freaky for Merlin's comfort, and then there was the time he went against orders and went to Texas to help me. I hoped that wouldn't come up in the hearing.

Sam flew into the office and perched on the back of the sofa. "Me and the boys have been talkin', and we think we could probably pull off a jailbreak. I got it all planned how we could get in, but I'm still workin' on how to get him out."

I didn't think Sam was joking, but I expected Merlin to take it as a joke. Instead, he said quite seriously, "I would be interested in hearing your thoughts. I have some ideas on managing the escape." That response didn't instill me with confidence.

Gloria stood. "Very well, we will return home to prepare as well as we can from our end. Katie, you will come stay with us Sunday night so that you will be there for the hearing." It didn't sound like I had much choice in the matter.

I stayed behind at the office when they left. It was too bad that the enforcers had come to take Owen before he had a chance to get to the fire station, I thought. I was even more convinced that we needed to know what was in that envelope. At the very least, it might be proof that Owen hadn't known who he really was. Unfortunately, we needed Owen to get the envelope.

Or did we?

With a burst of inspiration, I ran to Rod's office, hoping he might still be at work. He was at his desk, looking tired and grim. "I take it you've heard about Owen," he said.

"I was there."

"I wish there was something I could do."

"There might be." I told him about what I'd learned at the fire station and the envelope that the firefighters would give only to Owen. "You're good at illusions—it's probably second nature to you, after that one you used to use all the time." He ducked his head and broke eye contact, and I groaned. "You're not still using it, are you? You dropped the attraction spell, so I thought maybe you'd decided to go natural."

"Katie, this isn't the time," he said with a wince.

I held up my hands in surrender. "Okay, okay. Anyway, you're our expert with illusion. I showed them a picture of Owen, so they know what he looks like. As well as you know Owen, you could probably give them a good Owen, just long enough for them to hand over the envelope."

He shook his head. "It won't work."

"You think any of those firefighters are immunes?"

"No, but can you imagine that envelope going unopened all those years or not being mentioned at all to Children's Services?"

"I'm sure the envelope is enchanted so they wouldn't give it away to just anyone, but they might be able to give it to someone they *think* is Owen."

"If it's as important as you think it is, then she'd have protected it to make sure it didn't fall into the wrong hands. It's not just a compulsion on the firefighters that keeps them from giving it to anyone but Owen. If she did the magic the right way, no one but Owen would be able to open the envelope or take it out of that fire station. If I tried to do it, it would only make the firefighters suspicious of you for bringing an imposter there. The spell could even have negative effects if the wrong person tried to take it. Remember, Mina Morgan was known for using dark magic. Owen was right to be cautious."

My shoulders sagged into a slump as I sighed. "Oh well, it was worth a shot. But what else can I do?"

"Go home. Get some rest. Pray. Think. To be honest, I'm not sure there's anything that you or I could do other than be there. This is a job for Merlin."

"Merlin's talking seriously with Sam about a jailbreak."

Rod let out a low whistle. "That does *not* sound good."

*

By the time I dragged myself into my apartment, I was ready for a long bath, a good book, and about a pound of chocolate. I'd thought Wednesday was bad, but this had been one of the longest days of my life. "Oh, there you are," Gemma said as I headed for the bedroom I shared with Nita. "You'd better hurry and get changed."

"Changed for what?" The only thing I felt like I might change into was a pumpkin.

"It's Nita's night out, remember? And I don't think you want to go looking like that. Did someone try to drown you?"

"I got caught in the rain." For a moment, I thought about finding an excuse to bow out, but Nita was currently the only normal thing in my life. It might be nice to spend a whole evening without discussing how to beat the bad guys or wondering whether my boyfriend was really the spawn of evil—or if he'd be convicted of it whether or not he was. It wasn't as though I'd be doing anything to help Owen if I didn't go. "I'll be ready in a few minutes," I promised.

I was glad I'd taken the time to change when Gemma, Marcia, and I met Nita in the lobby of the hotel where she worked because Nita had gone all-out with the glam. She wore a spangled camisole with dark, low-rise jeans and stiletto heels, and she had on more makeup than I'd ever seen her wear, even back in high school when she did her face in the school bathroom before class and then washed it off before going home. "What do you think?" she asked, giving a catwalk turn.

"Very hot," I said. I felt like the country cousin in the simple sundress and flat sandals I'd thrown on.

"Yeah, you've already caught the fashion vibe," Gemma said.

"And this is a really nice hotel," Marcia added. I had to agree. It had the hushed elegance of a classy hotel lobby, with Art Deco furniture and a big chandelier overhead.

"I know! It's a pretty far cry from the Cobb Motel. They may have been built around the same time, but it's like they're in totally different universes." She jumped up and down and squealed. "I can't believe I'm actually here! It's so great!"

The hotel's cocktail lounge turned out to attract more than just business travelers. It was a popular neighborhood post-work watering hole. "It's just like on TV," Nita said as we entered. "There are actual single young people here! And drinks in fancy glasses!"

Her enthusiasm was contagious enough to make me temporarily forget my worries. After we'd found a table and ordered drinks—Nita got a cosmopolitan, of course—Marcia asked, "How did your parents take the news about your move?"

Nita tossed back her hair. "Not well at first. There was some screaming and crying, but then my brother reminded them that I'm an adult, and if they took me home against my will, it would be kidnapping. Once I described the hotel, my dad got excited. Now he's bursting with pride that his daughter works in such a fancy place. He's convinced I'll end up running it. Telling my mom about all the Indian men here worked on her. She thinks I'll be married soon." We all drank to parents realizing that their daughters had grown up.

When Nita had her fill of pink drinks and scoping out New York singletons in the bar, we went to a restaurant with a sidewalk café for dinner. After the earlier rainstorm, the evening felt fresh and cool, so it was pleasant outdoors. "This is so awesome!" Nita gushed, staring around the sidewalk. "I feel like a rock star." Then her jaw dropped as she gasped. "Oh my gosh! I totally forgot to tell you! I saw that guy from that band today. They must be playing in New York."

"What band?" Gemma asked.

"You mean Katie didn't tell you? Well, not long before she came back here, this rock band stayed in our motel. They must have been getting away from it all or writing an album, or something, but they caused some problems and my brother threw them out."

"That band?" I blurted as my heart sped up and got stuck in my throat. When Idris had come to my hometown to teach magic to previously undiscovered wizards, Nita had decided (with some nudging from me because I thought it might explain some of his eccentric wizard behavior) that Idris was a rock star hiding out in a small town. It took all my self-control not to sound demanding as I leaned across the table and asked, "Where did you see him?"

"Not too far from the hotel, when I went out to lunch. I thought about going up to him and saying something, but then I remembered that my brother kicked him out of the motel, and I didn't think he'd be all that thrilled to see me."

Marcia got a look of sudden revelation, her mouth opening into an O, but I kicked her under the table before she could say anything. I'd told her about my adventures back home, and I could tell she'd figured out who the rock star really was.

I wanted nothing more than to jump up right then and run to the hotel to search that whole area, but I reminded myself that Nita had seen Idris around noon, and he probably wasn't still hanging around. Then I remembered that I still had Owen's cell phone. "I'm going to make a quick trip to the ladies' room," I said. "Be back in a sec."

It was counterintuitive to head inside to talk on the phone, since it was noisier and the signal was weaker indoors, but this wasn't a conversation I could let Nita overhear. I scrolled through the directory. Surely Owen had Sam on speed dial. Ah, there he was. I placed the call and hoped that Sam had whatever communications technology or magic he used working.

The gargoyle answered on the second ring. "Hey, Katie!" he said.

"How'd you know it was me?"

"You're calling from Owen's phone, and he's not in a place where he can make phone calls at the moment. Who else would it be? So, what's up, doll?"

"I've heard about an Idris sighting earlier today." I gave him the time and approximate location as Nita had described it. "We need to check it out. If we can capture him and get him to talk, that might help Owen's case. And I'm sure I could think of some ways to make him talk. I'd certainly enjoy trying."

"You and me both. I'm on it, sweetheart."

The evening ended early, since Nita was working mornings, and her eyelids were growing heavy by nine. As we left the restaurant, Marcia grabbed my arm and said, "Want to go do something else?" She didn't let go until Gemma said she was heading home with Nita to call Philip. When they were gone, Marcia said, "What's going on? You and Rod have both been acting weird since Wednesday, and I can't get him to tell me why. You won't talk in front of Nita. So now that Nita's gone, spill."

I gave her the short version, to which she responded with a low whistle and a shake of her head. "No wonder Rod's been nuts, and I'm amazed you're as sane as you are. You think this guy Nita saw is Idris?"

"It sounds like it. Or it could be a real New York wannabe rock star who looks like him."

"Let's go check it out."

I wasn't sure what I'd do if I found Idris, aside from maybe knocking out a few teeth and sitting on him until Sam got there, but I was tired of inaction. Marcia and I headed back to the hotel to canvass the neighborhood, and as we walked, I brought her up to date on all the recent happenings. By the time I was done, she was ready to go after Idris with her bare hands, too.

I took mental note of the businesses in that general area. There might have been a Spellworks store Idris was visiting, but I wouldn't see it because those stores were mostly illusion, and Marcia wouldn't see it because the stores were veiled against the nonmagical. However, I didn't see any cheap-looking, nearly blank storefronts with no signage—the way Spellworks stores looked to me—so I doubted that was what brought Idris to the area. No, he must have been going to one of the hundreds of restaurants and delis, which didn't mean he frequented the neighborhood. "We're probably wasting our time," I said after we'd been walking for an hour.

"It was a thought," Marcia said with a shrug.

My shoulders sagging from weariness and futility, I turned to head home and ran smack into Idris.

"You!" we both said simultaneously. I hurried to grab his wrist before he could run, and Marcia grabbed his other arm. "I ought to knock your lights out," I said.

He smirked. "For what? Telling the truth?"

"Truth? What truth? Do you even have any proof, or were you just parroting what Ramsay told you?"

He froze in shock. "How did you know that?"

"How else would you have known about Owen? You would have been a toddler when all that happened, and there aren't any records about Owen's identity in the company. Besides, it became pretty obvious when Ramsay announced he was taking over Spellworks."

"He what?" Idris shrieked.

I couldn't hold back a laugh. "You mean, you didn't know? His whole scheme was to get you to stir up trouble, and now he's swooping in and taking over, probably shoving you to the curb because your name's as tainted as Owen's. You're too associated with the bad spells they're now selling protection against and you spoke out against Spellworks. I don't think he'll welcome you back."

"Ah, but didn't you hear? I was falsely accused by MSI. It was all a cover-up by Owen, who was hiding his own evil schemes by blaming me, and they forced me to speak against Spellworks. But now the truth is out, and, you know, if something happens to Merlin, we'll know who has evil in his blood and probably decided to take out his biggest rival."

I tightened my grip on Idris's wrist and dug in my fingernails. Now I really wished I had Sam's talons. "Oh, really?" I said. "Is that the plan, take out Merlin and blame Owen? Then I suppose Ramsay will deal with Owen and look like a big hero."

Idris gasped and tried to back away. I got the feeling he wasn't supposed to have shared that.

"When's this murder supposed to take place, huh?" I demanded, tightening my grip to the point I was probably drawing blood. "Because Owen was arrested today."

"You never know what might happen when a desperate criminal tries to escape."

The burst of panic that shot through me then was so strong I couldn't come up with a snappy response. Could they possibly know that Merlin was seriously considering helping Owen escape? Where was Sam? Had he sent someone yet? Although Idris couldn't use magic on me, I didn't think Marcia and I were physically capable of subduing him and bringing him in on our own, and I was worried what he'd do to Marcia if he bothered to notice her.

"You must really hate Owen if you were willing to give up a salary," I said, hoping that would distract him from casting a spell on Marcia or from trying to escape.

"What do you mean?"

"As I recall, the deal you made with Merlin when they decided to let you speak means any money you make from Spellworks will just vanish," I reminded him. "And in case you were wondering, that clause was Ramsay's idea. Your boss was setting you up. If things went wrong, then you were the one left to look bad, and you don't even get anything out of it."

He closed his eyes and groaned. "Oh, damn. I forgot about that."

"If you come with us, I'm sure we could work something out," I said. "What's the point of sticking with the bad guys when you don't get anything out of it?"

A flash of terror crossed his face. "I can't. I won't," he stammered as he started shaking. He looked like a person trying to fight a compulsion—or else like a bad mime attempting to do the "walking against the wind" routine.

That's when I realized what had to be going on with him. "He put the whammy on you!" I said. "Ramsay's got you under a compulsion of some kind, right? He was using one of those attraction or charisma spells—" I barely cut myself off before adding "like Rod used to use" in Marcia's presence "—on everyone else, so of course he'd have you under a spell. You really couldn't tell us who you were working for. It wasn't all just an act."

"Stop, stop, stop, stop, stop," he whimpered, moving his arms like he wanted to put his hands over his ears, but Marcia and I hung on and kept his hands down.

"We can help you," I said. "Now that we know about it, we could break the spell. You could help us beat him, and then you'd be free."

He gave a scream of fury and lunged away from me, but I refused to let go even as he tried to wrench his arm from my grasp. My purse slid off my shoulder and I couldn't get it out of the way without releasing him.

"Hey, buddy, drop the purse and leave the ladies alone," a guy passing by said, raising his fists at Idris in a threatening way. Idris took advantage of the distraction to worm away from us and take off. Of all times to run across a chivalrous New Yorker who wasn't willing to look the other way, I thought with a groan. "You okay, ladies?" the guy asked.

I curled my fingers up so he couldn't see the blood under my fingernails. "I'm fine, thank you."

"You need to call someone? Or need someone to walk you home?"

"No, thank you, I'm okay. It's not far. Thank you for coming to our rescue."

He reluctantly let us go, and we hurried away. I fumbled for Owen's cell phone as we walked, then hit redial and got Sam. "I found him," I said. "Idris. He got away, but he can't have gone far." I gave the location and the direction Idris had run. "But Sam, it's worse than that. They're planning to make it look like Owen kills Merlin trying to escape."

"Just relax, doll, we're keeping the boss safe, don't you worry, and we do have a plan."

"Katie, it'll be okay, right?" Marcia said when I got off the phone. I couldn't tell if she was looking for reassurance or offering it.

"I don't know. Everything's out of control, and I have no idea what we can do."

CHAPTER NINETEEN

I took the train to James and Gloria's town on Sunday afternoon, and James met me at the station. When I got to their house, I saw that there were new family photos on the fireplace mantle and bookshelves in the living room. On my first visit, I'd thought it odd that there were no pictures of Owen growing up, but they seemed to have decided that showing pride in their foster son could no longer be held against them, and they'd gone all-out. Gloria left me in there to get settled while she made tea, so I took the chance to study the pictures.

As Rod said, Owen had been a small, skinny kid with thick glasses. Until his late teens, he'd shown only hints of the good looks he'd grow into. The family portraits had a distinct sense of distance to them, as though he felt he didn't really belong in them. He didn't smile in many of the pictures, only in a candid shot where he was playing with a large German shepherd and seemed unaware of the camera and in one that must have been taken at Halloween with an older boy I recognized as Rod, with both of them wearing costumes. Owen was dressed as Robin Hood, while Rod wore a tux and carried a toy gun, so I assumed he was James Bond.

"They cannot tell me I'm not allowed to feel like a mother anymore," Gloria's voice said behind me, and I turned to see her standing straight and upright, a tea tray in her hands and her chin raised defiantly. I knew I wouldn't want to be the Council member making accusations against her boy. Her expression softened a little as she added, "I heard what you said to him at his house the other day. Thank you. I hadn't thought of it that way before, but you were right."

"Well, he is a special guy, and I think you had a lot to do with that."

It was a more comfortable visit than my first one, but it was still awkward staying in the Eatons' home without Owen there, especially given the reason that Owen wasn't there. I'd hoped that they might know something about whatever Merlin had planned, but they didn't know any more than I did. I had a feeling none of us got much sleep that night.

The next morning, they made me drive their ancient but perfectly maintained Volvo, since James said his eyesight wasn't up for driving outside their village. I had to move the seat forward and then adjust to driving something other than an old pickup truck with a stick shift. Having Gloria in the front seat watching everything I did didn't help matters.

The Council's headquarters was farther up the river in one of those mansions built by nineteenth-century robber barons—at least, that's what it looked like, but the building seemed so ancient that it could have been transplanted directly from Europe. It looked like a spooky old-world abbey, and the entire place reeked of magic. My skin hummed from the power, and I wondered what it felt like to magical people.

The entrance was innocuous enough, with a butler meeting us in a foyer that wouldn't have been out of place in any old mansion, but then he led us deeper into the house to a great hall, and I knew this wouldn't be a pleasant social occasion.

The room was beyond imposing. The ceiling went higher than I would have thought possible in the building I'd seen from the outside, and it was braced with heavy beams the size of giant trees. The floor was made of flagstones worn smooth with time, and the walls down one side were paneled in dark, intricately carved wood, while the other side held stained-glass windows depicting the history of magic.

At the head of the hall stood a massive rectangular table set on a stage so that it loomed over everything. The chairs behind that table were equally massive, the backs going well above the height of even the tallest man, and they had magical symbols carved into them. I noticed that the floor also contained those symbols, formed out of a darker stone, but they were difficult to see unless you were standing back and got a broad view. In the middle of the pattern, directly in front of the high table and reaching almost to the front row of wooden spectator benches, was a circle formed out of the darker stone. I wondered what those symbols did—maybe they were wards or one of those magic-dampening fields?

Gloria turned to James and said, "Go help him get ready." James nodded and left, carrying a garment bag. "They had best let him prepare to face this," she said, her tone making it clear they would answer to her if they didn't. She led me to the front of the room, where we took seats on the front row of benches. She sat with her back perfectly straight, her hands braced on her knees.

James joined us a few minutes later, sitting on Gloria's other side. "He said he was thankful for the suit, but he was perfectly capable of dressing himself," he reported.

Gloria took his hand and asked, "How is he?"

"Calm. He doesn't look like he's slept much, though. He did have all his limbs and fingers, and I didn't see any bruises, so I don't think they've mistreated him."

"They wouldn't dare." She checked her watch. "I cannot wait to get this farce over with."

More people trickled in. I recognized some of the Eatons' neighbors, along with many of my friends from MSI. Rod sat by me, and then Ethan sat by him. Ethan leaned across Rod to say, "I offered to provide representation, but they assured me my law degree wouldn't be of much use here."

"I'm sure he appreciates the gesture," I said with a weak smile.

"The situation is insane, anyway," he said, shaking his head. "I don't get it."

"That's because it's entirely trumped up," Rod muttered. He glanced over his shoulder and said, "Uh oh, my parents are here." I felt a faint burst of magic, and I assumed that meant he'd dropped his handsome illusion, or at least adjusted it so it didn't affect his parents. I could see why, since he looked just like his father, and it wasn't exactly a compliment to change his appearance so drastically.

I managed not to respond too strongly when Owen's boss entered. I knew that meant things were quite dire, since Mr. Lansing rarely left his office, thanks to a magical industrial accident that had turned him into a giant frog. He had an illusion that made him look human to most people, but it took a lot of effort, so he usually sent Owen out on his behalf. I saw the frog, since illusions don't work on me, and seeing a giant frog walking around is more than a bit disconcerting.

Jake came in and sat near the back. He wore a conventional suit and had his hair neatly combed, so it took me a moment to recognize him. Isabel sat next to him, and Trix was with her. Sam and a few other gargoyles perched in the rafters. The whole gang was there.

But it wasn't just familiar faces filling the hall. The place was packed, and I didn't recognize most of those people. Many of them craned their necks, looking like sightseers, and I wondered if this was the magical trial of the century, something people attended out of curiosity.

"Do you think Ramsay or Idris will show?" I whispered to Rod.

"Idris, no. He was in legitimate custody and escaped. Ramsay, I don't know. He lost his seat on the Council when he handed the company over to Merlin, so he has no official standing here anymore, though he certainly has kept his hand in the game."

"Speak of the devil," I muttered as a stirring in the crowd heralded Ramsay's arrival. It was like a cross between the pope and a popular politician as he made his way down the aisle. The people he didn't shake hands with reached out to touch him, like they thought some of his magic might rub off on them. That charisma spell of his must have been a doozy, I thought. He nodded cordially to us as he took a seat on the front row on the other side of the aisle. I reminded myself that the way he'd arranged things, I'd only make myself look like a villain if I launched myself at him and knocked his lights out. That didn't stop me from forming fists and fantasizing about doing so.

Gloria elbowed me sharply in the ribs as a hush settled over the room. I turned to see that the Council members were filing in to take their seats.

I wasn't sure quite what to expect, since nothing in the magical world ever turned out to be what I expected. Robes would have been a good guess, maybe with stars and moons on them, like something out of a storybook, or maybe just solid black, like judges' robes. Tall, pointy hats would have been appropriately magical. In short, they should have looked like Merlin's "Merlin" outfit.

Instead, it pretty much looked like a city council meeting, aside from the Old World setting. The Council members wore regular business attire, but with elaborate chains of office draped over their shoulders and floppy beret-like hats, like some faculty members wear for college graduation ceremonies. I was surprised when Merlin was the last one to enter. He paused to shut the door before taking a seat on that end of the table. I hadn't realized he was also on the Council, but it did make sense, given his position in MSI, which was the commercial arm of the magical establishment, as well as the fact of who he was. They couldn't possibly have a magical council without Merlin being on it. His being an actual Council member explained why Ramsay rankled him so much with all his talk about being privy to what was going on with the Council. I scanned the faces of the wizards on the Council to get a sense of the people sitting in judgment, but Merlin was the only who looked familiar or friendly.

The feeling of magical power in the room intensified, and I got the impression the entire room was being put under a spell. That was confirmed when the man sitting in the middle seat stood, pounded a carved staff as tall as he was on the floor, and said, "This room is now sealed. No one may enter or leave until the proceedings are concluded, except by special escort, and the world outside is now separated from us. No one outside may observe or listen to these proceedings, and those inside may not speak of them outside these walls."

Well, except for me. And Ethan, I couldn't help but think. I wondered if they'd bother with an oath to hold us to that or if they even realized there were magical immunes in the room.

"This meeting of the North American Magical Council is now in session," the wizard in the middle said with another strike of his staff on the floor. A large ceremonial gavel sat on the table in front of him, but it looked like the staff was the real sign of power. I'm sure Freud would have had something to say about that. "There has been a request to add an agenda item: A petition from Mr. Ivor Ramsay to grant a seat on this Council to the chairman of Spellworks and to reconsider the MSI seat, as that organization has failed to provide proper leadership to the magical world. We will address that issue after we deal with the primary matter that brings us together today. Now, bring in the accused." He pounded his staff again.

There was a shimmer in the air around the doors beside the Council's table, and then the doors opened. The black-clad men came in, guiding Owen by the elbow. He was dressed in a dark suit, and if his hands hadn't been bound behind his back, he'd have looked like he was having just another day at the office. Even the dark circles under his eyes were all in a day's work for him.

They brought Owen to stand in the middle of the circle in front of the elevated table, and he looked very young and very small with the Council looming over him. I'd seen what he could do using magic, and I still didn't think anyone could imagine him to be a threat given the way he looked. The crowd murmured, like they were discussing Owen's appearance, and I hoped they, too, thought he looked harmless. I felt Gloria tense next to me. She reached to take my hand and clutched it fiercely.

Merlin stared Owen down with a glare that made me squirm uncomfortably, and it wasn't even aimed at me. Owen seemed to be studiously avoiding looking at Merlin, but that wasn't the kind of glare you could ignore for long. Even if he didn't see it, he had to feel it. Once he finally caught Owen's eye, Merlin's expression changed. His lips moved ever so slightly, but I couldn't make out any words. I couldn't see Owen's face to get a sense of what he was doing, but his head nodded a fraction of an inch before he turned away from Merlin. I got the feeling that something had been communicated between them, but I wasn't sure how. They both had a tendency toward eerie knacks, but I'd never heard about either of them being able to communicate telepathically.

The head wizard peered through his reading glasses at a sheet of paper he held and said, "Owen Morgan."

"Palmer," Owen corrected, in a voice that rang through the room. "My legal name is Palmer. I was adopted by Stan and Lisa Palmer when I was an infant. Their parental rights were terminated and I eventually became a ward of this Council, but my name was never legally changed. As far as I know, there is no proof of my parents being the Morgans. That is merely an allegation. I have no record of who my birth parents were." That was one upside of not having had the chance to get that envelope from the fire station, I thought. He could say with absolute honesty that he didn't know his parentage.

"Very well, then, Owen Palmer," the head wizard said, "you stand accused of conspiracy to commit magical crimes, namely that you have engineered a variety of incidents around New York City in which magic has been used to cause trouble and create a state of fear among the magical population so that you can then come to the rescue and make yourself appear to be a hero. How do you plead?"

"Not guilty."

"On what grounds?"

"I thought that the way this court worked was that *you* had to have the grounds to charge me. We've had that in our law longer than it's been the law of the land. After all, we've suffered too much from witch hunts to conduct them on ourselves. *I* don't need grounds for anything. *You* have to present the grounds for the charges, and I must admit that I'm extremely curious to hear what you've come up with." Owen sounded almost cocky, like Idris on one of his more annoying days. Merlin was fighting so hard not to smile that he ended up looking very stern indeed.

"That is true, Rudolph," a woman at the opposite end of the table from Merlin said. "Surely you had evidence before you had Mr. Palmer arrested."

"But we can ask you questions as part of these proceedings," Rudolph said.

From the way Owen's shoulders shifted, I got the feeling that he would have crossed his arms in front of his chest if his wrists hadn't been bound behind his back. He did lean his weight onto one leg and cross the other in front of him, in a fair approximation of the way he might casually lean against a wall. "Then ask me a question."

Ethan made a strangled noise, and I couldn't help but glance at him. He looked like he had to bite his tongue to keep from shouting, "Objection!" My experience with the ordinary legal system was limited to jury duty a couple of times back home and watching the occasional episode of *Law and Order*, but even I could tell that there was something funny about the way this hearing was going. The low rumble of murmurs from the audience verified this.

Rudolph let the crowd mutter for quite some time, possibly because he couldn't think of a good question to ask. After a couple of minutes, he banged his staff on the floor to demand silence. Merlin caught Owen's eyes and held them, then leaned forward and said, "I have a question for Mr. Palmer."

"Yes, Mr. Mervyn," Rudolph said, sounding rather relieved.

"Mr. Palmer, have you ever used unauthorized magic?" Merlin asked.

I was fairly certain that this was part of whatever Merlin had planned, and that Owen was somehow in on it. Owen's head snapped toward Merlin like he was shocked, but his posture looked far too relaxed. Someone whose mentor was questioning him about a crime should have been a lot more tense. He should have looked like he was barely holding himself back from jumping at the man.

Gloria, on the other hand, went tense enough for both of them. "What does he mean by this?" she whispered, and she moved as though she was about to go after Merlin, herself.

"I think Merlin's up to something, and Owen knows what it is," I said. "Look at him." She stared at Owen's back for a moment, then turned ever so slightly back toward me, one eyebrow quirked upward.

Ramsay's reaction was even more interesting. He actually twitched, probably from being torn between impulses. If Merlin went on the attack against Owen, it could undermine his attempt to make Merlin look like he was out of it, but if Ramsay came to Owen's defense, that ruined his chances of setting Owen up to take the fall for killing Merlin.

"Could you be more specific?" Owen asked.

"You have used questionable magic in my presence. I don't know that it is strictly illegal, but I suspect that is because no one believed it could be done, and therefore it hasn't been included in the magical code of conduct. You have interfered with time itself."

That set the crowd going again. If this was part of a plan, I thought they were heading into risky territory, since Owen *had* interfered with time, and I knew it made Merlin intensely uncomfortable when he did it.

"Nonsense! No one can do that," the youngest-looking member of the Council said.

"I have seen him do it," Merlin insisted.

Rudolph glared down at Owen. "Can you do it?"

Owen stared back up at him, and he must have given a glare worthy of Gloria, since Rudolph pressed himself against the back of his chair, like he was moving as far as he could from Owen without getting up and fleeing. "You mean you can't?" Owen asked.

"Of course I can't! It's impossible." Rudolph addressed the other wizards on the Council. "Can any of you?"

They all shook their heads. I got the feeling that claiming the ability to do that time-stopping thing was the magical equivalent of a nonmagical person claiming the ability to fly or see the future.

"Would you like me to demonstrate?" Owen asked, sounding too innocent for this to be good. If any of the Council members, aside from Merlin, had known him at all, they would have known better than to let this go any further. They'd have dismissed the trumped-up charges, issued an apology, and let him go. But they played right into Merlin's plan. At least, what I assumed was Merlin's plan.

"The wards on the circle make a demonstration impossible," Merlin said. "There is a reason we prevent the use of magic by prisoners."

"The wards on the circle would have to be altered for a demonstration, but we do have other security measures in place," another Council member said.

"It would definitively prove that he is capable of everything for which he stands accused," Merlin said, as though he was being talked around to the idea.

I had to bite the inside of my lip to keep from laughing out loud. They were seriously going to let Owen stop time in the room for everyone but himself? That was like the prison guard handing the keys to an inmate and wandering off. But they didn't seem to believe it could be done.

Rudolph stood and held his staff over his head. There was a shift in the sense of magic in the room, and then he said, "Now, Mr. Palmer, if you would demonstrate."

"I'll need my hands free," Owen said. After a nod from Rudolph, the guard next to Owen touched the silver cord around Owen's wrists, and it vanished. Owen rubbed his wrists, then said, "Okay, here's how the spell goes." He knelt and put a hand to the ground before whispering a few words.

I knew what to expect because I'd seen it before in a more impressive setting when he'd frozen Times Square. No one else in the room, other than Ethan, would even know what happened. The room went silent as everyone in it but Owen, Ethan, and I were frozen in time. Owen turned to look at us, grinned, and said, "That was almost too easy." His grin faded, and he added, "Now comes the hard part."

"What will you do?" I asked.

"Try to remain free long enough to figure something out. I'll try to get to that fire station. I don't stand a chance in this hearing. I just hope they consider the circumstances when this is all over. I'd rather not spend my life on the run."

"What do you need us to do?" I asked.

He headed for the door behind the table, where the Council had entered—and where I'd have bet that Merlin had altered the wards—and with his hand on the doorknob, he said, "I'll need a diversion for a second or two."

"That's not what I meant."

"Don't worry, I'm sure you'll figure out something. Now, the diversion?"

"Okay," I said. "But take care of yourself. On the count of three."

He opened the door, said, "One, two, three." On "three" he broke the spell, and at that moment I faced the windows and screamed my head off.

"What is that—that thing?" I shrieked, pointing toward nothing. "It came through the window. Can't you see it? It must be veiled by magic. Someone has infiltrated this hearing!" I knew I was laying it on a bit thick, but most of the Council had never met me, so they didn't know that I wasn't the screaming, hysterical type.

The reaction was a lot like what you'd get if you shouted "Mouse!" in a crowded room. People in the general vicinity of where I'd pointed scurried away, the guards ran toward it, and a lot of magic flew through the air. By the time the guards and the Council decided that the thing had gone out the way it had entered, Owen was long gone. It took a moment or two after everyone settled down for Rudolph to shout, "Where did he go?"

Merlin pinned him with a glare. "You asked him to freeze time. And that meant freezing all of you, so that he was then able to escape."

"But he didn't…" Rudolph started to protest, and then his voice trailed off as he caught on.

Merlin nodded sagely. "Exactly. You wouldn't notice if you were affected."

"But he can stop time?" the wizard sitting next to Merlin asked. "That makes him even more dangerous than we thought."

"And he has just proved that these charges were valid," Rudolph said. Then he pounded his staff on the floor and added, "This hearing is dismissed and will reconvene when the accused has been returned to custody."

Merlin caught up with us outside the headquarters building as we left. Gloria whirled on him, and for a moment I thought she'd hit him with her purse. "That was the best you could do, accuse him and then turn him into a fugitive?"

"We could not have won today," Merlin said grimly. "I've bought us time. And now we should make use of that time. Miss Chandler, you are best equipped to find Owen. Any illusion he hides behind won't work on you. Then find out what his mother left at the fire station as soon as you can."

I wasn't sure how to go about doing that, but I had time to think while Ethan gave Rod and me a ride back to the city. Owen had a head start, but not a huge one, and if he'd managed to disguise himself, he might be able to stay undetected for a while. I'd likely be watched, though. That meant that I'd only put him in danger if I found him. I'd have to be careful.

By the time Ethan dropped me off at my building, I had an idea of where to look. I changed into jeans and sneakers, wandered the neighborhood for a while to see if I noticed anyone following me, then took the subway to Grand Central. I milled around the main concourse and flowed with a crowd toward a platform. Then I slipped away into the darkness at the end of the platform, toward Owen's dragon lair. He was supposed to have sent the dragons to a sanctuary after the conference demonstration, but there weren't too many people who knew about this location, and he knew that I knew.

Without the dragons, it was dark and quiet in the unused tunnel that opened to the side of the underground rail yard. I probably should have brought a flashlight, I thought, but since I was here without anyone magical to hide me, I'd worried it might draw unwanted attention.

I thought I saw a glint of light ahead, and I flattened myself against the wall. Was it a railroad worker, an untamed dragon, or something else?

And then I realized that there was someone next to me. I didn't plan to scream because that wouldn't do any good and would likely draw unwanted attention, but whoever it was got a hand over my mouth anyway while wrapping his other arm around my waist.

CHAPTER TWENTY

"It's okay, it's me," Owen's voice whispered into my ear.

He removed his hand from my mouth, and I said, "I know. And I wasn't going to scream." Then I turned to face him and threw my arms around him. He hugged me in return, holding me like I was a lifeline.

"That must have been a good diversion," he whispered as his lips brushed my temple.

"It was a real scream. So, now what?"

"We need to get to the fire station, but I'm being followed. I gave them the slip inside the terminal, but they're probably still waiting for me to leave."

"Merlin thought you might use an illusion."

"I did, but somehow they still spotted me. They may be tracking my magic, so I'm just as recognizable with an illusion as I am as myself. I may have to resort to the hat and funny glasses kind of disguise. I definitely don't want to lead them to the fire station."

"You need a safe place to stay. You can't stay down here."

"I'm open to suggestions. I made a quick run by my place to pick up a few things before they caught up with me, so I'm set for at least a couple of days."

"Nita!" I said with a burst of inspiration.

"What about Nita?"

"She works at a hotel—she handles registration. I could probably get you a room there under another name—maybe say you're a celebrity involved with a charity thing I'm doing at work. Nita would totally go for that. Since my friend works there, it wouldn't look suspicious for me to go to the hotel. Could you do that teleport spell you did with me that time? Or does that only work to a familiar place?"

"Anything familiar would work. I can travel to you if you're there. But doing that would wipe me out magically for hours."

"You could probably use the rest, and if you vanish for a while, maybe that'll throw off the bad guys. Meanwhile, I could find a hat and some funny glasses for you."

"Okay, sounds like a plan." He released me and conjured up a small, glowing orb of light that hung in front of his shoulder, then bent to dig in the duffle bag at his feet. "We'd probably better use cash for the hotel because credit cards can be traced." He stood with a wad of cash in his hand, which he then handed to me. "Two nights should do it, and that ought to be enough."

"This is a couple of thousand bucks," I said, thumbing through the bills in the dim glow of the orb. "You keep that much cash lying around?"

"My house is warded, so it's safe, and you never know when you might need cash."

I split the wad, sticking some in my front pocket and the rest inside my bra. "I just hope I don't get mugged between here and the hotel. Now, how will I let you know I've got the room? I've got your cell phone, but that can be traced, too."

He pulled a phone out of his pocket. "Pre-paid, and paid in cash," he explained. "All the best spies and criminals use them." He wrote the number on the back of a cash register receipt and handed it to me.

"Wow, you've spent some time planning what you'd do if you ever became a fugitive."

"I had a lot of time to think over the weekend."

Before I could leave, he caught me in another hug. "Thanks, Katie. I should have listened to you and gone to the fire station sooner."

"They'd have probably arrested you the moment you left your house, whenever that was," I said.

"Or we might have this whole thing wrapped up by now." He bent to give me one last kiss, then reluctantly released me. I didn't let myself look back over my shoulder as I ran down the tunnel and then eased my way back onto the platform and then into the terminal. I noticed a number of men dressed all in black in the concourse, but at least two of them appeared to be Hasidim, not magical law enforcers. Unless maybe they were Hasidic magical law enforcers. I didn't plan to stick this in the Council's suggestion box, but their guys would be a lot less conspicuous if they wore something else. I supposed they were used to dealing with people they could fool magically.

There was another man in black leaning against a nearby wall, and out of the corner of my eye I noticed him shove away from the wall and follow me once I'd gone a few feet past him. I ignored him, pretending I didn't see him at all even though the space between my shoulder blades itched with the sense of being watched. I knew he was technically one of the good guys, but that didn't make it any less creepy to be followed.

I went up to the level where the shops were and spent some time browsing in the bookstore, just to pretend that I had a reason for being in the building. I bought a spy novel I thought Owen would like, then went down to the food court in the lower level and bought a slice of pizza that I ate at a nearby table while pretending to read the book.

My follower was still with me when I left the terminal and headed up Lexington Avenue. I was so busy glancing at store windows to see if he was still there that I almost bumped into a tall, thin man wearing an overcoat and a hat that were both entirely inappropriate in the summer weather. I caught only the slightest glimpse of a face beneath the hat brim before the man whirled away from me, but I could have sworn there wasn't a face there, just a skeleton. Either the Grim Reaper was on my case, or my old buddy Mr. Bones, one of Idris's creepy creations, was also tailing me. Suddenly I felt better about having the magical law-and-order squad watching me. Mr. Bones wouldn't dare do anything while the magic cops were around. Good or bad, I needed to lose all my followers before I went to the hotel.

I walked uptown to the next subway station, then caught a train heading back downtown and got off at Grand Central, this time leaving through the front entrance instead of going through the main concourse. I didn't notice Mr. Bones or the man in black behind me in the shop windows as I hurried uptown, but just to be safe, when I got to the hotel, I entered the hotel's coffee shop through the street entrance, then joined a crowd leaving the shop to go into the hotel lobby.

There wasn't a line at registration, so I went straight up to Nita's position. "Hey, this is a surprise!" she said. "What are you doing here? I'm going on break in half an hour, so we could go have coffee if you can hang around that long."

"Yeah, that'd be great, but first I need to ask you for a favor. Do you have any rooms available?"

She grinned and winked. "Oh, you naughty girl. But I thought Owen had his own place."

"That's not why I need it." I launched into the celebrity charity story I'd developed while leading my followers on a merry chase.

Nita was just as excited as I expected to hear about a mystery celebrity staying at her hotel. "Oh my gosh! Who is it? No, wait, you can't tell me because it's top secret. It's Bono, isn't it? No, don't tell me."

"But can you get me a room?"

She tapped at her keyboard. "Let's see. I don't have any of the super-fancy rooms available, but I do have a mini suite. What name do you want to put it under?"

I couldn't resist. "Yankee Doodle."

She typed some more. "Okay, I've got a mini suite under the name of Yankee Doodle." She frowned and tilted her head. "If he's 'Yankee Doodle,' then it's probably not Bono, huh?" Her eyes went wide. "Oh my gosh! It's Bruce Springsteen, isn't it?"

"I can't tell you."

"This is going to drive me crazy, you know that, right? How many nights do you need?"

"Two to start with. I hope it doesn't take longer than that."

"And how will you be paying?"

"Cash—so it can stay top-secret, you know." I pulled out the wad of bills Owen gave me, angling my body so it wasn't visible throughout the lobby when I took the cash out of my bra.

"Wow, this is really unusual," she said as she took the money from me.

"You won't get in trouble, will you?"

"Just as long as the bill is paid in full by checkout, the police don't come looking for a list of registered guests, and your celebrity doesn't trash the place, I should be fine. Now, do you have any special requests?"

"Special requests?"

"You know how celebrities are—stuff like white orchids, M and Ms—but only the green ones—bottled water at a particular temperature."

"No, that won't be necessary. He's not picky."

"Well, let us know if you need something." She ran two plastic key cards through the machine, then stuck them in a folder and wrote the room number on it. "There you go. I hope Mr. Yankee Doodle enjoys his stay."

"I'm sure he will. Now, I'll go sneak Yankee Doodle in, and then I'll be back down when your break starts for coffee."

"Tell him I'm a huge fan!"

The mini suite was about the same size as the regular rooms in Nita's family's old roadside motel, but far plusher. There was a small living area with a sofa, television, and desk; a kitchenette with a mini fridge, coffeemaker, and microwave; a bedroom with a king-sized bed; and a decent-sized bathroom. The windows had a nice view of the midtown skyline, but I closed the drapes in case there was aerial surveillance.

Then I got out the receipt with Owen's new cell phone number and called him from the room's phone. "I've got the room," I said. "Sorry it took me awhile. I was being followed, so I had to lose them."

"Are you sure you lost them?"

"Even if I didn't, I'm about to have coffee with Nita, which gives me an excuse to be here."

"Okay, then, I'm on my way." I was about to ask how long it would take when I heard a cracking sound, and there he was. He swayed, and I moved to steady him. He shook his head like he was trying to clear it, then said, "Oh boy, I'm out of practice."

"You're tired and you've been under a lot of stress." I helped him over to the sofa, where he collapsed bonelessly against the cushions and dropped his bag on the floor. "Now, is there anything else you need?" I asked.

"A nap."

"What about food?"

"If my stay here is top-secret, room service is probably out of the question."

"I'll see if Nita can do something. By the way, she said she's a big fan."

He looked confused. "What?"

"I may have given her the impression that you were Bruce Springsteen. When I gave you the code name Yankee Doodle, she drew her own conclusions."

"You *what*? Are you going to tell everyone in the city about that?"

"Oops, I've got to go. Go take a nap. Close the bedroom door, and I'll have them deliver something to the living room." I tossed him the book I'd bought. "And here's something in case you get bored."

"We will discuss this further," he warned as he dragged himself to his feet, picked up his bag, and headed for the bedroom. Then he turned back. "Oh, and would you mind looking after Loony?"

"Already covered."

I got downstairs just as Nita was going on her break, and then we found seats by the window at the hotel's coffee shop—in full view of a man wearing black who stood on the sidewalk outside. I may have overacted the "girlfriends getting together for gossip" role as we shared a giant slice of cake and had lattes, but Nita didn't notice. That was the way she always acted.

When I headed to the subway station to go home after arranging for a meal to be delivered to the "celebrity," I recognized my follower. "Hi, Mack," I said cheerfully when I heard him fall into step behind me. "How's it going?"

The footsteps behind me faltered, and then he came up alongside me. "How did you know?"

"Remember, I'm immune to magic. Whatever you were doing to hide yourself, it didn't work. Owen's not a criminal, you know."

He sighed heavily. "I know. But I've got to go through the motions until my boss orders otherwise."

"Have you noticed the freaky skeleton thing following me?"

He gave a startled flinch. "The what?"

"That must be veiled from you. For what it's worth, the bad guys are also following me. I feel so popular."

"Shout if you feel like they're a threat, and I'll take care of it."

"Thanks, Mack."

He faded back into the background behind me and stayed there until I made it home. My entourage complicated matters. There wasn't a lot I could do while everyone was watching me, and while I was being watched, it was dangerous for me to go near Owen. How would we ever get Owen to that fire station to find the mysterious envelope that could be our only clue to resolving this situation?

*

The next morning, I figured my best strategy was to act like this was a relatively normal day and go to work. With any luck, that would bore my followers into complacency. I left early to stop by Owen's place and feed Loony before I headed to the office. The protesters hadn't come back after James and Gloria's scolding—or perhaps Owen's arrest—so that was one less hassle to deal with. While I was in his home, I looked around for anything that Owen might need me to bring him. It would have to be small enough for me to smuggle, or else it would be too obvious that I was bringing something out of the house. Owen's moving spell would come in pretty handy, I thought. All we'd have to do was set it up, and then Owen could zap anything to where he was.

Then I gasped as an idea hit me that was so good it made me dizzy and made my ears tingle. I had to lean against the kitchen counter for a moment until I felt a little steadier. "That's it, Loony!" I said. "I know how to get the envelope." The cat flicked her tail, but otherwise didn't let her excitement over my brainstorm get in the way of enjoying her breakfast.

The question was, where did Owen keep the supplies for the spell? I went into the living room and searched around the desk. I wasn't sure whether Owen's recent cleaning spree was a blessing or a curse. There was less clutter to sort through, but that also meant he might have put away the supplies instead of just leaving them in his satchel.

Where was the satchel? I tried the hall closet and found it hanging on a hook on the inside of the door. "Jackpot!" I said when I discovered the vials of powder and the spell booklet. The recent upsetting events may have led Owen to the unprecedented action of putting away his books and papers, but he hadn't emptied his satchel before putting it away. I selected one of the powders and put that vial and the booklet in my purse.

Now I needed to think of a way to get that powder on the envelope. I was so eager that I wanted to go straight to the fire station, but I knew that would alert my followers. Instead, I headed to the office with representatives from both sides in tow.

As I approached Sam's awning after weaving through the usual mob of protesters outside the office building, he said, "Looks like you've picked up an entourage."

"You can see them?"

"It's hard to hide completely from someone who knows to look for you."

"That's good to know. I'll need to chat with you about that inside in a little while."

"Got it, doll. I'll find you in a bit."

I went to my office first, as though it was any other working day. Perdita was doing her nails when I entered, and she immediately sat up and dropped her nail file. "Wow, you're here!" she said. "I heard about yesterday. That must have been exciting."

"It was more scary than anything."

"But I heard the boss accused Owen."

"Not everything is as it seems."

She winked. "Okay, gotcha." Then she leaned back in her chair and crossed her legs. "You know, it's kind of sexy having a boyfriend who's a fugitive."

"More like nerveracking."

"Do you think he'll be able to clear his name?"

"There's nothing to clear. He hasn't done anything wrong." Well, other than escape from custody, but there were extenuating circumstances. "Do people really think he's, well…"

"Evil?"

"Yeah. That."

She tilted her head to the side and frowned as she considered. "Not evil, really. But I think a lot of people who don't know him might be worried that he could become evil, like he won't be able to help himself."

"So his chances of ever having a normal life among magical people are pretty slim, huh?"

"People will have to see that they can trust him. And his big prison break isn't helping. I am trying to tell everyone I know that he's a good guy."

"Thanks, Perdita."

"Is there anything else I can do to help?"

I looked at her, with her long, shapely legs and perfect ringlets, and remembered her talent for disaster. "Maybe," I said thoughtfully. "Let me get back to you on that, okay?"

My e-mail had piled up to the point it was tempting to just delete the whole in-box and start over again, but I figured anything other than defeating Ramsay would fall into the low-priority category, so I skimmed the headings, checked my voice mail, then went up to Merlin's office. "I hope you don't have anything to report to me on Mr. Palmer's whereabouts," he said as soon as I set foot in his office. I paused, shaking my head, and he added with a wink, "Since I am a member of the Council—Rudolph seems to have forgotten that additional agenda item in the confusion—I would have to report the location of a dangerous fugitive."

"Of course," I said. "You probably don't even want to know that he's safe and okay, for the moment."

"No, I certainly would not want to know that. However, I might have some interest in the status of your assignment."

"The status hasn't changed and has been complicated by recent events, but I have some ideas and should have progress to report soon."

Jake and another guy in a lab coat then ran in, shouting, "We did it! We did it!"

"That's very nice to hear," Merlin said. "But what did you do?"

"We've cracked the spell behind those charms and amulets. We can negate it entirely. Want us to do it?" Jake said, panting in his eagerness.

Merlin thoughtfully stroked his beard. "No, I think it would be best to wait for a truly opportune moment. We'd like them to think they've got control, or else they might come up with something new. But good work, lads."

That bit of news was encouraging. It felt like things were coming together for us. I headed back to my office, where I found Sam chatting with Perdita. "So, whaddaya need, doll?" he asked.

"I need to lose my followers a couple of times—not enough that they'd know they'd really been lost, but enough for me to slip away for a while."

The three of us hashed out a plan, and then when lunchtime rolled around, my new accomplice Perdita and I headed out for a Chinatown shopping trip. We tried on hats and sunglasses, and I bought some things I thought might work as disguises. Then Perdita's natural clumsiness kicked in, and she lost her balance, tripping and falling against a sidewalk display rack, knocking it over—right in the path of both Mr. Bones and Mack. The shopkeeper came out, yelling in Chinese, while Perdita stammered apologies and set about helping put everything back in place. In the commotion, I darted around the corner.

It was a couple of long blocks to the fire station, and I slowed to a walk for the last block when I was sure I wasn't being followed so I wouldn't be too out of breath when I got there. Corelli was out in front again, and he waved as I approached. "Hey, Katie, couldn't get enough of us, huh?" he called out.

"You know it. Is Vinnie in?"

"Yeah, come on. He's been wondering what happened to you."

"It's not me. It's my boyfriend getting all weird now that we seem to be closing in on where he came from."

"I can see that," he said with a nod. "To be honest, there're days when I wouldn't mind not knowin' the rest of my family."

"I know what you mean."

Vinnie was in the kitchen again, and he grinned when he saw me. "So, you got my boy with you?"

"Sorry, Vinnie, no. I can't seem to talk him into coming down here. But I think I have an idea for making him curious. I know you can't give me that envelope, but I thought maybe if I showed him a picture of it with those instructions on it and a picture of you, then he'd want to know more."

He wiped his hands on his apron. "Sure thing, doll. Right this way." He led me to an office, where he pulled open a file cabinet and shuffled through some folders, finally coming up with one, from which he took a somewhat yellowed business-size security envelope.

I took Owen's cell phone out of my purse, making sure I got some powder on my fingers as I did so. "Okay, first a picture of you with the envelope. Smile!" I took the picture, then I reached forward to adjust the envelope in Vinnie's hand so that the handwriting on it was visible—and so that I got a good dusting of magical powder on it. I felt the tingle of magic when I touched it and knew that getting it out of Vinnie's hand really would be impossible.

I tried to read the note on the outside in the quick glance I got. Owen certainly hadn't inherited his mother's penmanship, but then again, the woman had just given birth and was in a hurry, so I cut her some slack. I took the picture, then said, "That'll do it. Thanks, Vinnie. Now, if this doesn't work, I'll have to just club him over the head and drag him down here."

Hoping I'd done enough to make this work, I hurried back to the place where I'd left Perdita. With either her natural charm or magic, she'd managed to soothe the shopkeeper and had roped in a few bystanders to help clean up. I slipped in among the helpers as though I'd been there all along. Perdita bought a couple of watches, a handbag, and a scarf, and then after exchanging several bows with the shopkeeper, we headed back to the office.

I'd wanted to go straight to Owen as soon as I'd rigged the envelope, but Sam convinced me that wasn't the best idea. I needed to convince my followers that this had been nothing more than a lunchtime shopping trip, which meant going back to the office for the rest of the workday. Once we were safely back in our office, Perdita burst into giggles. "That was so much fun!" she said. "I like using my clumsiness as a power for good. And, you know, it's hard to be deliberately clumsy."

"You were brilliant," I said.

"Did you get your mission done?"

"I think so."

Sam joined us a moment later. "My guys say you made a clean getaway. Your shadows never left that area."

The next trip was even riskier because I didn't dare lead them to Owen. I left the office a little early and walked up Broadway, stopping to window-shop my way through SoHo. I bought a new blouse at one store and hoped I was thoroughly boring my followers. I went into the subway at Prince Street and caught a train to Union Square. While I was in the maze of the station, I put the new blouse on over the top I was wearing and twisted my hair up into a bun before catching another train toward Grand Central. Meanwhile, Trix, wearing a Katie illusion, left the station and headed to my apartment building.

I left the subway at the station nearest the hotel and put on one of my new pairs of sunglasses before going up the stairs to the street level. The glasses were only lightly tinted, so I kept them on as I went through the hotel lobby to the elevators. It was a relief to be the only person on the elevator. I hit buttons for the floors above mine before I got off, just to muddy the waters.

I knocked on the door before using the key card to let myself into Owen's room. He was lying on the sofa, reading the book I'd left him. "I think I may have something," I said, by way of greeting.

He sat up, and I sat next to him. I got out the vial of powder and the spell booklet. "I got some powder on the envelope. Do you think you could use the moving spell to get it here?"

He pondered it for a moment. "It's worth a shot. The specifics might be a little different, but I can adjust." He sprinkled the outline of a square on the coffee table using the powder, then read through the booklet before putting it aside. He held his hands out palm-down over the square, said a few words in a foreign language, and then snapped his fingers. There was a flare of light and the square of powder vanished, but the envelope lay in the middle of where it had been.

I couldn't resist a fist pump. "Yes! It worked."

He blinked. "It did. Wow." His voice quavered. "So, I guess I have to open it now, huh?"

"If you don't, I will have wasted my day and Perdita will have terrorized a Chinatown shopkeeper for nothing." At his confused expression, I said, "I'll explain some other time. It's a good story." He studied the envelope lying on the table in silence, and when at least a minute had gone by without him doing anything, I said, "I noticed there's magic around it."

"Yeah, there's an enchantment, but it feels benign enough. Just a mild compulsion that's not aimed at me." He frowned and chewed on his lower lip. "There's something else, but I think it protects the contents. I don't feel anything beyond that."

"So it's not going to suddenly possess you or unleash terrible evil on the world?"

"I don't think so." He took a long, shaky breath. "Well, here goes," he said. I put my hand on his back in support as he bent forward and picked up the envelope. He read the writing on the outside first, then took another couple of breaths before sliding his finger under the envelope flap.

The envelope remained sealed, and Owen's soft "ouch" told me he'd got a paper cut. There was a tiny flicker of light as a drop of his blood hit the envelope, and the envelope opened by itself. I didn't know how he stood the suspense because I was about to die of anticipation and it wasn't even about me.

He slid out a folded piece of paper, then he shook the envelope, and a key fell into his palm. He placed the envelope and key on the table, then unfolded the paper.

CHAPTER TWENTY-ONE

I would have expected Owen to consider this a personal moment, something he'd want to absorb on his own before sharing it with me, but he cleared his throat and began to read aloud, "'My dear son, I hope you never read this. I hope you grow up healthy and happy and far away from the troubles we brought on ourselves. I don't want to think that your parents' actions will go on to harm you, but that's the way the world works, isn't it? He isn't getting what he wants this time, so he'll try again, and I'm afraid he'll try to use you. If he does and you find yourself in trouble because of who you might be, I hope you'll think to research your origins and come across this note.

"'I probably don't have to tell you this, if you've reached a place in your life where you needed to find this note, but the one who led us isn't what he appears to be. Your father won't listen to reason, but ever since I realized the path we were on and that there was no way out for us, I've been gathering evidence and documenting his actions. I hid everything in a monument in the park by the office. I hope you know what I mean. I will do everything I can to secure this note, but I'm afraid to take chances. If you need this, you'll know what the office is. This key will lead you to what I've hidden. Only you will be able to open it.'"

Owen read silently for a few minutes, then he read out loud, his voice rough, "'I am so sorry I won't see you grow up. But my last hope is that you will be able to undo the evil your parents did. You've already saved me, no matter what happens to us tonight. It was because of you that I started thinking and asking questions. I couldn't be selfish anymore when I had a baby depending on me. Perhaps it was your power that gave me the strength I needed to pull away.'" Owen's voice broke, and I rubbed his back as he finished. "'Know that you were wanted and loved, and if I thought I could take you and run away somewhere safe, I would, but I have to see this through.'" He turned to look at me. "It's signed 'Your mother, Mina Morgan.'"

He was silent for a while after that, and I put my arm around him and rested my head on his shoulder. He put his arm around my waist, and we sat, hugging each other. After a while, he said, "Well, now I know. Idris was right. And you were right. It's the smoking gun."

"Not entirely. It just tells us how to find the smoking gun. The letter on its own isn't much good, since she doesn't actually mention Ramsay's name. I assume she's talking about the park by the MSI building. It's going to be tricky getting to it, with the protesters and with people from both sides following me and ready to arrest you the moment they find you."

"But I have to go. I'm the only one who can find her stash and get into it. Since my blood from the paper cut opened the envelope, I'm guessing she used blood magic."

"Blood magic? That sounds dark."

"Some kinds are. This is more accurately DNA magic, but that doesn't sound nearly as dramatic. It's the best way to tie something directly to a specific person. Think of it as magical biometrics."

"So, now we need a plan for getting you out of the hotel and all the way downtown without getting caught." I thought for a moment, then said, "That close to the office, maybe we could get Sam to set up a security perimeter around the park. You could get the stash without an audience."

He shook his head. "I can't get Sam involved. I'm a fugitive. If he knows I'm there, he's duty-bound to hold me."

"That makes things more challenging."

"It's easier to hide among a crowd, so we should do this during rush hour, when all the city employees will be in that area." He checked his watch. "It's almost five, so I suppose it's now or never."

I got out my purchases from the lunchtime shopping trip. "I don't know how good a disguise these will be, but I do have hats and funny glasses. And 'I Heart NY' obnoxious tourist T-shirts."

"This would be a lot easier in winter, when we could really bundle up and hide ourselves," he said, taking a shirt from me.

I went into the bathroom to change shirts. I wished I'd thought to pick up some hair rinse at a drugstore to darken my hair, but I settled for stuffing it up under a "Big Apple" baseball cap. When I came back out, Owen had also changed. He hadn't shaved that day, and with a baseball cap, sunglasses, and a touristy T-shirt a size too large so that it looked sloppier than he usually did, he was almost unrecognizable. Someone who knew him well would spot him if they knew to look for him, but in a crowd, he might not obviously be Owen. I was naturally invisible in crowds, which made ditching followers in a busy city easier. Utterly average blends in nicely.

"Okay, let's do this," I said, trying to talk myself into courage.

He picked up the key, then folded the letter, slipped it back into its envelope, and then slid that into the book he'd been reading. "You've got a key to the room?" he asked. "I think it's probably safest if I don't have one on me." I didn't like the way he made that sound. It reminded me of the note of fatalism in his mother's letter.

"You think they're going to catch you?"

"Let's just say I'd rather plan for the worst-case scenario and then be pleasantly surprised. And I do think the odds of me making it there and back are slim." He took both my hands in his and faced me. "Listen to me now. Our priority—our only priority—is getting those documents. If we get ambushed or caught or chased, get the documents and don't worry about me. Go straight into the building and give them to Merlin. Once we have those, I'll be okay eventually, whatever happens, even if they catch me. Do you understand?"

I nodded and tried to swallow the lump in my throat. "Yes, I understand."

"Now promise me."

"Owen," I whimpered.

He squeezed my hands tighter and looked me square in the eye. "Promise me," he repeated, his voice firmer.

"Your magic doesn't work on me, you know. This isn't binding. But, yes, I promise. I know what the priority is."

He held my hands a moment longer, then said, "Are you ready?"

"Ready as I'll ever be." On impulse, I stood on my toes and threw my arms around his neck to give him a tight hug. "You will be careful," I whispered into his ear, making it an order.

He hugged me in response. "I will. Trust me, I have no desire to end up back in one of those cells."

"I'd better go down first and scope out the situation," I said. "I'm pretty sure I wasn't followed, but they saw me come here yesterday and may be on the lookout. You sit tight, and I'll call the room when the coast is clear."

I was glad I'd thought of checking out the situation because there were black-clad men at every exit in the lobby, and I didn't think they were doormen. Before I could sneak out of the lobby, one looked directly at me. *Oh, crap*, I thought. We were trapped. I couldn't even act like this was just another visit to Nita because they'd seen me leaving the elevators. They had to know Owen was hiding somewhere in the hotel.

Nita was my only hope. Maybe she knew another way out of the hotel. Pasting on a carefree smile, I went up to Nita's station at the registration desk and said, "Surprise!"

"Hey, you!" she said with a grin, then she looked at me and frowned. "What's with the look? Surely you know better than to go out in public looking like that. We have got to go shopping. I'm off Saturday afternoon.

Put it in your calendar, in ink. Don't argue with me, Katie. This is an intervention for your own good."

I glanced down at my tourist gear. "This is actually for that event I was telling you about."

"Oh, the secret celebrity thing?" She made a face like she was smelling something nasty. "You poor thing, having to dress like that around a big star."

"He's dressed like this, too. Speaking of which, he's got a thing about crowded hotel lobbies, and I have to get him to this event, but he doesn't want to come down with all these people here, and the event's going to start soon, so I'm desperate." I dropped my voice to just above a whisper and leaned forward. "Plus, there are a couple of people in this lobby who are on my list of people to look out for. One's a tabloid reporter and the other is a known industrial spy who works for our competition. Can you think of a way to get us out of here without being seen?"

You'd have thought I'd offered her an audience with Sarah Jessica Parker from the way she reacted. "You need me to help sneak a celebrity out of the hotel?" she gasped. "Oh, wow! I've always dreamed of something like this. I started coming up with plans as soon as I came to work here. Just go back up to the room and leave this to me."

I glanced over my shoulder and noticed that the men were still watching me. "Can you think of a way I could get up there without them following me?"

"Which guys are you worried about?" I pointed them out by location, since I didn't know what they might be doing magically to change their appearance. She nodded. "Okay, got it." Then she picked up the phone and punched a button. "Hi, Javier, it's Nita at the front desk. We've got an Operation Smile in progress. Phase one, you know what to do."

It was like watching a room full of undercover CIA operatives spring into action. An overburdened bellboy hurrying across the lobby tripped and dropped several suitcases—including one that fell open and spilled a cascade of lacy lingerie—right at the feet of one of the men. Meanwhile, one of the front desk clerks coming back from a coffee break bumped into the other guy and spilled his drink. I took advantage of the diversions and ran for the elevators.

I found an anxious Owen pacing in the room. "What took you so long?" he asked.

"They're here in the lobby. Nita's coming up with a way to sneak us out."

"You got Nita into this?"

"Remember, she thinks you're a celebrity traveling incognito." I chewed on my lower lip and looked at him. "I don't suppose you could do a Bruce Springsteen illusion."

"I'm not sure what he looks like."

"You don't know what Bruce Springsteen looks like?"

"I'm not really into music. I could probably pick him out of a lineup if you showed me pictures, but I couldn't begin to describe him, and I can't do an illusion without having a specific mental picture of what I want to look like."

Now that I thought about it, I wasn't sure I could describe Bruce Springsteen well enough to create an illusion. "Well, then, just do something that makes you not obviously Owen, in case Nita gets involved personally. You don't need to fool the enforcers, just Nita."

"What is she doing?"

"I have no idea, but apparently she had contingency plans."

There was a knock at the door, then a voice called, "Housekeeping. Nita at the front desk sent me." I opened the door to find a hotel maid and a large laundry cart. She gestured at the cart. "Hop in and cover yourselves."

Owen and I exchanged glances, then he shrugged. "After you." He gave me a boost into the cart and then swung himself over the side. We pulled a layer of sheets on top of ourselves as the maid got the cart rolling.

I heard elevator doors open and close, and then had a sinking feeling as we went down. The cart was a bit cramped with the two of us in there, but there were enough towels at the bottom to cushion us. "I had no idea celebrity life was so glamorous," I whispered to Owen.

The elevator came to a stop, then the doors opened and the cart moved again. A moment later, it stopped and the maid's voice said, "You can come out now."

We threw off the sheets and climbed out of the cart to find ourselves in the hotel's laundry room. The laundry staff applauded us, and I hoped Owen had thought to put up some kind of illusion because Nita was there, too. "Yay! It worked!" she said. "Now, we'll go out through the kitchen. There's a service entrance there."

She guided us out of the laundry area and down a dark, narrow hallway. "I don't think they're on to us," she said as we ran. Then we crossed another corridor, and I saw men in black at the other end.

"They're on to us now," I said, and we picked up speed.

We hit the swinging doors into the kitchen at a full run, Nita shouting, "Code red!"

The people nearest us immediately threw white chef's coats over our clothes and bustled us deeper into the kitchen. I eyed a rack of knives and wondered if it would come to that, but Nita's plan apparently covered this sort of situation. When the men in black entered the kitchen, an angry chef was on them in an instant, berating them for violating his inner sanctum. Meanwhile, the kitchen erupted into chaos, with people running back and forth carrying knives, pans of hot food, and dirty pots. Under cover of this mayhem, Nita hustled us out another door and into a small alley.

"The gate to the service entrance is open, and there's a car waiting there for you," she said as we handed her the chef's coats.

"Thanks so much, Nita," I said.

"Glad to be of service." She gave Owen a saucy wink. "I'm a huge fan. Not that I have any idea who you are, of course." With another wink, she was gone, and we ran to the metal gate at the end of the alley.

A limousine waited there, the driver holding the door for us. We dove inside, he shut the door behind us, and then he went around to the driver's side and got in. "City Hall," I called out through the window to the driver's compartment. "And make sure we're not followed."

"In this traffic, that may not be easy, but I'll see if I can confuse them," he said. "Now sit back and enjoy the ride."

I collapsed against the seat back and caught my breath. Owen took off his cap and sunglasses and rubbed his forehead. "I'll have to be sure to leave a huge tip when I check out," he said. "That was hotel service above and beyond the call of duty. Do they really have contingency plans for sneaking celebrities out?"

"I don't know if the hotel does, but Nita's been living for this, I'm sure. I'm impressed that she's already got the whole hotel working with her on it. Her dad may be right. She'll be running the place before long."

He found a bottle of water in a cooler and handed it to me, then opened one for himself. After a long drink, he said, "You've got to admit, this beats taking the subway."

"And it may be harder to track us this way. How will they know we're in here?"

The limo wove in and out of traffic on the way downtown, making a few abrupt turns along the way. Finally, the car stopped. "City Hall," the driver said. "I haven't noticed anyone following us, and there doesn't seem to be anyone here waiting for us."

Owen paid him for the ride while I scoped out the area. The fact that the driver didn't see anyone didn't mean anything. I wouldn't feel safe until *I* knew no one was there. But there was no one to see—no men in black, no Mr. Bones. We might stand a chance.

As the limo drove away, I turned to Owen. "Do you have any idea which monument the stuff is in?"

"None whatsoever, but this is supposed to lead me to it." He took his mother's key out of his pocket and drew the tip of it across his thumb, drawing blood, which he then smeared on the key. The key began glowing softly in his palm. "Let's hope this works," he said. He closed his hand around the key and paused, like he was listening for something, then said, "This way."

While he followed whatever signals the key was giving him, I kept an eye out for any possible pursuers. "I'm glad your mother thought of sending you a magical divining rod because there are dozens of monuments to everyone and his or her dog in this park. And wasn't the park renovated not too long ago? Things have probably been moved."

Instead of answering, he moved faster, and I had to hurry to keep up with him. Soon, he was on his knees in the grass, next to a brass plaque on a stone base. He touched the key to the plaque, then the plaque popped open. In a cavity underneath was a manila envelope. Owen reached in and pulled it out, then the plaque slid back into place. He hurried to open the envelope, and I leaned over his shoulder to see what was in it.

"There you are, Palmer," a voice said. "Turn around with your hands up."

Instead of turning, Owen grabbed the hem of my T-shirt and shoved his hands under it, sliding the envelope under there. I instinctively wrapped my arms around my middle to keep it in place. He stuck the key in my pocket, then he hissed, "You know what to do."

He jumped to his feet and ran toward the man, startling him. That gave me a second to get up and run in the opposite direction, toward the office. There were shouts behind me and the sound of a struggle, but I forced myself not to look back. That was the downfall of women in every horror or action movie ever made, and I'd sworn I wouldn't ever do the same thing if I were being chased. It grew harder and harder to keep my focus forward when I heard what sounded like blows landing behind me and when I became aware of running footfalls nearby.

I clasped the envelope tighter to me as I felt someone clutch at my shirt. There was a rushing sound from above, zooming over my head, and then I heard something hit the ground behind me. "It's okay, sweetheart, I got your back. Just keep runnin'," Sam's voice said.

I was gasping for breath, and still I had to keep going. Sam and his security gargoyles fought off a few pursuers, and then we neared the street. "Sam, the light!" I panted. I'd be taking my life into my own hands to dart across that street against the light, but I couldn't stop and wait for a walk signal with people chasing me.

"I got it, doll!" he cried out, flying ahead. The moment I reached the curb, the light changed. There was a squeal of tires and a chorus of honks, but I ignored them and dashed across the street. Then I faced the mob of protesters. If they were all controlled by the charms and amulets, that meant they'd likely try to stop me. I got a firmer grasp on the envelope under my shirt as Sam dive-bombed them, but there were too many for him to fight off. Hands clutched at my clothes, pulled off my hat, tried to grab my arms. Keeping one arm around my waist, I struck out and kicked, fighting in sheer animal desperation.

There was a crack of thunder and a roar of wind, and soon the crowd was being pushed away from me by an invisible force. I looked up to see Merlin standing, staff in hand, in front of the MSI doors. Sobbing with relief, I stumbled toward him. He escorted me into the building with an arm around my shoulders. The sound of those doors shutting behind me was more joyous to my ears than Christmas carols.

I turned to Merlin, words pouring out of me in fits and starts. "Owen, they got him, back in the park."

Merlin said calmly, "Intervening at this point would endanger my position on the Council, and I need to hold that position to be able to help Owen. I hope he had a good reason for leaving his place of safety."

I pulled the envelope out from under my shirt. "So do I. It all depends on what's inside this."

"Let us go to my office and find out."

He got me settled on the sofa in his office, where I got a sudden bad case of the shakes. He went to make tea, giving me a moment to pull myself together. I wanted to go to the windows to see what was happening in the park, but I knew Owen would be long gone by now. They'd probably zapped him to wherever the magic jail was the moment they brought him down. The only way I could help him now was to use the information he'd risked his freedom to find—and that his mother had probably lost her life for hiding.

I was a little less shaky by the time Merlin brought tea to me. At least, the cup only rattled slightly against the saucer when I held it. I took a few sips before telling Merlin what the letter had said and why Owen had to go to the park. "He opened the envelope before he gave it to me, I guess in case she'd sealed it magically."

"That was very good thinking under pressure," Merlin said with an approving smile. He picked up the envelope and pulled out its contents. It looked like a lot of documents, some on carbon paper, with a few Polaroid photographs, some regular snapshots, and a couple of cassette tapes. I didn't know enough about the magical world to know exactly what any of it meant, but Merlin whistled softly under his breath as he read.

"So, is it what we need?" I finally asked when I couldn't stand the suspense any longer.

"It appears that Owen inherited his attention to detail from his mother," Merlin said, looking up. "These first few documents are enough to prove Ramsay's role in the Morgan affair. I can only imagine what other incriminating evidence she recorded. It's ironic, isn't it, that Idris's seemingly baseless accusation about Owen's parentage—which he made under Ramsay's orders—turned out to be true, and that will be the key to Ramsay's downfall."

"What do we do now?" I asked. "How do we let people know about this stuff?"

"There will be a hearing, at which Ramsay will likely carry out his plan to make it appear as though Owen is attacking me. We can bring up this information then. But we should be prepared—he is ruthless and driven, and when we foil his plans to look like a heroic savior, he may resort to force."

"What do you need me to do?"

"You've done more than enough. You should rest and be ready for when they call a hearing. I don't think they know what you had or why you and Owen were in that park. With Owen in custody, the enforcers should leave you alone. I will assign a security detail to you, in case Ramsay tries to find out what you've discovered."

*

The next two days were sheer torture. I felt like I was going through the motions while life moved around me in a blur. I gathered Owen's things from the hotel room and checked out, leaving a huge tip to be shared among the people who'd helped us escape. I brought Owen's things to his house and took care of Loony. I think I carried on conversations with my roommates, but I barely noticed what they were saying. At the office, Perdita did her best to cheer me up and distract me, creating all sorts of new coffee concoctions—some more successful than others—before finally deciding it was best to leave me alone. Finally, on Thursday afternoon, Perdita stuck her head into my office and said, "The boss wants to see you."

I jumped up, nearly knocking over my coffee cup. This time, it was Perdita who rushed to the rescue and kept the cup from tipping over. I knew I was in bad shape when *Perdita* was saving *me* from clumsiness. I got up to Merlin's office so fast I might have beat someone who teleported if it had been a race. "What is it?" I gasped as I ran into his office.

"The hearing has been set for tomorrow," he said. "I will need you with me."

"Of course," I said, nodding. "What's the plan?"

"I think it depends on Mr. Ramsay's plan. I do intend to reveal some rather incriminating information about him as soon as possible. I will have Jake and the research team there to break the amulet spell at the most opportune moment. Other than that, we should be prepared for—how is it you say it?—all hell to break loose."

"And from what I've seen of Idris's work in the past, that may be literal," I said with a shudder. "You've found enough incriminating evidence, then?"

"I may have to propose a posthumous medal for Mina Morgan. Not only has she revealed Ramsay's role in that plot, but he was involved in a lot of other mischief within the magical world. For instance, he was blackmailing the Meredith family about their takeover of the Vandermeer firm. Your friend Philip will be interested in that information, I'm sure. There appears to be almost as much fear and blackmail involved in Ramsay's rise to prominence as there was magic. He is not as beloved and popular as he would like everyone to think."

"And what about that scheme to make it look like Owen's the one to kill you? What can we do about that?"

"I would hope that revealing Ramsay's perfidy will negate that. There is little point in creating another villain when he has already been revealed as one, himself." His eyes became steely and the air crackled with power. "Then he can face me one-to-one—wizard-to-wizard."

I had no doubt that Merlin could beat Ramsay in a fair fight, but I also had no doubt that Ramsay would cheat. Either way, I was afraid Owen would be caught in the middle.

*

Early the next day, I went with Merlin to the Council headquarters. The security guard was properly deferential to the distinguished Council member and allowed us into the Council chamber. "Now, we will search the room to ensure that nothing has been hidden," Merlin said once we were alone in the room. The two of us went over the chamber inch by inch, comparing what we saw. We didn't find anything out of place, which bothered Merlin. "I know Ivor Ramsay would not assume he could win without cheating," he said, frowning and scratching his beard. "But how does he plan to cheat?"

"He may bring something in with him. Too bad you don't have the magical equivalent of metal detectors at the entrances."

"Unfortunately, it would be nearly impossible to tell the difference between good and bad because it's the intent that matters, and I doubt we'd ever get this Council to agree to ban all magic from the chamber. How else would they show off? Some of these people don't know how to function without magic. Rudolph wouldn't be able to tie his shoes." He sighed wearily. "I suppose we have done all we can to prepare. We will have to remain on the alert."

A livid Gloria was the next to arrive, with James in her wake. "What is the meaning of this?" she demanded of Merlin, getting up in his face. "Why won't they let us see him? They wouldn't even let us bring him a suit for the hearing."

"I hadn't heard anything about that," Merlin said. "I suppose after he managed to escape from them so easily, they're worried about security."

"It wasn't a nice suit and a visit from his father that allowed him to escape," she said with a derisive snort.

Merlin promised to look into it, then left to go prepare in the Council offices. Gloria then turned her attention to me. "So, it is true about him, then?"

"Yes, it is." I'd brought the letter and the key with me, and I handed her the letter.

She and James read it, then she said with a sniff, "I suppose she couldn't have been all bad if she had a child like that." Her expression softened ever so slightly. "How did he take it?"

"The last time I saw him, it hadn't yet had time to really sink in."

More people began arriving. It was much like the previous hearing, but there were a lot more strangers. I was fairly certain I recognized a number of people from the mob of protesters at the MSI building and a few of the people James and Gloria had scared away from Owen's house. That left me with no doubt that Ramsay had something in the works. But what?

We took our seats in front, with Rod and Ethan soon joining us. Two minutes before the hearing was set to begin, Ramsay made his grand entrance, with the usual adulation from most of the crowd. His fan club was in for a big surprise, I thought with some satisfaction. He took the front-row seat across the aisle from us, and he knew better than to even pretend to give James and Gloria a friendly acknowledgment. He carried a briefcase, which he set on the floor in front of his feet. Had he brought his own evidence?

The Council members then took their places at the head table, and Rudolph stood and struck his staff on the ground while giving the ritual opening. I felt the wash of magic as the wards took hold. This time, I knew no one would drop the wards for Owen. He was stuck until we proved our case.

Then they brought Owen in, and James, Gloria, and I gasped in unison. He was dressed all in black, like the uniform of the enforcers, and it looked like they'd scavenged whatever they could find for him to wear. The dark, ill-fitting clothing made him look small and pale. The only hint of color on him came from his eyes—and from the ugly bruise under his left eye that spread over his cheekbone. It was a few days old, so it looked like sunset over the Grand Canyon, all reds and purples, with a hint of yellow. James had to grab Gloria's arm before she instinctively went to him.

The one improvement over the last hearing was that his hands were bound in front of him this time, which had to be more comfortable. Mack being his guard probably had something to do with that. I felt a little better about his situation.

Owen caught my eye as they brought him in. I could see the question on his face and realized that he didn't even know if what we'd found was useful. I nodded, and his shoulders relaxed ever so slightly.

And then the hearing began. Rudolph read off a list of charges, which included the earlier conspiracy to commit magical crimes plus charges of escape and evasion. He added, "And these crimes are even more alarming when taken in context with the allegation that Owen Palmer is none other than the son of Kane and Mina Morgan, who were so disastrous to the magical community. We know he can't help the accident of his birth, but we also know he has great power—a power he may have inherited from his alleged parents—and there is also the possibility that the capacity for darkness has been inherited, as well."

Merlin leaned forward. "As I understand, these were merely allegations made by someone with a personal grudge against Mr. Palmer. Has anyone presented any proof? The person who made the allegations doesn't appear to be present today, as he is also a fugitive."

Ramsay then stood. "I took the liberty of asking Mr. Idris to accompany me here today after he approached me to explain how he came by this information." A man in a hat and jacket stood at the back of the room and made his way down the aisle. He must have come in at the last second, or I would have recognized Idris. I wasn't sure what Ramsay's game was, since it was more than likely that Idris learned it from Ramsay.

"This is most unorthodox, Ivor," Rudolph said. "Mr. Idris has broken numerous magical laws and escaped from legitimate custody. In fact, he's known to have committed more magical crimes than even Mr. Palmer is accused of. It's hardly fair to have Mr. Palmer as a prisoner while we do nothing about Mr. Idris. We will listen to your evidence and take your cooperation into consideration, but Mr. Idris, I'm afraid we will have to take you into custody first." He waved a hand at one of the guards, who moved toward Idris.

"I was framed!" Idris screamed, suddenly breaking into a run and charging toward Owen. "It was him! He did it! It's all his fault!"

I shouted a warning to Owen, who whirled just in time to see Idris running at him. With his hands bound, Owen was practically helpless. Idris sent a magical attack in his direction and, acting as if on instinct, Owen threw his hands up in a defensive position, and his lips moved silently, like he was doing a spell. He was in the containment circle that kept anyone from using magic, so the spell was useless for defending himself or attacking Idris.

But then Merlin fell out of his chair with a cry of pain, like someone had hit him with a powerful spell.

"See, he's found a way to breach the circle!" Ramsay shouted. "He's attacking Merlin, even now! He has to be stopped!"

CHAPTER TWENTY-TWO

Owen went a sick gray color and froze. I thought Gloria would come right out of her seat and take on Idris herself, but the guards finally got to him and pulled him away from Owen.

"I didn't attack Merlin," Owen said, his voice so faint it wasn't much above a whisper. "I wouldn't, ever. I don't know what happened. I was just defending myself from Idris—and I did that without thinking. It shouldn't have done any good, since I'm in the circle."

"Likely story, when we know what he is," Ramsay scoffed. "We saw him do a spell, and we saw Merlin, not Mr. Idris, suffer the effects."

The audience erupted into arguments and discussion. Rudolph rapped his staff on the floor, and the room went silent. "We will deal with the alleged attack on Mr. Mervyn in a moment," he said. "Given his attempted attack on Mr. Palmer, I am not sure how seriously we can take accusations made by Mr. Idris. Obviously, there is a personal grudge, as Mr. Mervyn mentioned. Mr. Ramsay, I hope you have additional evidence."

"That won't be necessary," Merlin said. "I happen to have proof that Owen Palmer is the son of Kane and Mina Morgan. Miss Chandler, if you please?"

While the audience muttered in surprise at Merlin being the one to provide proof, I took the letter and the key out of my purse and brought them up to Merlin. "This note was left with Mr. Palmer when he was left as a newborn at a fire station," Merlin said, then he read the letter out loud. I watched Ramsay's face the whole time, as he first went red, then the color drained entirely from his skin. There was a gasp from the audience when Merlin read the signature, then Merlin said, "And now the key." I went to Owen, who held his hands out, and placed the key in his palm, giving his hand a squeeze as I did so. Then I stepped to the side so the Council could see the key glowing in his hand. "The Council will notice that the key glows at his touch," Merlin pointed out. "That is proof that he is, in fact, the child in question."

"Who did she mean when she said 'he' wasn't what he seemed, and what did she hide?" Rudolph asked eagerly.

"Fortunately, Mr. Palmer had the opportunity to obtain those materials before he was recaptured," Merlin said, his lips twitching like he was trying to fight back a smile. He waved a hand to start the recording, and Ramsay's voice rang through the room, saying, "The three of us can have unprecedented power, if you will just agree to play your part."

The voice of a young man said, "What do you want us to do?"

Ramsay's voice said, "I need you to play the villains—only for a while. You need to terrify the Council enough that they'll revive Merlin. Then the three of us can defeat him, and there will be no one left to challenge us."

The room exploded with shocked shouts. I would have expected Ramsay to deny it, but although his face briefly turned a purplish color, he sat totally still and looked almost casual. "These are very interesting allegations, Ambrose," he said. "But I must say, it's a clever bit of fakery. You can't trust anything Mina Morgan did. We know the kind of person she was."

Merlin, now smiling openly, said, "I have more documentation, as well as photographs. Mina was quite thorough. The current situation sounds rather familiar. Did you use Phelan Idris the way you used the Morgans? You certainly used him as an excuse to revive me."

The outraged yelling from the audience grew even louder. Rudolph pounded his staff for order, but everyone ignored him. Most of the people seemed to be aghast that their hero was turning out to be a villain, but then voices rose in support of Ramsay. It was the people I'd recognized as part of the protest mob, and they moved down the aisle in lockstep, practically in formation. Ramsay stood in the aisle, with them at his back. "You cannot diminish the support I enjoy with a few baseless accusations," he said as his supporters chanted his name.

I turned to look up at Merlin, who gave a subtle nod. Suddenly, the supporters reeled and blinked in confusion as the spell broke. Some of them didn't even seem to know where they were or how they got there. When they realized they were standing in the aisle in the Council chamber, most of them slunk away to take seats. That event sent a fresh wave of murmurs through the crowd.

"I would suggest that if you have bought any tokens from Spellworks, you discard them immediately," Merlin said dryly, raising his voice to be heard above the tumult. "They only leave you open to manipulation." There was a rustling and clattering sound as the former mob members emptied their pockets and tossed charms and amulets on the floor. Merlin turned to address the rest of the Council. "I believe that is evidence that Spellworks was not what Mr. Ramsay led us to believe. It was merely his vehicle for manipulating people and events."

"And so all of these charges against Mr. Palmer were part of that scheme?" Rudolph asked, sounding like he was waking up from a dream and wasn't yet sure what was real.

"Aside from the escape and evasion, yes. But I think you can see why escape and evasion were necessary," Merlin replied.

Mack vanished the silver cord binding Owen's wrists. I was just moving to go stand at Owen's side when Ramsay gave a roar of fury and rushed at Owen, magic shooting in violent sparks from his outstretched hands. Owen staggered backward, unable to defend himself, and Mack stepped in to shield him, counterattacking against Ramsay.

But Ramsay seemed entirely unaffected. He kept advancing on the circle. I heard Merlin cry out behind me at the Council table, and I turned to see him nearly fall out of his seat again. I whirled back to face the room. "Stop! Don't!" I called out to Mack while I tried to block out the noise and chaos to think.

Owen was within the circle of tile on the floor that kept prisoners from using magic, but he had used magic instinctively against Idris, and it had worked, but it had harmed Merlin instead of Idris. Mack was sticking close to Owen and had one foot still within the circle, and his magic had also hurt Merlin. That was it! It looked like instead of preventing magic use, the circle now turned magic used within it into an attack on Merlin. That must have been what Ramsay planned to make it look like Owen was the bad guy. But how? We'd swept the room before the hearing. Nothing had been altered or out of place.

The Council's guards rushed forward to grab Ramsay, but the remaining loyalists in the audience got in their way. James, Gloria, and Rod left their seats to help defend Owen. "Stay out of the circle," I called to them. They were able to protect Owen from most of the fighting, but Mack apparently didn't have the power to take Owen out of the prisoner's circle. Owen was stuck there as securely as if there were iron bars around him, and while he was, he couldn't do anything magically without hurting Merlin.

The Council members were now getting into the fray, mostly in a vain attempt to restore order. Merlin, looking a little pale and shaken but otherwise unharmed, came down from the high table and headed straight for Ramsay, and Ramsay turned to face him. "This is what you wanted, isn't it, Ivor?" Merlin said. "You wanted to face me so that nothing would stand in the way between you and total power." He held his arms out to the side. "Here I am."

I'd seen some big magical battles in the past, but this was a clash of the titans. Even though Merlin wasn't wearing his mystical robe, I felt like I could see the aura of it around him. He and Ramsay were more evenly matched than I would have thought. Ramsay held his own and showed no sign of tiring as they flung spell after spell at each other. Fights against Merlin usually didn't last very long, but this one kept going.

Idris moved to join his boss, which surprised me. He was the type to switch to the winning side, especially after learning that Ramsay was using him. It had to be that compulsion spell. He didn't have a choice but to fight—probably even to the death—alongside his master. I told myself that meant I was actually doing him a favor when I grabbed the ceremonial gavel from the high table and whacked Idris on the back of the head. He crumpled, and I dragged him under a bench, out of the way of the fight. I looked around for one of the enforcers to watch or bind Idris, but they had their hands full.

Apparently, there were some true Ramsay loyalists even without the charms and amulets—or else he had some people under more direct compulsion spells, like Idris—since there were still people trying to get to the front of the room, either to help Ramsay against Merlin or to attack Owen.

Since I wasn't much use in a magical battle and wasn't affected by all the magic flying around me, I focused on figuring out how Ramsay had rigged the circle to make magic deflect onto Merlin. If the spell wasn't there before the hearing, then he must have brought it in after our search. His briefcase, I realized. That had to be it.

I wove my way around combatants to get back to the front of the seating area, and there I saw the briefcase, which rested right on the edge of that tile circle. I kicked it to move it out of the way, but the only thing that happened was my foot going numb from the direct contact with powerful magic. If I'd been wearing my magic-detecting necklace, I'd have probably passed out. The case didn't move even a fraction of an inch.

Owen had dropped to the ground to get below the worst of the magical attacks, and he crawled over to the perimeter of the circle where I was. "What is it?" he asked.

I pointed to the briefcase. "Ramsay brought this in. See how it's sitting right there on the edge of the circle? And it won't budge—I tried. My guess is this has something to do with that redirect spell."

Frowning, he tried to move it, and I had to jump into the circle to grab him when he nearly collapsed just from touching it. He blinked rapidly and shook his head to clear it. "Whoa," he said. "That's not just redirecting power. It's also working something like an amplifier. The circle is part of this room's defensive and protective systems, and whatever's in that case is tapped into the whole system. He's drawing power from the building itself, and from all power being used in the building."

"So it's not just about making you look bad?"

There was a rumble overhead. The heavy wooden roof beams were shifting. Bits of plaster showered down. "It's about giving him an advantage over Merlin," Owen said.

A chunk of plaster fell not too far from us, and I turned at a loud popping sound to see a crack appear in one wall. "And I think it's about bringing the building down around us."

"Well, he is desperate," Owen said.

"We should get Rudolph to drop the wards. Maybe that will stop it, or at least let people escape."

"Do we want to give either Ramsay or Idris a chance to escape?"

I looked at him in horror. "So, it's a magical cage match—only the victor leaves alive? But Ramsay is cheating, and he's going to kill us all."

We both turned to check on the battle. Merlin was still holding his own, deflecting every burst of power Ramsay sent his way while shooting plenty of sparks and lightning bolts at Ramsay. He was tiring, but he was more clever than Ramsay, and he was still clear-headed, while Ramsay was desperate and panicky. "If only I could get out of here and help," Owen said wistfully.

"Let me guess, only Rudolph can let you out."

"I'm not sure even he could while this spell is tied into the wards."

One of the beams came loose and crashed to the ground. A split second before it fell, Owen grabbed me and threw me down, shielding me with his body. We came up, coughing from the plaster dust, to see the beam not far above our heads, resting across the benches on either side of the aisle. Chunks of rubble were all over the floor. Owen gasped, and I turned to see James kneeling next to a fallen figure that I assumed was Gloria.

On the other side of us, at the front of the room, Ramsay cackled madly. "Are you willing to let all these people die, just to defeat me, Merlin?" he spat.

"I am trying to prevent the many more deaths that will occur should I let you win," Merlin said, a little out of breath, but still calm. "I am merely serving my purpose—preventing evil wizards from seizing power."

Owen's jaw took on a stubborn set that I recognized all too well. "That does it, we have to stop this, now," he said. He glanced around. "Get me one of those amulets."

I crawled out of the circle, passing where Gloria was sitting up shakily. The ceiling swayed overhead, which I figured wasn't a good sign. I found an amulet and crawled back to Owen. "Gloria's okay," I reported as I handed him the amulet.

"Good." Then he caught my chin in his hand and kissed me. "Now, go."

"Go?"

"The wards won't stop you. You can get out of here before the building falls around us all. Go get help."

"What help? What would anyone from the outside be able to do?"

"Just go, Katie."

I shook my head. "No. I'm not leaving you trapped here. You may need my help. You can barely touch that case without passing out."

He clearly didn't like it, but he accepted it with a curt nod. "Okay, then, see if you can open it."

Although I hadn't been able to move the case away from the circle, I could lay it flat where it stood. Ramsay hadn't used blood magic to seal the case or even locked it, so it opened easily for me. He probably assumed that anyone not using whatever protective device he had wouldn't be able to touch it. Inside the case, resting in a velvet lining like a giant, evil jewel was a softly glowing crystal. "Maybe I can move the crystal if I can't move the case," I said.

"It's worth a shot."

I tried, but I couldn't lift it. The thing seemed to weigh a ton. I glanced back at Owen. "Sorry, no go. It's either bonded to the circle or it's incredibly dense."

Owen took a deep breath and let it out slowly. "Okay, Plan B," he said, scratching the back of his neck. He handed me the amulet and said, "Drape this across it."

I did as he said. "What'll that do?"

"I hope it'll make what I do next feed back to Ramsay. He's drawing power from the building, but I can give him more than he can handle, all at once."

"Won't it be dangerous for you?"

"A bit, I'm sure. No magic is entirely safe. There's always risk." He gave me a shaky smile. "But I'll be careful."

Ramsay got in a wild bolt of something that sent Merlin a few steps backward. "Get away from the circle, Katie," Owen said. "Get under a bench. Get everyone under benches. I don't know what will happen."

Reluctantly, I left his side to go warn everyone. Nobody needed much urging to take cover, since the one beam falling had really destabilized the roof. Even the magic making the chamber bigger on the inside than it appeared on the outside wasn't enough to withstand Ramsay's magic. When I was sure everyone else was safe, I crawled under a bench.

I couldn't see from my hiding place exactly what Owen was doing, but I knew it couldn't be easy since that crystal was channeling some serious power. It must have been like digging bare-handed in an electric generator. Whatever it was, he did it quickly. There was a loud explosive sound, a burst of white-hot bright light, and then total silence.

I waited a few moments more, then crawled out from under the bench. The building had stopped shaking, and nothing was falling from above. I first looked to where Merlin and Ramsay had been fighting to make sure the fight really was over. I didn't see Ramsay, but Merlin was kneeling in the circle, next to a motionless figure in black.

My heart started pounding so hard I could hear my pulse. "No," I whispered as I drew close enough to see Owen. He was so pale his skin was almost transparent.

"He's alive," Merlin assured me, "but very weak."

"And Ramsay?"

"He is unconscious, as well, and rather badly singed."

James, Gloria, Rod, and some of the others joined us. Gloria immediately knelt by Owen and brushed a strand of hair off his forehead. "Will he be okay?" I asked. "What happened to him?"

"He sent most of the built-up power surging into Ramsay, but some of it blew back to him," Merlin explained.

"And what does that mean?" I demanded.

"It means he received too much power for the human body to manage, though not as much as Ramsay left himself open to."

That still didn't mean much to me, but Owen was the one who was good at explaining magic using nonmagical metaphors. "So it's bad?" I asked.

"It could be," Merlin acknowledged. "The full impact remains to be seen."

Rudolph joined us. Almost as an afterthought, he pounded his staff against the floor to break the wards. Emergency crews then rushed into the chamber. I watched with a sense of despair as they carried Owen away.

James, Gloria, Rod, and I followed to the building's medical facility, where I sat holding Gloria's hand in a waiting room while the healers did their magical healing thing and James paced. "He'll be fine," I said, wishing I had the power to make that be true. "I don't think he'd have done something like that if he didn't know exactly what he was doing."

"I'm afraid he did know what he was doing. He knew what he risked, but he also knew the danger of not acting. I am very proud of him," Gloria said, holding her chin up, even though her voice trembled. Now I was worried. If Gloria was practically writing his eulogy, that was a bad sign.

The chief healer came out then and said, "We've done what we can for now. Physically, there appears to be no permanent injury. The full extent of the magical damage remains to be seen. He will likely remain unconscious for a day or so."

They let us in to see Owen half an hour later, and seeing him didn't reassure me. I'd never seen him so pale. The bruises on his face from his capture stood out in stark contrast to the pallor. When I tentatively touched his hand, I was surprised that it was warm—not normal warm, but he looked like he'd been carved out of ice, so I was expecting him to be frozen. Gloria straightened and smoothed the covers around him, then adjusted his hair so it didn't fall into his eyes.

We stayed there until the healers made us leave, then I went home with James and Gloria. I told myself it was because they needed someone there for them, but I also didn't want to be alone, and I wanted to be with people I could talk to about what had happened. Besides, they needed someone to drive them back and forth to the Council infirmary.

The next morning, we arrived at the infirmary to find Merlin already there. "It appears that both Mr. Idris and Mr. Ramsay have been stripped of their powers," Merlin reported. "The power surge was too much for Mr. Ramsay, and it both burned him and burned out his powers. The link between him and Mr. Idris that maintained the compulsion spell fed enough power into Mr. Idris to damage his powers, as well. The same thing happened to a couple of other people who must have been under a similar spell."

"What will become of them?" I asked.

"That will be for the Council to decide, but I can't think of a worse punishment for those two than to be forced to live normal lives."

"I'm not sure Idris knows the meaning of the word normal," I said, even as I worried about what this might mean for Owen. He hadn't received nearly the jolt Ramsay had, but he'd been the one controlling and directing that power.

Rod came running up to us. "He's waking up!" he said, panting. We didn't need to ask who he meant.

We all hurried into Owen's room to find his eyelids fluttering. I took his hand and gave it a squeeze, and he whispered, "Katie?"

"I'm here."

Gloria squeezed his other hand. "As am I. We're all here."

"You're okay?"

"Everyone is fine," Gloria said soothingly. "It's over, and we're all safe. How do you feel?"

He scrunched his eyes into a wince and groaned slightly. "I have a splitting headache. What happened?"

"You overloaded Ramsay's power draw," James said.

"Did it work?"

"Quite well," Merlin said. "The building still stands. Ivor Ramsay has no magical power left. He's completely burned out. There also seems to have been a similar effect on Phelan Idris."

"Remind me never to do that again." Owen finally opened his eyes, then shut them quickly against the light. He wriggled into a sitting position, and Gloria rushed to adjust the pillows for him.

"If we are fortunate, another situation like that will not arise during your lifetime," Merlin said.

The longer Owen was awake, the more he looked like his usual self.

There was even some color returning to his cheeks. He glanced around the room, giving each of us a faint smile, then he suddenly frowned. "Wait, who are you?" he asked Rod. "You look familiar, but…"

"Amnesia?" Rod asked.

"*Rod?* What happened to you?"

"I don't think he sees your illusion," I said, getting a queasy feeling in my stomach.

Merlin frowned and placed a hand on Owen's forehead, like he was checking for fever. "Odd," he said. "Try to do a spell—something simple and non-taxing."

Owen frowned and shook his head as his forehead creased in concern. "Nothing's coming. I can't find the power." His voice wavered ever so slightly.

Then Merlin did something with his hands and asked, "What do you see?"

"Nothing." Owen half closed his eyes, like he was running an internal diagnostic on himself. "Wait a second, there's no magic at all."

"What does this mean?" I asked.

"It means he's lost all magic," Merlin said, looking somber. "Not only can he not do it, it doesn't affect him."

The greatest wizard of his generation, now utterly without magic? It was a tragedy that didn't seem to have yet sunk in for Owen, who looked rather shell-shocked. I wanted to cry, hug him, and kiss him, all at the same time. Since I was in a room with his parents and our boss, I settled for blinking away tears. I wasn't even sure what I was crying about. I'd meant what I said when I told him I didn't care whether or not he was a wizard. I supposed I was crying for his loss.

"I am most grateful," Merlin said, his voice rough enough that it sounded like he was fighting back his own tears. "I do not think I could have continued defending myself while Ramsay drew power that way."

Owen tried for a smile that came out lopsided. "At least they can't be afraid of me or accuse me of trying to take over the world," he said, just a little too enthusiastically, like he was forcing himself to put a brave face on the situation.

*

Owen came home a couple of days later—that is, he went to James and Gloria's house. He was up and around but still shaky enough that he let Gloria fuss over him. I suspected he rather enjoyed the maternal attention, and there was no doubt that Gloria thoroughly enjoyed finally being able to fuss over him openly. Most of the time, it seemed like he didn't notice the lack of magic, since he seldom used it away from work, but every so often he'd move a hand ever so slightly, then blink and wince when nothing happened. He didn't talk about it, though, and I wasn't sure what to say. He seemed calm enough, but I suspected he was still in shock.

Merlin came by a couple of days after that to report that Ramsay had been given a lifetime sentence, while Idris was being exiled from the magical world. "And all charges have been completely dropped against you," he told Owen. "Including the escape and evasion charges."

Owen nodded. "That's good to hear. I wasn't looking forward to being a fugitive."

I smiled more than the joke was probably worth, but it was good to see his dry sense of humor returning.

"Did you have any particular plans for the future?" Merlin asked him.

Owen shrugged. "I haven't really thought about it. I know immunes are rare enough that you still need me, but I'm not sure I'd want to work in Verification."

"Believe me, you don't," I muttered.

"Yes, magical immunes are rare, but what you are is unprecedented," Merlin said. "I have not known of a magical immune who was fully trained as a wizard, and that may be incredibly valuable. You see, we have in our vaults some magical works that are so potentially dangerous that we cannot allow anyone with any magical ability to so much as read them. But you have the expertise to decipher them and understand what they might mean, with no risk of accidentally enacting any of the spells they contain."

He'd said words more magical than any spell. Owen's eyes lit up. "You mean the *Codex Ephemera*?" he asked breathlessly. "I thought that was just a legend. And you want me to read it?"

"If you are interested."

"If I'd known we had that, I might have wiped out my powers ages ago." He gave a wry half smile. "And that might have saved me a lot of trouble."

"I will take that as a yes," Merlin said with twinkling eyes. "Take some time off, and when you're ready to come back to work, report to the vaults."

That afternoon, Owen and I walked down to the park by the river. "You seem to be feeling better about life," I said. "Are you going to be okay—with all of it? Your parents, the magic thing, and all?"

He settled his arm around my shoulders, and I leaned into him. "Yeah, I think I'll be okay," he said after a while. "My parents were who they were. I can't change that. The magical world won't ever see my mother as anything but a villain, but at least I know what she did. As for the power loss…" He shrugged and sighed. "That's taking some getting used to. It may not be permanent. With time, the power could come back."

"On the bright side, they can't accuse you of being a magical supervillain when you're immune to magic," I said.

"No, and I can read things that are too dangerous for magical people to read. I could contribute a lot to our knowledge of magic." He glanced down at me, then smiled, "And I'll get to see the way the world looks to you."

"So you are going to be okay?"

There was a long pause, and then he said, "Yeah, I think so."

"If you're looking for more bright sides, they can't make you take the lead if there are any more magical threats. But then again, that didn't exactly help me, so maybe you're still stuck with being a hero."

He laughed and squeezed my shoulders. "Have I said thank you?"

"For what?"

"Where do I begin? For being a big help, for believing in me, for giving me a swift kick when I needed it."

I turned within the circle of his arm to face him and put my arms around his neck. "Any time."

"You mean the kicking part?"

"I mean all of it."

He bent to kiss me, gently at first, and then more ardently. When he broke the kiss, he whispered in my ear, "I know the circumstances were a little crazy when I said it the first time, but I meant it. I love you."

I kissed him, then said, "And I know I was yelling at you when I said it the first time, but I meant it. I love you, too."

We stood like that for a long time, our arms around each other and my head resting on his shoulder. Then he said, "I did say that we'd go away somewhere when all this was over, and it does seem to be over."

"Yeah, it's over. So, any vacation ideas? I mean, other than that motel in the Poconos. I don't think they'll let us come back."

"There's this library in an old abbey in Wales I've always wanted to visit…"

I laughed and kissed him. You could take the magic out of Owen Palmer, but I didn't think anything would ever really change him. And I was just fine with that.

ABOUT THE AUTHOR

Shanna Swendson is the author of the Enchanted Inc. series of humorous contemporary fantasy novels, including *Enchanted, Inc.*, *Once Upon Stilettos*, *Damsel Under Stress*, *Don't Hex with Texas*, and *Much Ado About Magic*. She's also contributed essays to a number of books on pop culture topics, including *Everything I Needed to Know About Being a Girl, I Learned from Judy Blume*, *Serenity Found*, *Perfectly Plum* and *So Say We All*. When she's not writing, she's usually discussing books and television on the Internet, singing in or directing choirs, taking ballet classes or attempting to learn Italian cooking. She lives in Irving, Texas, with several hardy houseplants and a lot of books.

Visit her Website at http://www.shannaswendson.com.

AN EXCERPT FROM
NO QUEST FOR THE WICKED

The Enchantment isn't over! Read more in Book Six of the Enchanted, Inc. series, *No Quest for the Wicked*.

Now that the Magic, Spells, and Illusions, Inc. team has defeated the nefarious Spellworks, the only "competition" in town, Katie Chandler doesn't have much to do as director of marketing, and she's starting to question her role at MSI. Her boyfriend Owen Palmer, on the other hand, is in hog heaven, translating an ancient and powerful magical manuscript.

But then he finds that the cryptic text describing the location of an enchanted gem known as the Eye of the Moon has radically changed. This deadly stone gives its holder enhanced power over others and a craving for more power. It once caused a terrible war before it was safely hidden and then lost – and now it seems to be in New York and set in an elven brooch that renders its wearer invulnerable. Whoever has this brooch could take over the world.

Katie and Owen must find it before anyone else does, and they're not the only ones searching. They'll need all the help they can get, including Katie's visiting grandmother. But who can they trust when their allies fall under its spell? Not to mention the new enemies who are deadlier than anything they've faced before.

An impossible mission …

I'd reached the part of my mission where stealth was most essential. One wrong footstep, one breath that was a little too loud, and the game would be up. The door ahead of me was ever so slightly ajar. It looked as though anyone could walk right through, but the door wasn't what kept out intruders. Anyone who tried to pass through that doorway would wake up in a body-shaped dent on the opposite wall.

Anyone, that is, who didn't have my particular qualities. For me, that slightly ajar door was the most challenging obstacle. I'd need to open it wider to get through, but there was the risk that would make enough noise to give me away. I slid my toe into the gap, shivering as I crossed the powerful wards. Moving my foot slowly forward, I eased the door open, bit by bit, then I paused and held my breath, listening carefully. The scratch of a pen confirmed my fear that the room was occupied.

At this time in the morning? How early did I have to get up?

At any rate, it was time to make my move. I slid my body into the gap in the doorway, edging sideways into the chamber. I'd made it all the way into the room when a crunching sound made me freeze. I glanced down and saw that I'd stepped on a wadded-up piece of paper. After holding my breath a few seconds without noticing any reaction from the room's occupant, I kept going, watching more carefully where I stepped.

I'd almost made it to the paper-and-book-strewn table in the middle of the room when the occupant said, without looking up from his work, "Katie, what are you doing here?"

CPSIA information can be ob
Printed in the USA
LVOW05s1613131114

413544LV00018E

510612